JOURNEY
to the WELL

JOURNEY
to the WELL

A NOVEL

DIANA WALLIS TAYLOR

R
Revell
a division of Baker Publishing Group
Grand Rapids, Michigan

© 2009 by Diana Wallis Taylor

Published by Revell
a division of Baker Publishing Group
P.O. Box 6287, Grand Rapids, MI 49516-6287
www.revellbooks.com

Printed in the United States of America

Library of Congress Cataloging-in-Publication Data
Taylor, Diana Wallis, 1938–
    Journey to the well : a novel / Diana Wallis Taylor.
      p.   cm.
    ISBN 978-0-8007-3309-4 (pbk.)
    1. Samaritan woman (Biblical figure)—Fiction. 2. Jesus Christ—Fiction.
3. Bible. N.T.—History of Biblical events—Fiction. 4. Women in the Bible—
Fiction. I. Title.
PS3620.A942J68 2009
813'.6—dc22
                              2008048716

Scripture is taken from the King James Version of the Bible.

To my husband Frank,
my children, Karen, Steven, and Brett,
and my family
who over the years have shown me
the many faces of love and
helped me on my own journey.

PART I

Reba

1

"Marah! Come at once!"

At the sound of her name, she paused from cleaning the ashes out of the clay oven and sat back on the ground to relieve her sore knees. Hearing the happy chatter of small children playing in the dust of the street outside the gate, she listened wistfully and sighed once again. She was nearly thirteen, a woman now, too old for such childish games.

Wiping her hands on her dark shawl, she rose slowly and stretched as she looked out over the village. The air seemed less heavy than the previous day. The village dogs that lay panting in the sparse shade most of the day would be seeking to quench their thirst in the water channels that cooled the street. While the surrounding valley of Shechem retained a verdant green, the town itself shimmered in the summer heat of Elul.

The time of noonday rest must be over. Marah heard voices and activity from the heart of Shechem. Picturing the streets as they came alive with shopkeepers opening their stalls for the afternoon trade, she smiled to herself as she allowed her imagination to take her through the marketplace. At each merchant's shop brimming with goods, she browsed leisurely, ignoring the persuasive pleas of the vendors. She would take her time, choosing carefully the things she wanted to buy—

She glanced reluctantly toward the house. Did her aunt have still another task in mind? She lifted her chin and strolled toward the gate to watch the children play. It seemed an eternity since she had been free to be a child.

"Marah! Come at once," the now angry voice called out again.

She had delayed too long. Lifting the heavy braids off her neck in an impatient gesture, Marah turned and walked slowly toward the house. A rivulet of perspiration ran down her back.

Like other things around the house, the wooden door to their dwelling was in need of repair. It hung loosely on worn leather hinges. Marah moved it carefully as she slipped inside and stood quietly.

A narrow ray of sunshine spilled into the darkness and fell upon the rounded figure of a woman leaning back upon the cushions of a pallet. The petulant face was deeply creased around the mouth from constant frowns and made the woman, who was in her late twenties, appear much older.

"I am here," Marah said softly.

Immediately the woman began to gasp, as if struggling to catch her breath. At the sign of such apparent distress, Marah moved closer and touched her aunt Reba's shoulder.

"Don't touch me!" Reba roughly brushed the girl's hand away. "I can't bear to be touched when I am suffering."

Marah quickly stepped back.

"Don't stand there looking foolish. Have you never looked death in the face? Just bring me some cool water." Reba moaned again.

Her aunt was not dying, Marah was sure, yet it frightened her to think it might be serious. Reba was all she had. Turning to the water jar, Marah averted her eyes lest her aunt see the fear that sprang so quickly to the surface.

10

As she lifted the dipper, Marah was surprised to see the jar was nearly empty. It had been full this morning.

She handed the dipper to Reba who, with much effort, raised her bulk onto one elbow to drink a swallow or two.

"Aunt, the water jar is nearly empty."

The woman fell back among the cushions with another round of pitiful moans. "I feel feverish. You must go and get more water or I shall not last the night in this heat. Go to the well of Jacob and fill the water jar before it grows later."

Puzzled, Marah stared at her aunt. "The well of Jacob? But Aunt, surely the village well is closer. I could go and be back quickly."

"Did I say the village well? Don't be a dull-witted girl. If I wanted the water from the village well, I would say so. Now go!"

Marah stiffened at the insult, but still she hesitated. Reba had become unusually strict in the last few days and had forbidden her to leave the house or speak to anyone.

As if reading her thoughts, Reba raised herself up again. "You have not been out in the last few days. The walk will do you good. Take Hannah with you. You shouldn't go alone."

Still Marah lingered.

"Must you stand there wasting precious time? Go!" Reba waved her hands impatiently.

"Yes, Aunt." Marah's voice was barely audible.

Reba covered her eyes with one hand and the other hand clutched her heart. "Go quickly," she moaned.

"Will you be all right until I return? Perhaps Dorcas could stay with you?"

"Did I ask for Dorcas? I will just rest until you return. Now go!"

Puzzled and yet relieved to be free of the confinement of the small house for a little while, Marah adjusted her shawl to cover her hair, lifted the water jar to her shoulder, and moved gracefully toward the door. Her body, curving into womanhood, filled out the simple garment she wore. Even

11

in her youth she was already tall, as were most of the women of Samaria.

Marah looked back for a moment at the woman on the pallet. There was something . . . but perhaps she only imagined it. She hurried from the house and quickened her step. It would be good to talk to Hannah today.

When Marah's mother died six years before, her father grieved deeply but eventually realized his daughter needed a woman's care. He sent for his only sister, Reba, to come to Shechem and care for their household. How could they have foreseen the change her aunt would bring to their lives? Reba's small, darting eyes had never missed an opportunity to point out a fault. Two years later, when her father also died, Marah was left in the care of her aunt. Though only in her early twenties herself, it was Hannah who became Marah's surrogate mother, and through the years, it was her warmth that had made Marah's life less lonely.

As Marah neared the house of Hannah and her husband, Simon, her friend stepped out of her doorway.

"So, you finally come to see me, and with your water jar? I have missed you these past few days."

Marah shrugged slightly. "Reba wouldn't let me leave the house."

Hannah's warm brown eyes highlighted a plain square face. A gentle smile made her appear almost pretty. "Is the time of women upon you again, child?"

"No, I'm fine." She looked at Hannah eagerly. "Reba said you could go with me to get water. It is cooler now. Can you go?" She looked hopefully at her friend and waited.

"Could I refuse you any request?"

Hannah turned back into the house and reached for her own water jar.

Suddenly, Marah hesitated. "Reba is feverish but has told me to go to the well of our father Jacob for the water. I am not to go alone."

"Jacob's well?"

12

With her hand paused in midair, Hannah turned and looked closely at Marah, then snorted. "If I should live to see a hundred harvests, God willing, I shall never understand your aunt."

Hannah reached again for her water jar. "Of course I will come. Your aunt is right. You shouldn't walk so far from the village alone."

Marah waited impatiently, anxious to be away lest Reba change her mind and fetch her back to the confines of the house. She thought of the many springs that flowed nearby that fed the village well. Why would Reba tell her to go all the way to Jacob's well when she felt feverish?

Hannah interrupted as though reading her thoughts. "If Reba feels the water from the well of our father Jacob will make her feel better, let us go quickly," she said with resignation.

Hannah cared little for Marah's aunt.

"You do all the work of the household while Reba spends her time in idle pursuits and walking through the street of the merchants," Hannah said more than once. "She takes advantage of you. And all those aches and pains are in her head!"

"She gives me a home" Marah replied once.

"A home?" Hannah snorted. "And what home have you got, Reba's? It belongs to a distant kinsman. It should have been yours. You are the only child."

Marah sighed. It was difficult to defend her aunt to Hannah.

"The Levirate law requires you to keep your land within the tribe, yet Reba claims there was not a kinsman redeemer to be found who could marry you," Hannah had stated flatly. "And what will be your dowry when you do marry? How will you live when the money from the sale of the house and land is gone?"

Shaking her head with righteous indignation, Hannah looked out at the street leading to Marah's home and folded her arms. "She brings more sorrow to the house. Have you not borne enough with the death of your parents and then to be saddled with that woman?"

Marah kept silent.

"A selfish woman, that Reba." Hannah rolled her eyes at the ceiling. "Who knows what she will do."

"I will be all right." Marah said gently, smiling back at Hannah with trust in her eyes. She understood Hannah's desire to protect her, for despite prayers and hopes, Hannah's marriage to Simon had not produced any children. Hannah poured all the mother love of her nature into Marah as if she were her own.

They walked quietly for a time, their sandals making a soft slap, slapping sound in the dust of the road.

"So what is Reba's ailment this time?" Hannah said.

"She gripped her heart and said she was feverish." Marah's winged brows knitted together as she recalled the strange confrontation with her aunt.

"Did you not get water this morning?"

"Reba was to go. I have been forbidden to leave the house."

"For what reason?"

"I'm not sure. Reba has been acting rather strangely lately, perhaps because she hasn't felt well. I was cleaning the ashes out of the oven, and she called me in to send me to Jacob's well. Does the well have medicinal properties?"

"Not that I know of, child." Hannah chewed on her lower lip. She seemed about to say something and then thought better of it. She glanced furtively at Marah from time to time and then sighed heavily, pursing her lips as they continued in silence. Each was occupied with their own thoughts.

As she and Hannah neared the town gate, some of the village women stopped to watch them pass. They regarded Marah and spoke among themselves.

She decided not to pay attention, listening instead to the barking of the village dogs and soft twitter of the bulbul birds. In the distance she could hear the chirp of tree crickets. As they began the mile-and-a-half walk to the well, Marah felt a sense of adventure. She had never been to Jacob's well before.

Away from the town they enjoyed the cooler air that began to blow down the vale of Shechem.

"Perhaps someone should have stayed with Reba while I was gone," Marah murmured. "This pain seemed to come upon her so suddenly. It was different. Perhaps she shouldn't have been left alone. I offered to get Dorcas, but she didn't want her."

Hannah glanced quickly at Marah. "She will be all right, child. We will be back soon with the water she desires. It will make her feel better."

Marah nodded, reassured by Hannah's confident tone. "I try hard to do as my aunt asks, but there seems to be no pleasing Reba. Perhaps she will be in a better mood when we return."

As they walked along in companionable silence for a while, Marah's thoughts tumbled over one another. "Hannah. How did you feel when you were to marry Simon?"

"So it is marriage that occupies your mind these days!" The tone was teasing.

Marah blushed. "Well, yes and no. I mean, I merely wondered. I know that one day I shall be a bride. At least I hope I shall . . ." Her words trailed off and she looked beseechingly at her friend.

Hannah paused, studying Marah's face for a moment. "It is in the hands of God."

Marah looked up at Mount Ebal. The hands of God. Were they like her father Jared's hands, gentle and loving, yet firm when she misbehaved? Her father had always said, "Doesn't the God of all the earth know His way?" What was God's way for her?

She thought of the dream that came to her from time to time. A man, a stranger, reaching out to her. He wanted something and when she tried to get closer he disappeared. Her grandmother had believed in dreams and visions. What did it all mean?

She shook her head. *I am only a maiden. Why would the God of all the heavens be concerned with me?*

Blinking, Marah looked back at Hannah who was still speaking.

". . . If your family has chosen well for you, a marriage can be a good thing. Simon has been a kind and good husband." Hannah looked off in the distance. "I was fortunate. As the youngest of three daughters from a poor household and plain, I was almost fourteen when my marriage to Simon was arranged."

"At least you were not a maiden forever!" Marah immediately regretted her words. Only one misfortune was worse than being an unmarried maiden. She knew how much Hannah wanted a child. To be barren was a disgrace. God had closed Hannah's womb and she sadly bore the stigma of it. Marah looked quickly at Hannah, but her friend did not seem to be offended. Relieved, she fell silent again, and then a possibility entered her mind.

"Do you think that Reba will arrange a marriage for me?" She hung her head. "We have very little money."

Hannah hesitated. "How much do you understand of the sale of the property to that distant kinsman?"

"I know it mustn't pass out of the tribe of my father. That is the law. Reba said that, out of respect for Jared, the kinsman allows us to remain in the house for a small rent. He was very old and married. As my father's sister, Reba has no inheritance. Reba had to act quickly and said I must trust her to do what is right."

Marah paused to see Hannah shaking her head in unbelief.

"That is like trusting a wild dog with a chicken!" Hannah muttered half aloud.

"Reba would do the right thing for us, wouldn't she?"

Hannah sighed and continued walking. "Yes, child, I am sure she will do the right thing. And she will arrange a marriage for you one day. She is your family now that your father is gone."

Though Hannah's tone did not carry a very positive note,

Marah was comforted because of her words. Hannah would know.

At the mention of her father, tears came to Marah's eyes. It had been over a year, and she still missed him terribly, longing to hear his booming laugh and feel his gentle touch.

She looked across the fields for a moment, imagining his tall figure striding through the stalks of grain. He would scoop her up in his strong arms and carry her home when she was small. She remembered candlelit evenings sitting at her father's feet while he repaired a tool or carved something out of wood.

Then Reba came, with her complaints.

"Jared, when will you fix the roof? Don't you care if I catch my death of cold?"

"The roof is fine, Reba. I repaired it only last month."

"Jared, do you not care that I struggle to keep up this house? Marah needs to help me more."

"She does most of the work as it is, Reba. Aieee, she is only a child yet!"

"She needs to learn her duties." Reba said sternly, her lips pinched tight and arms folded over her considerable chest.

Marah's father was no match for her.

He worked his fields and patiently endured Reba's tirades. Marah recalled that he frequented one of the inns more often as the months went by. Then, two years after Reba had come to live in their home, Jared was found dead in the fields. His great heart had given out. Some men from the village gently carried him home. In her grief, Marah had turned to her aunt for comfort. It was a mistake, for Reba had no comfort to give.

"Now which of the young men in Shechem will you have for your husband?" Hannah asked, breaking her reverie. When Marah just shrugged, she added with a twinkle, "I'm sure there shall be someone, a handsome young man. Probably there shall be a rich merchant passing through who cannot live without you."

Alarmed, Marah looked at her friend. "I would not wish to leave Shechem. I pray my husband shall be from our own town!"

"Most surely, child, he will be. Perhaps the son of the shammash?"

Marah's eyes grew wide for a moment and then they both laughed. The shammash, who assisted the high priest, was a strong influence in the community, but his son was an empty-headed young man.

"Perhaps a shepherd?" Hannah murmured with a knowing glance at her companion.

Marah blushed and made a face. She turned and breathed deeply of the smells of the rich earth stirred by a welcome breeze.

Jesse. When had she not known him? When had that moment come between them when the friendship of children had slipped into the shadows? When had they become aware of one another in a way that had suddenly made her shy and him protective? Each day when she took their few sheep to him for watching, they talked shyly, prolonging the time together. One day soon, Jesse would speak to his father.

As Marah pictured Jesse's father speaking to Reba, warmth spread through her heart and an unconscious sigh escaped her lips. She looked quickly at Hannah, but her friend was looking ahead, a slight smile tugging at the corner of her mouth.

"I shall probably not marry for years!" Marah cried defensively, lifting her chin. Then they both laughed again at the improbability.

The two women didn't hurry, but walked with purpose.

Marah looked over the dry fields and saw the date palms burdened with ripe fruit. As they passed through the narrow valley, she listened to the birds that perched in the groves of olive trees. It was nice to be carefree, even for a little while.

At the point where the road climbed slightly, they paused to rest and savor the view of the Vale of Shechem. With the valley curving behind the mountains, the walls of Shechem were hidden from view. The mountains seemed to give the valley strength, forming a barrier that protected the valley from the cold winds of the north and the hot winds from the south. The waters that sustained the valley poured forth in a benevolent flow from the side of the holy mountain, Gerizim, bringing moisture and balancing the dry air of Palestine.

Marah breathed deeply again, savoring the breeze at this peaceful time of the day. Ahead she saw the well of their ancestor, Jacob, whose men had dug the well to water his flocks and herds. It stood on a windswept hill that formed the crossroads for foot travelers and caravans passing through Samaria from other lands.

Many villagers still liked to come to Jacob's well to enjoy the walk and the cooler air that blew down the vale in late afternoon. It was a well of tradition more than convenience. Both a cistern and a spring, it was fed by surface water as well as an underground stream.

The well measured seven spans of a man's hand across. Over the years, the ropes used to raise the water pots from the well had etched deep grooves into the stones forming its rim.

As Marah and Hannah approached the well, they saw three women laughing and talking together. The latest gossip, no doubt.

The women stopped talking and looked up as the newcomers drew near. After showing Marah the ropes to lower her water jar, Hannah exchanged a few words with one of the other women.

Occupied with filling her vessel, Marah paid little attention, knowing that Hannah would share any interesting news.

When she had carefully drawn up the full jar, Marah turned to call to Hannah. The teasing words caught in Marah's throat as she beheld the startled look on Hannah's face.

"Hannah, what is wrong? What has happened?"

One of the women, Leah, started to speak. Hannah silenced

her with a sharp look and a slight shake of her head as she began to lower her own water jar.

"It is nothing," Hannah said quickly, and more loudly than necessary.

Leah tossed her head and went aside with the other women to speak in animated whispers.

Glancing briefly at the other women, Hannah said offhandedly, "Leah is always the bearer of bad news. Such a gossip. I think she must make up half of it just to shock us. Come, we've been gone long enough. We must return."

As Hannah lifted her jar to her shoulder, Marah stood dumbly watching her, questions filling her mind.

Hannah walked quickly past the other women and started down into the valley. Breathless, Marah struggled to carry the full water jar while hurrying to keep up with her friend. For a moment, her concentration overcame her curiosity.

When she at last walked by Hannah's side, her attempts at conversation were met with silence. Whatever was on Hannah's mind was not going to be revealed in spite of her persistence. Marah sighed audibly. The walk on the way to the well had been more pleasant!

As they neared the street of the merchants, they passed the shop of Zibeon the sandal maker. Marah wrinkled her nose. The smell of the new leather drifted out into the street.

Glancing at her companion, Marah saw Hannah looking at the shop with a strange, hard expression on her face.

Zibeon himself stepped out of the shop. He was not dressed for work in his leather apron but rather in his Sabbath clothes. How strange, Marah thought, for this was the middle of the week, not the Sabbath or a holy day.

Zibeon's dark, brooding eyes boldly met Marah's as he leaned his large frame against the doorway, his arms folded across his great chest.

Marah knew it was wrong to stare. She should have modestly looked away, yet his eyes imprisoned hers as if she were looking into the eyes of a serpent.

"Marah!" Hannah's sharp tone broke the spell. She shuddered and quickly looked away, hurrying once more to keep up with Hannah.

"I don't like that man," Marah whispered fiercely, and almost felt she could hear his low chuckle behind her.

Hannah had looked at her sharply and then, slowing her pace, said firmly, "We must not judge, child. Perhaps he needs a wife to make his life more pleasant."

Zibeon was a widower and had not yet taken another wife, though it had been three years.

"A wife?" Marah snorted. "I would feel sorry for the woman who marries the sandal maker."

"It is not for us to judge," her friend repeated doggedly. "All things are best left in the hands of God. Look, we are almost home. I am sure Reba will be feeling better by now."

Puzzled by Hannah's attitude and the meaning of her words, Marah shook her head.

Hannah did not care for Zibeon either, yet she defended him. This was a strange day.

At the end of the street, the two friends parted. When Marah was almost to her door, she turned and saw Hannah still standing at the end of the street watching her. She waved, but Hannah turned and went to her own house.

With a heavy heart and questions chasing themselves around in her head, she entered the doorway a little anxiously, expecting to see her aunt still lying upon her mat. To her surprise, Reba was up, her best shawl about her shoulders.

Her aunt jumped when she turned suddenly and saw Marah standing in the doorway. "Must you sneak up on me like a thief?"

"You are feeling better?" Marah inquired quietly. Her eyes met Reba's but she kept her face composed. Reba suddenly looked away.

"Yes. Of course I feel better. Can you not see it is so?" She waved her hand. "The pain went away, very suddenly. I saw no need to lie about."

"I've brought the water from the well of our father Jacob, as you asked." A statement, and a question.

"You did well to return in so little time."

Marah wondered at the sudden change in disposition, but she was used to Reba's many moods. She watched patiently as her aunt moved restlessly about the room, picking things up and putting them down again, glancing from time to time at Marah as she did so.

Then Marah saw the small exquisite leather box. It was beautifully designed with little inset jewels. Her eyes widened. Never had they owned anything so costly.

"Oh. It's beautiful!"

As Marah reached out to touch the lovely box, Reba snatched it and placed it on a higher shelf.

"It was a gift," she said possessively.

Marah heard a metallic sound as Reba picked up the box. It was full off coins.

Reba turned to face her. "Marah, you may as well know. I am returning to my family in Haran." She paused, letting the words have their desired effect.

"You are going to Haran? Shall I be coming with you?" Marah felt panic rise. Reba was the only family she had.

"I am returning alone. I cannot leave you here by yourself— of course it would not be the right thing to do, would it? It has become necessary to make arrangements for you."

"Make arrangements for me?"

Reba waved a hand impatiently. "Must you echo every word? You must be about your own life, with a good husband to provide for you."

"Husband?" A shadow passed through her mind.

"Yes, child, a husband. You are of age and it is my duty as your, ah, family, to see that a marriage is suitably arranged for you. I promised your father, may he rest in peace. You should be grateful that such a fine man has asked for you at this time."

Someone had asked for her. Jesse? Had he gone to his

father? Now the full meaning of Reba's words struck her. Jesse! She caught her breath and looked expectantly at Reba.

Reba turned away from her again. "You must trust me that I know best."

Marah waited, thinking of the last time she and Jesse talked when she brought the sheep. Had Jesse asked his father to speak to Reba? Her aunt had already made the arrangements! Hope grew in her heart as she waited impatiently.

Reba took her time speaking. "He is a good man, and an able provider," Reba went on.

This was news Marah should have welcomed, yet she began to feel uneasy.

"You shall be mistress of a good house. He has done well at his trade and has only an aging mother and younger brother to provide for."

An aging mother? Younger brother? Both of Jesse's parents lived. And Jesse had no brothers or sisters. Marah's brain whirled and she thought back to the well and Hannah's face.

A strange sense of foreboding gripped her as, with a small, almost inaudible voice, she asked, "Who is to be my husband?"

"Zibeon the sandal maker!" Reba crowed triumphantly.

2

"Zibeon has chosen you of all the marriageable girls in the village," Reba declared brightly, ignoring the look of horror on Marah's face. "Think how lucky you are!"

Marah stared at her aunt and felt tears fill her eyes. "The sandal maker? Please, let it not be Zibeon!" she implored. "He frightens me. He is not a kind man. I have heard things. Please, I will do anything . . . anything! I do not want to marry him. I could stay with Simon and Hannah. They would welcome me."

Reba's eyes narrowed. Taking Marah by the shoulders, she shook her. "Be still. Why should Hannah's husband be burdened with an extra mouth to feed? You know nothing of these matters. Where is your respect for your elders? The matter is already settled and I have agreed. Zibeon is a fine choice. You are a foolish girl to listen to groundless tales!"

Terror gave Marah boldness. Shaking her head she cried, "I cannot marry him, I cannot!"

Reba's grip on Marah's shoulders tightened. Her voice grew firmer. "Who are you to tell me you cannot?" Reba demanded. "You will do as I tell you! I have assured Zibeon that you are an obedient girl."

Marah cowered as the truth of Reba's words penetrated. Reba was all the family she had now. Hannah was right. Her aunt had the right to arrange the marriage.

She had fooled herself into thinking that Reba cared for her. After her father died, it had helped somehow. She tried to believe that Reba's coldness only covered her grief. But now, as she looked at the pinched face in front of her, she saw desperation and something more—resentment. Had Reba resented that much having to remain and care for her? Marah shuddered.

Desolation swept over her and she sobbed quietly.

She remembered a girl of the village the year before whose parents had, out of necessity, chosen a man old enough to be the girl's father. The women of Shechem had gossiped and tittered, and Marah recalled the face of the girl, stricken and pale, as she went dutifully to her wedding.

Reality filled Marah's heart like a heavy weight. Her mind raced. Zibeon was old. He was almost twenty-five. Maybe he would die before the betrothal year ended.

Drying her tears, Marah drew on all the inner strength she possessed. She would go to Hannah. Hannah would know what to do.

Reba stepped back and dropped her hands, watching her as if waiting for any further rebellion.

Marah felt her childhood drop away like a discarded garment. Resentment and pain blazed out of her eyes as she looked back at her aunt. Turning toward the door, she stood tall and, with all the strength she could muster, lifted her chin defiantly.

"I would tell Hannah of my news," she said and waited.

For a moment her aunt barred her way. Then, resigned, Reba stepped aside. She suddenly looked much older.

"Yes, by all means, go to Hannah," she said sarcastically, "but return shortly, as it is nearly time for the evening meal and you have your work to do."

Marah nodded woodenly and saw the look of relief on her aunt's face. She started slowly for Hannah's house, but with a smothered cry, broke into a run.

The sun was setting and the dry wind from the land had

begun to blow. Hannah opened the door before she could knock and gathered the sobbing girl to her.

"Hush now, child, hush," she murmured, drawing Marah into the house and closing the door against prying eyes. "So it is tears you bring to me. What can be so terrible?"

"I am to be married." Marah felt miserable.

"So, to be married. My little Marah, you shall be a bride. That is news for rejoicing, not tears."

"Hannah, you don't understand," Marah sobbed. "It is to be the sandal maker!"

Hannah's arms dropped to her side and she hung her head. "So it is true, then?"

"Why didn't you tell me at the well, Hannah?" Marah looked at her friend in disbelief. "How could you keep such news from me?"

"Oh child, I had hoped it was only gossip of Leah's making. I didn't wish to frighten you, if perhaps it wasn't true," Hannah said gently.

Marah sank down on a wooden bench and looked at her friend. She felt hopelessness draining the color from her face. "He is cruel. I have heard stories how his first wife died. All of Shechem must be whispering behind my back. No other family in the village would approach Zibeon for their daughters. Only Reba. She doesn't care for me. I saw it in her face. She only wants to be rid of me so she can return to Haran. She told me she is leaving."

"She is returning to Haran? Good riddance, I say to that woman."

Hannah continued to pat Marah's shoulder as the words poured out.

"There was a beautiful leather box. It had jewels on it. I could hear the sound of coins when Reba snatched it away. I only wanted to look at it. Zibeon has paid the bride price for me!" The words tumbled over one another.

"I am to marry Zibeon and I am afraid! I thought—I thought it was to be Jesse. I thought, I mean, we talked. I've always known that one day Jesse would go to his father; that he would ask for me. What can I do? I must get away. I must leave Shechem."

"Marah." Hannah's voice was firm as she held the girl gently by the shoulders. "And where would you go, a girl alone? How far would you get before thieves or someone worse found you? You must obey Reba or face the elders."

The thought of the elders caused her to jerk her head up. A disobedient son or daughter who defied their parents could be stoned! Reba was her aunt, but she was as her parent.

She stopped weeping and looked sadly into the face of her friend. "Is there no other way? Couldn't you or Simon speak to her?"

Hannah released Marah and looked with compassion at her tear-streaked face. In a voice full of pity and love, she said, "Child, you have no choice. Reba has taken the bride price and agreed. The *Ketubah*, the marriage contract, has been arranged. She has the right. You have no other family to speak for you."

She held Marah to her again. "A cunning shrew that one. You can't have much of a dowry, but there is not a young man in the village who hasn't looked your way more than once."

Putting a finger gently under Marah's chin, she tilted her face up and looked at her earnestly. "Marah, I had hoped Leah's gossip was not true, but word went out across the village this afternoon that Zibeon was on his way to Reba's to ask for you and that Reba had already spoken to him. His bride price was four minas!"

Marah gasped. A mina was worth sixty shekels! Two hundred forty shekels was an unheard-of price for a poor girl with no family to speak of.

Then her mind reeled. The journey to the well, Reba's sudden pains, and Zibeon in his Sabbath clothes. The picture came to her clearly. She shuddered with grief and felt hatred for her aunt.

"Reba laid her plans carefully," Hannah continued softly, yet angrily. "No one knew, until today."

Least of all me, Marah thought.

Then she remembered. Jesse would be coming in from the hills with the sheep. Had he heard the news? Jesse's parents could never afford a bride price of 240 shekels. Surely if his father had spoken to Reba, Jesse would have told her. She pictured Jesse receiving the news of her betrothal. The anguish on his face would mirror her own. Marah's young heart ached for him. She remembered the look on Zibeon's face earlier in the day and shuddered again.

When Marah was calm, Hannah dried her eyes and gave her a small cup of wine for strength. Then Simon kindly led her home through the now darkening street.

Later, as Marah and her aunt shared the evening meal, only the occasional sounds of the animals settling for the night broke the silence between them. Marah dipped her bread in the vegetable stew, but as she swallowed, the bite seemed to stick in her throat. She stared at her meager meal.

Reba, after attempting conversation once or twice and receiving no response, left her alone. Marah started to dip her sop in the stew again only to put it down again.

Reba was in one of her rare good moods. *Why shouldn't she be?* Marah thought bitterly. *She's gotten what she wanted, to be rid of me and have money to return to Haran.*

"There is much to do," Reba said, ignoring Marah's tearstained face and silent desolation. "In the morning be sure the bread is set out to rise and then take the sheep out to the shepherd."

The shepherd. Jesse. It was dark now and the sheep were already back in their pen. He'd come and gone while she was at Hannah's.

She must talk to him!

"You may also straighten the house tomorrow," Reba continued. "You may as well get used to my choice. You'll see it is for the best. I promised your father I would arrange your marriage when the time came, if anything happened to him.

I have done so. You should be proud of the status you will have in the village."

Reba got up and began to busy herself with her things. Marah knew she was thinking of Haran and her journey.

My status in the village. Marah shook her head. *They are full of pity for me. No girl in the village wishes to be in my place.*

She got up quietly and began to straighten their few meal-time vessels. Marah could not trust herself to speak to Reba with tears so close to the surface. Only her strong will forced them back to the confines behind her eyes. Reba would not have the satisfaction of seeing her tears again.

When her evening tasks were finished, Marah crept up the steps to the roof of the small house where her meager pallet lay. At least with the warm weather she had a place to herself and on this night especially, she wanted to be away from her aunt.

Marah knelt down on her pallet and looked up at the night sky. A bird sang its bittersweet song and the moon poured its light on her face as the unbidden tears came once again and journeyed in wet furrows down her cheeks.

She saw Jesse's face as they spoke so earnestly only a few days before. His parents must not have agreed, she told herself miserably.

Then a thought came to her. Perhaps they had come. Had they approached Reba but the bride price had not been enough? Zibeon was a prosperous merchant. Jesse's parents were poor. Reba must have refused Jesse's father if she had already approached Zibeon. Two hundred forty shekels. It was more than enough to buy the bride of Zibeon's choice.

Thought after thought raced through her mind until, exhausted, Marah lay quietly in the shadowy darkness. In the stillness she listened to the beating of her heart and thought of her father. She pictured herself sitting on his lap, in the protection of his big arms. How safe she had felt when troubles came into her small world.

"Oh Papa," she whispered in the darkness, "what is to become of me? You would have picked Jesse. You would not want me to be so unhappy."

Warmth came softly over her like a presence. She had felt it before at the death of her mother and then her father. Like loving arms wrapped around her. Filled with a small sense of peace and somehow comforted, she fell asleep.

Marah awoke as the cock crowed the dawn.

During the restless night, the dream had come to her again. She was walking down a long, dusty road and there was someone waiting for her. His face seemed shadowy, but there was no fear. He reached out his hand to her, and as she in turn reached out to him, wanting to speak to him, the dream faded. She shook her head as if to clear away the wisps of memory and sleep.

Dressing quickly, Marah paused, looking out over the parapet at the quiet town. She went down the narrow steps reluctantly, each step bringing her closer to something that loomed before her like a nameless dread. She went to the small courtyard to grind the grain for bread flour. As she took a handful of kernels and began to crush them on the smooth stone, the events of the previous evening played through her mind. It all seemed like a bad dream. Perhaps today she would find it was only that.

She mixed the coarse meal with water, salt, and a little fermented dough from the previous day for leaven, then kneaded the mixture and set it aside to rise. She sprinkled feed for the few chickens and thought about what to do. She knew she must talk with Jesse when she took the sheep to him today. Did he know about Zibeon? He must, if the rest of the village knew. What would he say?

She was gathering the sheep from the small pen when Reba at last appeared in the doorway. Marah looked at her warily, but Reba smiled benignly, as if she could afford to be gracious on this morning of all mornings.

She bustled over to Marah. "I have important matters to attend to in the marketplace. These things take great care."

She fussed with her shawl, brushing imaginary things from it. "There are neighbors to invite since your betrothal will be sealed tonight. After you have taken the sheep to the shepherd, look for some wild mustard and bring home a large bunch. Our supply of mustard oil is almost gone."

Then as an afterthought, "You may go alone. No one will bother you. They would answer to Zibeon!"

Something in the way she said his name, the way she drew it out, caused Marah to look more closely. Reba had a faraway look on her face. She heaved a large sigh before she looked down at her niece again.

Marah lowered her eyes quickly, her mind racing. Reba had eyes for him! Marah's heart pounded. Reba wanted him. But if Reba had set her eyes on Zibeon, why had she not sought to marry him herself?

Suddenly it became clear. He had refused her. Had Reba arranged the marriage to save her pride? Was it revenge? Against Marah or Zibeon? He would not consider it revenge. She had seen it in his eyes. He wanted her.

Overwhelmed at the revelation, Marah barely heard Reba's final words.

"We will have guests this evening for your betrothal ceremony. The wedding will take place when the harvest is in."

Marah only nodded her head dumbly and looked away lest Reba see what she knew.

Reba turned toward the marketplace. Marah looked back and watched her as she walked briskly down the road, and fought the hatred that burned like a fire in her belly. It was only about seven months until harvest. Reba was not even going to give her the full year of betrothal!

After checking once again on the rising dough, she quickly tucked her mantle into her girdle and grabbed her staff. Calling to the sheep, she began to lead them hurriedly toward the hillside. She knew where to find the wild mustard, and Jesse.

3

The young shepherd sat on a rock and looked out over the sheep without seeing them. He was tall and slender with warm brown eyes beneath a shock of golden blond hair. The hair was a rarity that occurred infrequently among the Samaritan tribes. His high cheekbones and firm jaw were accented by the scowl that creased his face.

The scowl seemed to melt as Marah approached. He jumped up eagerly. "You have not brought the sheep for many days," he said with a forced smile.

"Reba would not let me leave the house. She was feeling ill."

"She is ill when it pleases her," Jesse growled.

"Oh Jesse, let's not quarrel. I came to talk to you. I have sad news."

Jesse looked away from her toward the hills, his fists clenched tightly. "It is all over the village that you are to marry the sandal maker."

"I am afraid of him. I know God chooses His own way, but I had not wished for Zibeon. I had thought . . . I thought . . ." She searched his face beseechingly as he turned back to her.

"I did speak to my father," Jesse said slowly. "It was too late. Reba had accepted the bride price from Zibeon and agreed to the marriage. I didn't know. If only I had spoken sooner, if only . . ."

Jesse told her of the scene with his father the night before.

He asked his father to go to Reba and speak for him. It all seemed so simple. They would not be surprised in his choice, for Marah was favorable in their eyes.

"I know we are poor," Jesse told his father earnestly, "but they are also poor and I know you can reach a bride price her aunt will accept. Now that their property is sold, I do not have to worry about the Levirate law. I will work hard to take care of her." He had looked at his father confidently, sure that they would follow his wishes.

A look passed between his parents and Jesse was bewildered as his father hesitated before speaking.

"Is she not acceptable, Father?"

"She is truly an acceptable maiden, my son. Had you spoken earlier, I would have gone without hesitation. But it is not possible to speak for her now."

Elon looked sadly at his son, and put his hand on Jesse's shoulder. "She is betrothed as of this day, to Zibeon, the sandal maker."

"No!" Jesse cried out from the depths of his soul. "No! How can this be? She would not choose Zibeon . . . When could this have happened?" He searched one face and then the other.

His mother spoke gently, "The village has known since this morning, my son. Zibeon boasted that he had waited for her and the bride price would be acceptable to her aunt. The *mohar* is more than we could possibly pay. Two hundred forty shekels! There is nothing we can do."

"Two hundred forty shekels? Reba has *sold her* to Zibeon! How could she do this?" Jesse cried to his father. "There must be something you can do!"

Jesse's father drew himself up and looked at Jesse sternly. "My son, it is God's will. You must now not covet that which belongs to another. Reba has the right to arrange a marriage as she feels best for Marah. You will not interfere! Your mother and I will seek a bride elsewhere for you. There is a young woman from among our cousins in Sebaste. Her name is Tirzah. I have heard that she is a virtuous and worthy young woman. Your mother and I will travel to Sebaste to speak to her parents."

Jesse's father gripped his shoulder in a gesture of understanding and then left Jesse to deal with his feelings alone.

Now, looking at Marah, his anger made him bold. "I don't want another bride. You have lived in my heart since we were children. How can God take you away from me?"

Then Jesse hung his head. "I knew it was useless to argue with my father."

Like Marah, he had been raised to be obedient, respecting his parents and the law. "If my thoughts against Zibeon were so many poisoned arrows," he growled, leaving the sentence unfinished.

Trying to think of something to say to him, Marah's eyes grew misty. "Do you remember how we met, Jesse?"

He nodded. "You were only about six. I was much older and wiser—ten," he smiled ruefully. "You had wandered away from the mourners after the death of your mother. You were sitting in the tall grass, weeping."

Marah smiled at the memory. "You wiped away my tears and gently led me back to my house and the arms of my father. He was so overcome with grief, he hadn't seen me go."

"He was nearly beside himself with worry when they couldn't find you," Jesse said.

As he looked down at her face, Jesse paused a moment, his eyes revealing his feelings. "I saw in the child the beauty of the woman to come," he murmured huskily. "When you looked up at me so trustingly, I gave you my heart. I knew even then, you would be the one I would marry."

They stared at each other a long moment.

"I hurried to bring the sheep to you each day just so we could talk." She smiled shyly.

34

"We were children. We were friends."

Marah nodded, thinking back to those years that seemed to have passed so quickly. She too had known that Jesse was the one who held her heart. Somehow between them there was an understanding, but her aunt had changed that now.

"How I hate her!" Jesse said, clenching his fist.

Marah, startled by his vehemence, suddenly realized he was also thinking of Reba. She shook her head sadly. If only Jesse had spoken sooner. God did not will them to be together.

"My parents travel even now to Sebaste to make the arrangements for my betrothal to a cousin. Her name is Tirzah." He shook his head. "If only I had not waited. If only I had gone to my father sooner. How could I know about Zibeon?" He sat down suddenly on a nearby rock.

The pain in her heart was tempered by a small gladness. He had gone to his parents. It was just too late. She sighed. There was nothing that either of them could do. How could they have foreseen what different paths their lives would be taking?

"There is so little time, Jesse. Reba has set the wedding date for after the fall harvest."

"She does not give you the full year?" His face showed the anguish he felt.

Marah watched him struggle with his emotions. He remained quietly regarding her, and then with a sigh, he smiled at her.

"Marah, I have something for you. You must take great care." He bent down and lifted a stone near the tree. Taking out a small bundle wrapped in lambskin, he held it out to her.

Her eyes grew wide as she anxiously unwrapped the gift. Jesse had carved another flute. She thought of the first small flute Jesse had carved for her out of olive wood, and of her joy when he placed it in her hands.

"Oh Jesse, you can carve anything! It is so beautiful," she had cried, her face radiant as she carefully took the little flute. She had few possessions, making this a wondrous gift.

35

Covering the small holes with her fingers, Jesse showed her how to hold it and blow gently, producing the notes. She had kept it hidden under her pallet, taking it with her when she took the sheep to the fields. Then, one day, as she returned, it had fallen out of the folds of her mantle. Reba had snatched it up and noted the fine workmanship.

"Where did you get this?" she demanded.

"The shepherd made it for me. He carved it." Marah waited anxiously for Reba to return the flute.

"You have more important duties to attend to while looking after the sheep, such as making sure we have enough yarn! You can spin from your distaff to the spindle if you have that much free time. You are too old for such foolishness!" Reba chastised.

Marah watched helplessly as her aunt bore the beautiful little flute away and hid it somewhere among her things. With a sigh, Marah turned away, wondering what to tell Jesse.

When Jesse noticed the absence of the flute, she had told him sadly where it had gone.

Anger blazed on Jesse's young face. "Reba took the flute away?" He would not let Marah make excuses for her. "Are you the only one in the village who cannot see what kind of a woman she is?"

"Reba is all the family I have," Marah reminded him.

Jesse snorted in disgust.

It seemed like only yesterday. Then, aware Jesse was speaking again, she turned from her thoughts.

Venting his anger, Jesse almost spat the words. "So now Reba arranges a marriage for you to Zibeon. He is too old for you! When I think of the two of you together and the wedding." He paused and Marah lowered her eyes. "If Zibeon hurts you—" His voice trailed away as if he could not speak the thoughts he contemplated in his heart.

The bleating of the sheep brought Marah back to reality.

She ran her hands gently over the new little flute, feeling its smoothness. "Oh Jesse, I shall treasure it always." Wrapping the flute gently in the lambskin, she would have taken it with her, but then she remembered Reba. She looked sadly from the flute to Jesse.

Sensing her dilemma, Jesse gently took the flute and put it back under the stone. "It will be our secret. Reba shall never know."

Marah nodded and tried to smile. "It will be our secret, Jesse. I will always remember you as my friend."

"And I shall remember you as my friend," he answered.

Marah looked into his earnest face. She could not touch him she knew, but like gentle fingers, her eyes caressed his face.

Rising slowly, she adjusted her mantle. "I must cut some wild mustard to take home."

Jesse glanced at the sheep, grazing peacefully, and surveyed the surrounding pasture. All was peaceful.

"Let me help you," Jesse offered. It would prolong the time.

They walked together on the hillside, cutting the wild plants and glancing back from time to time to make sure all was well with the sheep.

"I must return. I am to prepare the house for our betrothal ceremony tonight. Oh Jesse, I . . ." She strove to hold back the tears and be strong for them both.

The anguish in his face nearly broke her, but she knew she must not allow Jesse to embrace her. She was a betrothed maiden, and if anyone saw them, she would be compromised.

Greater than their longing to touch one another was the fear of consequences. She knew Jesse would protect her every way he knew.

"God go with you, Marah," Jesse said, stepping back. He stood tall and straight. Marah thought he had never looked so handsome.

"God be with you also, Jesse," she said. Turning away, she held her tears until she was far enough away. She did not look back.

4

Zibeon was in fine spirits. He and his brother Shimei had consumed several cups of wine. Usually Shimei skulked about the house and stayed out of Zibeon's way. They had never gotten along, even as children, and there were frequent quarrels between them. Zibeon had taken out his temper on Shimei on more than one occasion, but Shimei never told on his older brother. It wouldn't have done him any good. Their mother, Athaliah, doted on her eldest son and catered to him. He was the image of her late husband. Shimei, on the other hand, was secretive and spent a great deal of time to himself. He had been a sickly child who wearied her as she struggled to raise two boys alone. She was fortunate that Zibeon, already big for his years, had been taught well by her husband and could keep the sandal shop going. She had not been forced to seek another husband.

Enjoying the respite from Zibeon's temper, Shimei toasted his brother, flattering him over his good fortune. Zibeon was so pleased with himself he didn't seem to notice that it was Shimei he was slapping on the back and boasting to.

"A wife to make a man's senses turn. More wine, woman!" he bellowed at Athaliah.

It was the closest the brothers had been since they were children. While widowed several years before, Zibeon had ignored Athaliah when she brought up the subject of re-marriage. Tonight she was delighted that her favorite was to finally marry again.

Athaliah poured more wine. She had cooked Zibeon's favorite dishes and bustled about the house bursting with pride. She bragged to neighbors that at last she would have the grandchild she longed for.

When Zibeon married the first time, Athaliah had jealously berated the girl, Rizpah, and reproved her for her constant sad face. Zibeon scowled for a moment as he recalled the frail, long-faced girl his parents had chosen for him, forever weeping. In spite of his lusty efforts, she shrank from him always. Rizpah's constant weeping, and cries of pain any time that he sought the comforts of a husband, frustrated and angered him. After two years of marriage, Rizpah had shown no signs of producing the son that Zibeon wanted so badly.

"I shall go into my old age with no grandchild to comfort me," Athaliah wailed until Zibeon finally threatened to wring her neck.

"Am I God Himself that I can give you grandchildren?" he flung back at her angrily.

Rizpah became gaunt and hollow-eyed. His mother continued to chide her for her weakness.

"You must eat. You will become ill. Don't be a foolish girl. You must make up your mind to get well and take up your duties as a wife to Zibeon."

Day after day, the ungrateful girl lay quietly on her pallet. Athaliah's rebukes fell on deaf ears for the girl's eyes remained closed and there was no answer. Frustrated, Zibeon came each evening after his work to stand at the foot of her bed, watching for some sign. Then after a few moments, with a snort of disgust, he would sit at the table and nurse his cup of wine, muttering about the frailty of women. At last, one early morning, in spite of all Athaliah's efforts, Rizpah turned her face to the wall, gave one last, long sigh, and died.

"No maiden in the village interests me," Zibeon bellowed at Athaliah when her nagging became too much.

"You do well in your shop, my son. There is not a maiden in the village who would not be pleased to be chosen," Athaliah wheedled.

"Silence, woman. I will choose when it suits me. No more of your incessant chatter."

Zibeon drew himself up and scowled so fiercely that Athaliah backed quickly away. He threw a bowl at her feet and stormed out.

Now Athaliah hovered over him. "She will give you strong sons. I shall have my grandchildren at last." She beamed. "That Rizpah, always so pale, and always with such a sad face . . ."

"Be still, woman," Zibeon growled.

His mother ignored the warning. "She was bound to make you unhappy with all that weeping. Two years of marriage and not a child to comfort me in my old age, the shame of it." Athaliah raised martyred eyes to the ceiling. "And the foolish girl would not eat. I told her a hundred times a day she should keep up her strength so she could be a proper wife to you." She shrugged her shoulders and spread her hands in puzzlement.

Shimei, seeing the thunder building on Zibeon's face, feared an explosion. Hurriedly grabbing the wine, he proposed another toast to his brother's good fortune. Fortunately for Athaliah, she was easily distracted and hastened to put more food on Zibeon's plate.

Zibeon stared at his wine, thinking of the mothers that hurried their daughters past his shop as though he had some great plague, daughters who averted their eyes.

"Simpering, useless females," Zibeon had grumbled to Shimei. "I don't need any of them."

Then he had seen Marah. Her face stayed in his mind for days. Zibeon watched for her and tried to be friendly, but like the others she averted her eyes and hurried past his shop. Day after day his frustration grew.

Reba came to the shop on a day when Zibeon was angry with Athaliah. He was pounding forcefully on the leather with a mallet, trying to make a hole with his awl. Weary of his mother's constant nagging, he was taking his anger out on the thick leather. From the corner of his eye, he saw Reba coming toward the shop and cursed under his breath. She came many times, too many times it seemed, to purchase small leather items. She was cunning and brash, but they understood one another. Her attentions flattered his ego at times, and he let her flirt. She hinted at marriage, but she didn't appeal to him. Now her niece, Marah, that was a different matter.

"She no longer has the figure of a child," he had murmured one day to Shimei. "Soon she will be eligible for marriage. She dislikes me, I know, but it only makes her more interesting." Like the lion that waits and watches its prey, waiting for the right moment to strike, Zibeon would bide his time.

With a nod from Zibeon, Shimei moved back into the shadows of the shop as Reba planted herself in front of Zibeon.

"You must work every moment?" she had asked coyly.

With great care, Zibeon put down his tools and looked at her. "There is something you need?" he asked in a low voice.

She did not miss his meaning as he rose to his full height and looked down on her, enjoying her momentary discomfort.

"Would I interrupt such a man at his work for no reason?" she said with a slow smile. "You are a strong man, Zibeon. It is a shame for you to be alone. You should have a wife to comfort you after a hard day at work." Reba almost smirked.

Zibeon sighed irritably and sat down again, picking up his tools. He was not in the mood to be bothered with Reba's barely disguised hints at marriage today. Perhaps if he ignored her, she would go away.

"I have a proposition." Her voice had been low, conspiratorial. "Is there someplace we can talk?"

"Say what you have to say now. I am a busy man," he growled.

She smiled, anticipating his reaction. "It concerns my niece. Do you wish to talk here?"

At the mention of Marah, Zibeon's head came up sharply. She had gotten his attention.

Reba looked around to be sure no one was near, and didn't see Shimei. "She is now of an age to be betrothed. I wish to return to Haran to my family. I am tired of this village. Perhaps we can do business?"

Zibeon licked his lips. So his interest in the girl had not escaped Reba's attention. She was shrewd. She knew how to get to the heart of a matter.

"What do you need to return to Haran?" He also got to the point.

"A large sum, Zibeon, a worthy price for such a beautiful bride."

They looked at each other for a moment in their unity of thought.

"You are right. We cannot talk here," Zibeon murmured, knowing Shimei was listening to the entire scene.

"I will send the girl for water to Jacob's well tomorrow at this time. It is a long walk. I'm sure she will be gone long enough. I will be waiting," Reba smirked.

"Tomorrow at this time," Zibeon answered, his gruff voice dangerously soft.

Two women were headed their way and Reba pretended to examine a pair of sandals. "I have not seen anything that interests me," she said loudly. "Perhaps tomorrow."

"I'm sure you will find something tomorrow," Zibeon answered in the same tone and watched her walk away, her ample hips twitching as she walked. As he moved to the back of the shop, he eyed Shimei, daring him to mention a single word. Shimei spread his hands in a depreciating gesture and moved away. Zibeon looked through one or two baskets until he found what he was looking for. He unwrapped the soft leather covering and held up a beautifully carved leather box with inset jewels. He examined it carefully and nodded his head. He stood for a moment, savoring his thoughts, and then returning to his stool, he picked up his tools. He brought the mallet down again forcefully on the awl.

Now the betrothal ceremony was over. He had only to bide his time. Zibeon continued to muse, ignoring his mother and brother. He had what he wanted. Let his mother's words flow over and around him like a small breeze. Let her celebrate. He had the wife of his choosing and Athaliah would have her grandchildren. He nodded to himself and lifted his cup of wine.

Across the village, Marah also thought of the betrothal ceremony. She had served the guests with downcast eyes, her mind troubled. Even when the betrothal scrolls were signed, she couldn't bear to look at Zibeon. She had already determined to be a dutiful wife, and tried to convince herself that perhaps the rumors about his first wife were untrue. Perhaps he had changed. Casting about in her mind, she sought for all the positive things that she could find, yet that night she trembled inwardly when he was near her. She watched Zibeon partake freely of the wine that was offered, and now and then he would glance her way from under his heavy brows. She looked away. Whenever he tried to get near her, she would find an excuse to move elsewhere.

Reba circled Zibeon, laughing a little too quickly at his remarks, bending a little too close as she fussed over him pouring the wine, exclaiming how pleased she was with her new nephew. Marah wondered if their neighbors and friends saw through the transparency as easily as she did. Once or twice she caught some of the women whispering among themselves and nodding knowingly toward Reba and Zibeon. Then their eyes turned toward Marah who looked away and busied herself. She did not need or want their pity!

Suddenly, Marah looked up to find Zibeon directly in front of her. The smell of the wine was strong, and he bent over her with a smile that turned to a scowl when he saw the fear in her eyes. He bent to whisper a few words and then with a laugh turned away.

Marah went white and Hannah, standing with Simon as witnesses to the betrothal, saw the brief scene and moved quickly to Marah's side.

"Child, you are pale. What has happened?"

Marah felt she was going to be ill. She wanted to scream and run out of the house, losing herself in the dark hills. Hannah took her arm and hissed, "Smile!" in her ear as she firmly propelled Marah to her aunt. Hannah looked Reba in the eye.

"Our bride-to-be is clearly overcome with all the excitement. Perhaps she should rest?" It was more of a demand than a question.

Reba was at first irritated and then, seeing that Marah was on the verge of fainting, chose to be benevolent. It would never do for the girl to be visibly sick at this moment. She dismissed them with a cursory wave of her hand.

"It is time for our bride to rest. So much excitement," she purred as she moved among the guests, urging more wine and food as Hannah and Marah went quickly up the steps to the roof of the house. They could hear as the guests began to drift away to their own homes.

"Ah . . . a fine match, Reba."

"You have done well for the girl."

As though there had never been such a betrothal event and never a more gracious hostess.

Marah heard Zibeon's voice as he too departed, but it was low and she could not make out the words.

Marah stood quietly, with Hannah's hand upon her shoulder. She calmed herself, taking deep breaths of the cool evening air. Staring out into the night, she was rigid with unshed tears.

"Child, what did he say to you?" Hannah whispered.

"Oh Hannah, I am so afraid." Marah looked up, shuddering slightly as she relived the moment, and bitterly repeated the words.

"'Soon, little bird, you will not be able to flee from me!'"

5

Marah knew Jesse would be leaving soon for the village of his father-in-law. Still, she hoped to speak with him one last time. She had waited until the middle of the day when the village was quiet. Reba slept in the heat of the day and Marah watched to be sure she was asleep. Reba snored loudly. Quietly, Marah slipped out the door and with one last fearful look about, covered her head with the dark shawl and hurried away by a path behind the village. She took a water jar to cover her steps should Reba wake and miss her.

Her heart pounded as she moved quickly through the trees to the hillside where she could hear the soft bleating of the sheep. Was Jesse still there? Had the new shepherd taken over the flocks? Marah chewed her lower lip as she thought of Jesse's betrothed. She knew he had already met Tirzah at his ceremony.

"Is she . . . pretty?" Marah asked Hannah.

"She has a kind face," Hannah replied tactfully. "She is not too plain, and seems to have a good temperament. She will make him a good wife."

Now Marah climbed the hill and saw to her relief that it was indeed Jesse with the sheep. He was playing the *kinnor*, a small lyre, to soothe the animals. It reminded her of the small flute he had carved for her. She wondered if it was still

46

hidden. As she watched him from behind a tree, she looked cautiously behind her to see if she had been followed or anyone at all was in sight. There was no one.

Jesse must have been thinking of the flute also, for in a moment he put down his lyre and walked over to the rock. He stood looking down for a moment and then after glancing around, lifted the rock and took out the lambskin bundle. He was standing there, looking down at it when Marah walked up quietly and stood in front of him.

"I also wanted to see the little flute. I'm glad it is still there."

"Marah!"

She looked furtively around. Her head was covered with the dark shawl to keep from being recognized as she went to find Jesse. Now she felt like there were eyes hidden in the trees and behind the rocks. Someone would see them. After hesitating for a moment, with a show of boldness, she set down the water jar and eased back her shawl. The sun made highlights in her hair.

Jesse almost reached out to touch it and pulled his hand back as though burned by the fire of her dark tresses.

"Jesse. I . . . I wanted to speak to you. I knew I would find you here."

He looked down, a bit embarrassed by being caught looking at the flute.

She spoke again. "I know we should probably not talk, but I heard you were leaving the village. I wanted to say goodbye."

"Yes, I'm leaving," he said, his eyes still on her shining hair, "to be an apprentice to Tirzah's father. I will be learning to be a carpenter." He shrugged self-consciously. "Can you imagine me, a shepherd, making tables and tools?"

Marah smiled. "You'll be a good carpenter, Jesse. You are very good with wood. I know you will do well. I . . . ah . . . wish you good fortune in your marriage and that your wife will bear you sons." She stumbled over the word "wife."

Jesse tried to return the blessing but found the words stuck in his throat. Marah realized he could not wish her well in her marriage, nor could he wish her children by Zibeon.

"Thank you," he answered lamely.

Marah ran her fingers over the smooth surface of the little flute. She wanted to put it to her lips and play on the beautiful instrument that had been carved by Jesse's gentle hands.

But knowing it would call attention to them, she sighed and carefully wrapped it in the lambskin. Jesse placed the flute back in the hole and moved the rock over it.

"It will be our secret," Marah repeated as before. "Perhaps someday I'll be able to come for the flute and play it." Then she sighed again. "Flutes are for shepherds and children, and I'll be a married woman. There will be no time for playing a flute."

His longing reached out to her like tangible warmth, but he did not touch her. For a long moment they looked at each other, and then she turned and covered her hair with the shawl. Jesse must not see her tears. He also turned away, looking out over the sheep for a long moment.

"Goodbye, Jesse." She struggled to keep her voice from quavering.

"Goodbye . . . Marah." His voice was muffled.

Marah grabbed the water jar and fled.

6

The time of the barley harvest was nearly over. Every farmer in the village was harvesting his crop. The women exchanged bits of news and gossip as they worked. Some tossed the grain into the air from their baskets and let the wind float away the chaff. Others used a threshing board, letting the children ride on it for extra weight as the oxen moved in wide circles over the grain. Some gathered the sheaves and other women cooked, bringing out the food at midday when everyone would stop for a noontime prayer and refreshment. It was a time when the whole village worked together.

The workers harvested the family fields. As Marah moved gracefully about her tasks, she was aware that she was pleasing in the eyes of the men, young and old. During the harvest, many a maiden had been caught in the fields alone by an amorous young man and a hasty wedding had ensued. Simon watched over Marah as a father would, and Hannah stayed close by, but no one in the fields would bother her—they were all afraid of Zibeon. Many of them had been the recipient of his temper on occasion, and it was not an incident to be easily forgotten.

The days passed far too quickly. The last of the harvesting would be over and the time of the wedding was approaching. Working from dawn to dusk, Marah fell upon her pallet at night in exhausted sleep. Sometimes she slept soundly out of sheer weariness, but from time to time her strange dream occurred. It was always the same. Walking down a long road with that mysterious person waiting for her. It was not a person to be feared. As she walked toward the man, she felt only peace. He held out his hand to her and smiled, but as she went to reach for his hand, she awoke. Marah puzzled over the dream, but was strengthened when the dream occurred. Soon, with the preparations for the wedding, she put it out of her mind. She had no time to think of strange dreams.

Reba remade her beautifully embroidered wedding dress for Marah. A garland of leaves was woven for Marah's head and soft embroidered slippers waited for her feet. Even though remaking the dress was a way to conserve the bride price for herself, Reba was a prideful woman and did not want anyone to say that she had not done her best for her niece. Reba was already aware of gossip in the streets when she went by. She held her head high and played the role of the gracious aunt to the end.

"I will be shaking the dust of this town of Shechem from my feet soon enough," Marah once heard her mutter to herself.

A craftsman made the headband of coins that would be part of Marah's dowry. It waited in the jeweled leather box. There was little that Marah would bring with her except for her wedding coins, the animals, and the candlesticks. The candlesticks! Marah thought of how Hannah had related the incident and smiled in spite of herself.

Hannah came in search of Marah and saw Reba with the candlesticks, trying to quickly put them out of sight. Fortunately, Hannah knew they had belonged to Marah's mother.

"Ah, Jerusha's candlesticks!" she proclaimed loudly. "Marah shall be proud to bring these to her new household."

Hannah gently but firmly took the candlesticks out of Reba's hands. Ignoring the woman's sharp look of anger, she held them up and praised their fine quality.

"I was merely putting them in a safe place," Reba blustered.

"Of course Zibeon will be pleased!" She shot Hannah a look of pure hatred, but placed the candlesticks among Marah's household goods.

The day before the wedding, Shimei came to take the small flock of sheep and the three goats to Zibeon's pens. One of the sheep was killed and dressed for the wedding feast. Reba wanted to keep the sheep and goats to sell, but she dared not go against Zibeon, and he made it clear he expected the animals in his pens. The chickens were carried away squawking. He didn't miss anything that would add to his wealth. And there had been a scene over them.

Marah was on the roof the day Zibeon came, and she crouched back from the parapet not wishing to give her presence away.

"Why haven't the animals been brought to my pens?" Zibeon demanded.

"Ah, Zibeon, surely you can spare a goat and a few sheep?" Reba's voice was wheedling.

Then Marah heard Zibeon's low growl of anger and saw him take Reba by one arm, pressing his fingers painfully into her flesh.

"That was not our agreement. Were you trying to sell them, Reba?"

"You are hurting me, Zibeon. Let go of my arm. It was only a thought. Of course I will see that the animals are brought to you. They will go into your pens tomorrow. Of course you are entitled to the animals."

"Thanks to your bride price, you have enough money to return to Haran. As far as I am concerned, the sooner you are gone, the better!"

Marah heard the small cry of pain as he released Reba's arm and strode angrily out of the courtyard. Marah had warily glanced down and saw Reba standing there, rubbing her arm and then shaking her fist in a defiant gesture at the empty gate. Ducking down, Marah remained still until she heard Reba go into the house and then crept down from her hiding place and walked toward the door of the house as if she had just come into the courtyard.

Reba was slamming things down in the house and muttering to herself when she saw Marah come in. She stared at her as if to determine if the girl had witnessed the previous scene, and when Marah gave no indication of having seen her humiliation, she turned away again to sort and pack her things. She picked up the jeweled box and stared at it a long moment. Then she smiled and opened it, taking out the headband of coins. She laid it with the other wedding garments and, with a defiant look at Marah, rolled up the box in a bundle of clothing and placed it in her own basket.

It had been a gift, Reba had told her, so Marah shrugged and turned to help with the evening meal. Marah could not anticipate Zibeon's rage when he found out Reba had taken the box for herself.

The two women ate quietly, each absorbed in their own thoughts. Marah ate slowly as if she could somehow hold back this last night hour by hour. Finally, as she lay on her pallet, she realized that though tomorrow would come, tonight was hers alone. She looked up at the stars and the constellations that had taken their places in the night skies since the beginning of time. Was the great God of the universe aware of who she was? A simple girl of Samaria? Did He not order the heavens and the seasons that came and went year after year? He must know of the anguish in her heart and her unhappiness, yet it was He who ordered their lives according to His plan. As her father had said many times, "Does the God of all the heavens not know His way?" Somehow, her life to come was His way, and she accepted it simply. In the months that had passed, with Jesse living in Sebaste, it was easier to put him out of her heart. The friendship between them was a moment that was to be only a memory. She would close that door tightly within her. No one would touch that inner place, ever again, especially not Zibeon. He would have her body, but her spirit could never be taken by force.

7

Marah could hear Reba moving around in the house below. She stood and dressed slowly, but now the thought struck her like a knife in her heart. It was her wedding day! It had come at last in spite of her desperate thoughts willing it to wait. It would take all of her courage to get through this day and the night to come. As she stood at the parapet and looked out across the village, heaviness lay upon her heart. She stood quietly, lost in her thoughts, but her reverie was quickly interrupted.

"Marah! Come down. You will be expected to be ready for your attendants!"

Putting her few personal possessions in a small pouch to be taken by Hannah to Zibeon's house, she looked around at the small area that had been her own. The house had once echoed with laughter and love. But love was not to be hers. Jesse's face came to mind, and with all her will she pushed it away. She must not allow herself to look back. She gathered her things and slowly went down the steps.

There was a knock at the door announcing that Hannah and several neighbor women had arrived along with two of Marah's friends, Timnah and Atarah. Behind them came other women of the neighborhood. They all looked over Reba's preparations with a practiced eye. Gathering the wedding garments, they exclaimed over them in animated whispers. One woman counted the coins in the bridal headband. Marah unbound her hair as they began to dress her. Since her wedding feast was the only time she would appear in public with her hair down, her friend Atarah carefully combed the rich tresses that tumbled down.

"Such a bride, may this day be the greatest of all days, may she have many sons!" The women mouthed the expected phrases.

"Chattering chickens," Hannah murmured in her ear.

The headband of coins was carefully placed above her forehead. The veil was drawn over her face and the crown of leaves was wound around her head by Timnah and Atarah. Marah watched Reba as she glanced from time to time at her own small pile of belongings. Tomorrow the cousin would claim the lands. The house had been rented to a man in the village. Reba had made arrangements at the caravansary with a merchant's caravan that would be traveling through Haran; they would leave early in the morning. Marah knew she would probably never see her aunt again. Contemplating the thought, Marah found she had no emotions at all in regard to the woman she had shared her home with for these past few years.

"You are such a silent bride!" Timnah scolded. "It is no fun to dress someone who will not even talk to you!"

Marah turned toward Timnah. She had not been an attractive child, and as she had grown older, her long face and narrow eyes gave her the appearance of a frail bird. Her parents were seeking a husband for her, but as yet, they had not been successful. It was an important event in Timnah's life to be an attendant. Marah reached out and touched her arm.

"You are a help to me, Timnah. I know you have done everything very well. Thank you for being with me today."

Timnah brightened and blustered a little, but easily distracted, she went over to indulge herself in the food.

Atarah had a round face, a smooth complexion, and a

tendency toward plumpness, but she possessed a genuine good nature and sense of humor. Her parents had just announced her betrothal to a young man in the village. He was plain and stocky and was learning the pottery craft from his uncle. Atarah was happy enough. At least she would not be an unmarried maiden, as seemed Timnah's fate.

Marah watched the scene around her with detached curiosity. She lapsed back into silence when Timnah wandered away. She answered questions when asked, but mostly listened to the women chatter to one another as they helped Hannah and Reba see to the last-minute preparations. Marah sat in her lovely bridal dress—an oasis of silence in a desert of commotion.

Hannah spoke to her from time to time to reassure her. The girls checked and rechecked their small clay oil lamps and the small vials of extra oil that hung from their waists on cords. They must be ready with lights if the bridegroom should tarry and come after dark.

More neighboring women came. It would seem to be the one wedding all wanted to observe, to the last detail. They looked over the simple preparations with practiced eyes.

They exclaimed over Marah's dress as Reba bustled about importantly.

"The Lord be praised that you have a veil to hide such a long face! You should be more courteous to our guests!" Reba hissed in Marah's ear when the others were occupied elsewhere for a moment.

From time to time someone peered through the gate into the street. Mothers fussed at small children who ran about. Timnah and Atarah arranged and rearranged Marah's garments and fussed over her until finally Hannah shooed them away. The women whispered to one another as they observed the bride. They made a great show of being joyful for her, but Marah did not wish to meet their eyes.

As the day wore on into late afternoon, some of the older women and children dozed. A small rivulet of perspiration ran down Marah's back. Time seemed to stand still as she let her mind wander to other things. Once again she and Jesse were walking through the fields; talking while he watched the sheep. She heard the song of the little flute and the sound of the *kinnor* Jesse played to soothe the restless animals. Now and then a shrill laugh or cry from one of the children would bring her back to reality. The day seemed endless and even her attendants lapsed into silence. Timnah or Atarah would get up from time to time to see if the bridegroom was coming, but all was still.

Zibeon magnanimously furnished the wine for the men of the village who came into the inn from the fields at the end of the day. Darkness had fallen by the time the men left the inn with Zibeon. Torches lit the procession and each man carried his own candle. Villagers along the way called out greetings and good wishes, crowding upon their rooftops to get a better look at the procession. Farther down the street as they approached the home of the bride, the cry went up, "He is coming! He is coming!"

All eyes were focused on Zibeon as he approached the door. Some of the women came out to welcome him. Marah steeled herself to face her groom.

At last there was a loud knock at the door and Reba hurried to swing it open. Zibeon stood outside, dressed in his Sabbath clothes with a garland about his head. His great beard was trimmed. Forgotten were the gossip and rumors of earlier days. It was a wedding and the groom was more than presentable.

"I would see my wife!" cried Zibeon.

Marah was brought to the doorway and waited, trembling, as according to tradition, he lifted the veil.

"Ah, a treasure indeed! Rejoice with me, my friends, for a more beautiful maiden cannot be found!" The guests smiled and nodded at the expected words as Zibeon placed Marah's arm on his, holding his large hand tightly over hers as though she would run away. The bride thus captured, the procession began the walk to the house of the groom.

As the noisy wedding party approached Zibeon's house, Athaliah stepped forward to greet her new daughter-in-law, her narrow eyes boring into Marah's. Marah greeted her new mother-in-law respectfully, bearing the shrewd inspection patiently. Athaliah might not be any easier to live with than Reba, she thought, but after two years with her aunt, she felt no fear of Zibeon's mother.

"Welcome to the house of Zibeon, Daughter. We have awaited your coming with great expectations." Athaliah stepped back to allow the bride and groom to enter the house and then turned to the crowd. "May our guests enter and be welcome."

The invited guests also entered the house for the wedding and the marriage feast, and the door was shut. With more noisy good wishes and comments, the rest of the village dispersed to their homes.

Marah's attention was drawn to Zibeon's brother, Shimei. She had not seen much of him and was only vaguely aware of who he was. She knew he was unmarried as he still lived in Zibeon's house. His long sharp nose, piercing deep-set eyes, and high forehead, along with his thin body and long arms, reminded her of an owl. He had a way of hopping with a strange bouncing gait when he walked. She was trying to decide what kind of a person he was when he edged his way up to her.

"I am Shimei, Zibeon's brother," he said almost apologetically, in a soft, breathy voice. "You are very beautiful." He peered at her as one would examine a curiosity, then spoke again, half to himself, "Rizpah was beautiful too."

Marah stared at him. Was he simple-minded? Again she felt apprehensive about her new household. She knew who Rizpah was. Why in the world would he mention her at this time?

Shimei caught Zibeon's eye and, with a murmured "Welcome," melted into the crowd.

With many toasts, the wine flowed freely. Marah viewed Zibeon's drinking with alarm. Hannah tried to tempt him with more food to balance the wine. Dear Hannah. In all the celebration it was good to have one friend, at least, who knew how she really felt.

Finally the guests began to depart and her attendants came to escort Marah to the bridal chamber. As they passed Reba, Marah paused and they looked at one another. Reba's face was a mask in the candlelight. She did not move to join them. Reba opened her mouth to speak, apparently thought better of it, and remained silent. For a brief moment, Marah thought she saw compassion on Reba's face, and then Reba glanced briefly at Zibeon out of the corner of her eye and her face hardened. Regret perhaps? It was only fleeting, but Marah felt Reba would have exchanged places with her if she could. The moment passed, and with a brief nod to Marah, Reba turned away.

Stifling the fear that pounded in her throat, Marah moved woodenly toward the bridal chamber. She scarcely heard the forced cheerfulness of her companions. The embroidered wedding dress was carefully removed and she was seated on the bridal couch, clothed only in a simple shift. The girls laid the veil and garland aside with her dress. Timnah and Atarah murmured good wishes and stood awkwardly watching her. Marah knew no one wanted to be in her place tonight. They too had watched the groom as he partook of the wine and pounded his great fist on the table. Atarah and Timnah remained speechless. With a few words, Hannah excused them, and the attendants awkwardly left the room, whispering among themselves.

Hannah put her hand on Marah's shoulder and she covered the hand with her own. There was no need for words. They had already shared all that could be said many times in the last few months.

"I must go."

"Hannah . . ."

"Yes?"

"Nothing. Just thank you, for everything."

"I will pray for you, and for Zibeon." There was nothing more to do now.

Marah felt somehow abandoned.

Hannah turned to the closed door and, as if Zibeon could hear her warning, shook her fist and spoke vehemently. "If you do nothing else worthy of this child, be kind tonight!" Then, with a sigh, and one last glance back at Marah, she left the room.

Marah sat with her thoughts tumbling about her. Surely the wedding guests who still remained could hear the pounding of her heart. She gazed at the small high window. A thought passed briefly that she could climb out the window and run. But where would she go? Hannah was right. There was no place to go, nowhere to run. Then she thought of her dream. It had come again last night and thinking of it calmed her. Who was the man in the dream? Would she ever know? She sighed. Her life was as God willed. She must not question His designs.

With a start she heard the latch on the door lift. It swung open forcefully and Zibeon stood in the doorway.

PART II

Zibeon

8

Marah kneaded the bread slowly and glanced from time to time at the clay oven to check the fire that was beginning to burn down as it heated the oven for baking. Athaliah was at the marketplace to buy vegetables. It was pleasant to enjoy the peace of the morning since she didn't have to face Zibeon until late afternoon when he closed the shop. She moved her shoulders to stretch and put a hand in the small of her back. The child within her grew large as she neared her sixth month. Her belly was stretching, and as women do, she moved her hand back and forth across the taut skin. As the babe moved to her touch, she smiled.

In spite of her own barrenness, Hannah was happy for her.

"God smiles upon you, Marah. He has given you a child quickly to please your husband and make your way easier."

Marah sighed. At least the pain of that first week with Zibeon was behind her, and being practical in nature, she had accepted her lot in life. Sometimes, though, when she thought of that first night with Zibeon, she shuddered. The smell of the wine, his eager hands, and the pain within her that rolled and ebbed, the cries in the darkness that seemed to come from beyond herself. Mercifully she had fainted. She had awakened in the wee hours of the morning, her mouth dry.

Zibeon was asleep beside her, snoring noisily. Slowly, biting her lip at the jabs of pain, she had made her way to the corner of the room where a large jar of water had been placed. She drank greedily from the dipper, looking back toward Zibeon lest she make a noise that would awaken him. In the dimness of the room, she glanced down and saw shadows on her shift. As she touched one, she stifled a cry. It was dried blood. She dipped water into a small clay basin and washed herself as well as she could. Standing quietly in the darkness, she bowed her head. She was a wife now and there were duties she must bear. No one had told her what to expect. Reba would not, and Hannah must have thought Reba had borne the task, for she had not brought up the subject. Was it this way with all women, Marah wondered. Had it been this way for her own mother? Suddenly, without warning, a longing for her mother swept over her. Tears stung her eyes, but she straightened herself, willing the tears back to the depths from which they came. Her mother was gone and she herself was no longer a child. She was now Zibeon's wife and she must work hard to please him. Quietly she crept back to the bed and lay down beside Zibeon. She was so weary. Zibeon still slept soundly, and in spite of her fear, she fell asleep again.

When Marah awoke, it was with a start. Zibeon was gone. Why had he not awakened her? Her mother-in-law must think her a lazy wife not to be up before her husband and about her tasks. Feeling stronger, she got up, and looked toward the water jar. The basin of water in which she had washed herself had been emptied. For a moment she felt a rush of gratefulness toward Athaliah. Perhaps she was not all she seemed. Marah washed her face quickly in fresh water and dropped a clean garment over her head, winding the woven belt around her waist.

As Marah entered the main room of the house, she found Athaliah busily sweeping.

"Mother-in-law, forgive me. I did not mean to oversleep. What can I do to help?"

The old woman looked at her a moment with her bright eyes. "Zibeon has had his breakfast and gone to the shop. You will do the washing and see that the water jars are kept full. I will see what other tasks you are capable of. I trust Reba trained you well in the matters of a household."

"Yes," Marah answered quietly. What good would it do to tell Athaliah that she had been doing most of the tasks of their household since she was ten.

The day passed quickly with Athaliah assigning many jobs. She followed Marah around and watched everything she did.

"Have you checked each garment carefully that it is clean?" Athaliah asked needlessly. "You must hang the garments so . . ."

Each task was carefully scrutinized. It would be hard to please Athaliah. Marah bore the comments in silence. Perhaps it was difficult to have another woman come into a household. Even though Athaliah wanted a wife for Zibeon, she had cared for him for so long it was probably hard to yield to another woman. *I must let her see that I know my place*, thought Marah. *Surely in time I will gain respect in the eyes of my mother-in-law.*

❧

Now the morning sun rose higher and already she felt the warmth on her back. The chickens scratched about the yard and the goat was loudly proclaiming her need to be milked, for they had sold the kid. Dibri, the young son of a neighbor, had come and collected the sheep to take to the shepherd. Marah looked around her. She had a home, a husband, a family, and soon, a babe of her own. Her life could be worse, she reasoned to herself. Tomorrow would be the Sabbath, and Zibeon would go with the other men to the temple to pray. Since no work could be done, she would have a day to herself.

It was getting more difficult to kneel down at the stream

and wash the clothes. The day before, as she worked on the cloth, Marah looked up and smiled as she saw Hannah put her basket down.

"You are well? The child grows."

"I am well, Hannah, but I feel like a great cow!"

Hannah laughed and set about her own washing. "Your friend Atarah marries soon. It may be a race to see which comes sooner, the babe or the wedding."

Marah laughed aloud with an exaggerated shrug.

"Zibeon is treating you well?" Hannah did not look up, but though the question was casual, Marah heard her concern.

"He is pleased about the child. He does not seem like such an angry man." Marah paused, reflecting. "I was so afraid of him, Hannah. And those first few weeks I did not know how to behave. He was so unpredictable. Yet now," she murmured thoughtfully, "he does not seem like such a bad man. Perhaps it is as you said that day on the way back from Jacob's well. Perhaps he needed a wife to make his life easier."

Hannah nodded. The two women talked as they worked, sharing the latest gossip, and finally parted to their respective homes. As Marah carried the basket of clothes, she noted that the afternoon shadows were beginning to stretch over the yard. Zibeon would be returning from the shop soon. She remembered that first day when she had braced herself to face Zibeon's return. When he came, he strode boldly into the house and sat down by the small fire. Marah and Athaliah moved swiftly to set his dinner in front of him. He did not greet his mother or Marah but lustily consumed his food. From time to time he watched her. It was as if he were waiting for something.

At last Marah had taken a deep breath and blurted, "Your day went well, Husband?"

Zibeon paused and appeared to be surprised. Then he let out a great bellow of laughter.

"That is good, Wife. Yes, I had a fine day." His eyes narrowed and he looked at Athaliah. "She is adequate in her duties?"

Athaliah had been hovering over him. "She will learn."

"Mmmmm," Zibeon murmured. Then he looked at Athaliah again. "Shimei has not returned?" he growled.

"No, my son," she answered quickly. "It could be that the skins you sent him for took longer—"

"You make excuses for him?" Zibeon bellowed and both women trembled.

Zibeon leaned back on his elbow and belched. "Eat, old woman. I have had my fill." As Marah hesitated, he indicated her with a wave of his hand. "You also, Wife. You will need your strength," and he grinned. He unplugged the wineskin and took a great gulp.

"Did Reba leave with the caravan, my son?"

"Yes, Zohar the silversmith saw them leave at first light. Good riddance to that one!"

He spat. For once Marah could agree with him.

She waited, almost holding her breath as she helped Athaliah clean up the remnants of the meal. As Athaliah turned to her pallet at last, Zibeon picked up the small lamp.

"Come, wife," he ordered.

Marah bowed her head and followed her husband from the room.

9

Marah stretched her shoulders again in the warmth of the morning sun and resumed kneading the bread. She continued to ponder the events of the last few months. When the pain of that first week had passed, she felt she would survive. Athaliah watched her every move. When the time of women came to her that first month, Athaliah had sighed loudly, shaking her head. When the second month passed and Athaliah did not see her washing her women's rags, she began to watch Marah's every movement.

One particular night Marah wrestled with the nausea that came and went. Marah turned from Zibeon, feeling she was about to retch. It angered Zibeon, for he had raised his arm as if to strike her.

"I am that repulsive to you?" he roared.

"Forgive me, Husband," Marah cried in desperation, "I am with child." She covered her face with her arms to ward off the blow. She hunched herself on the pallet and made herself small, feeling wretched.

Zibeon's reaction had been instantaneous. His hand stopped in midair as he stared at her.

"You are ill due to carrying a child? You are sure of this?"

"Yes, my lord. I am sure." She had passed her second month.

Zibeon stroked his beard, savoring this new thought. Then his chest swelled noticeably.

"So, I am to have a son at last!" He sat down suddenly on the edge of the bed, smiling to himself. Then he lay down, crossed his arms over his chest, and went to sleep.

With a small sigh of relief, Marah lay down also. This man she had married was very unpredictable! Zibeon was pleased. She had done what was expected of her, but it was no small comfort.

The next morning Marah was preparing the morning meal when he strode into the room, grabbed Athaliah, and swung her around.

"I am to have a son," he announced.

The startled old woman barely caught her breath. Her mouth worked but no words came out. As he put her down again, she huffed, "Oh that I should have borne such a man. Did you think I did not know I was to have a grandchild?"

Zibeon grinned as he took some bread and cheese. "I am to have a son," he almost shouted and strode out the door.

Marah slowly shook her head. Men. How could he be sure it would be a boy?

Marah stared down at the bread she had been kneading as a thought struck her. Zibeon had been almost kind to her these past months, as had Athaliah. Her mother-in-law wanted a grandchild as much as Zibeon wanted a son. Marah prayed fervently that it would be a boy. If she gave Zibeon a son, who knows, life with him might just be bearable.

The babe is sturdy, Marah thought as she felt the child move powerfully within her.

Shimei came quietly through the courtyard and went into the house. Marah had become used to Shimei's elusive comings and goings. She saw that he feared Zibeon as did Athaliah, but for different reasons. "I wonder why he has never married," she mused, half aloud. As far as she could recall, Athaliah never mentioned finding a wife for him. Those large, sad eyes watched her from time to time. When Zibeon was at the shop and Athaliah was not around, he made life easier by doing small tasks for her. When his mother and brother were around, he studiously ignored her and faded into the background. A strange man, Shimei, he would often disappear for days at a time. Marah understood that he went to the next village. Yet when she ventured to ask about Shimei, if he had friends he visited there, her mother-in-law had given her a strange look.

"There are some things best left alone," she rebuked her daughter-in-law sharply. Marah asked no more questions about Shimei.

The chickens squawked, bringing her out of her reverie. Athaliah returned from the marketplace and approached to inspect Marah's work. Marah put the dough on the paddle and set it to rise by the earthen oven.

"Did you knead it long enough?"

"Yes, Mother-in-law." It was the same question every day but Marah answered patiently. Athaliah still had a criticism for every task, even after all these months, but Marah brushed them off. In spite of herself she had become fond of the old woman.

Athaliah patted Marah's belly. "The child grows."

"Yes, Mother-in-law, he grows." She knew that to mention any other gender in the house caused severe displeasure.

Observing her strange new family, it was obvious that Zibeon was his mother's favorite. Athaliah adored him and in spite of his manner toward her, doted on his every wish. As far as Marah could see, he never seemed to return the affection. He treated Athaliah like a servant and seemed to enjoy seeing her hop to do his bidding.

Once Marah had asked about Athaliah's husband and saw the old woman's face soften. Zibeon must have been the first child of their marriage.

"So strong was my husband. Zibeon is just like him. He was a beautiful boy and the delight of our hearts. Zibeon worked in the sandal shop with my husband and learned the trade from the time he was a young boy." Athaliah studied her hands, lost in thought.

"What happened to your husband?" Marah ventured, sensing that Athaliah was in a talkative mood.

"He died of a fever when Zibeon was thirteen. Shimei was six months in my womb. When he died I nearly lost Shimei." She paused, her face grown hard again. "Perhaps it would have been better if I had."

"Was he a difficult birth?" Marah prodded, her curiosity aroused.

"Two days the pains lasted and he was jaundiced when he was finally born. He was pale and sickly from the first. His constant crying nearly drove Zibeon and me mad. God willed his birth, but I do not see the purpose of it."

Marah began to see Zibeon in a different light. A young boy, grieving for his father and forced to take over his father's business and do a man's work to support his mother and baby brother. With her husband gone and Shimei fraying her nerves with his crying, Athaliah had turned to Zibeon, focusing all her love and attention on her firstborn. She had spoiled Zibeon outrageously and now paid the penalty for her attention. Yet Athaliah didn't seem to notice.

In her eyes he could do no wrong. There was much about this family she wanted to know.

When Zibeon returned home that evening, he noticed something in Marah's demeanor toward him and seemed to watch her curiously. Then he did something out of character.

"Wife, join me at my dinner."

Marah looked at Athaliah, but Zibeon ignored his mother and patted the cushion next to him. Clearly Athaliah was not included. Marah lowered herself carefully. Zibeon picked up a piece of cheese and ate it slowly, watching her speculatively from hooded eyes.

"So . . . my little bird is no longer afraid of the snare?" he asked softly.

Marah's eyes grew wide. It was true. She did not fear him as before, yet something told her to be cautious. "I seek only to please you, my husband."

"Please me?" Zibeon growled. "My mother seeks to please me, my brother seeks to please me . . . and my little Marah, what would you know of what pleases me, hmmm?" His face was close to hers and he had taken her arm, gripping it tightly. She did not flinch, but bravely looked back at him. The expression in his eyes was unreadable. After a long moment, he released her arm.

"You have spirit, Wife. I like that." He brought his face close to hers again. "My little mouse gets bolder." He chuckled to himself.

Athaliah watched furtively from across the room. She did not hear his last words.

That night, Marah lay awake on their pallet listening to Zibeon's heavy breathing as he slept. He had turned to her that night, but there was something different about his love-making—he seemed almost gentle. Was it because of the child? He had put his great hand on her belly and felt the child move. It seemed to please him. Marah sighed. A strange man, her husband. Why did he seem pleased that she did not fear him as before? He was a man of many moods and his temper was like a sudden sandstorm in the desert, appearing out of nowhere. Yet, briefly she had seen another side of Zibeon. A side she was sure even his mother did not see.

With the time of birth drawing near, Athaliah took over more of Marah's household duties. Marah still went for the water up to her last few weeks, for it was the only time that she and Hannah could meet and talk. This past week she had missed Hannah's company, but Athaliah kept her so busy she had little time to think of her wants. An air of expectation had come over the household and even Shimei appeared to stay closer to home. Marah still puzzled over Shimei and once asked him, "Why do you not work in the sandal shop?"

Shimei had shrugged. "My brother does not wish my

assistance in the shop. I procure the leathers for him." He sighed. "It pleases Zibeon to send me on many errands."

Marah thought she detected a bitter note, but when she looked at Shimei's face, it was as bland as usual.

The pains began suddenly one day as she was mending. Dropping the garment, she clutched her belly. All the stories she had heard of the ordeals of the first birth came to her mind. She didn't know what to expect and suddenly she was frightened.

Her cry of pain brought Athaliah running. Alarmed, the old woman helped Marah to her pallet, then ran to the doorway. "Shimei, get the midwife, Shelomith, quickly!" Then, for all the neighbors to hear, "My grandson makes his way into the world today!"

But the child was not born that day or the next. Time had no meaning, for day and night were as one. The pains ebbed and flowed. Cool cloths were placed on her head. With eyes glazed with pain, she saw Shelomith take Athaliah aside and caught snatches of their low conversation.

"Her passageway will not give for that great babe she carries."

"You must save my grandchild!" Athaliah had hissed. "Is there anything you can do?"

"I can give her something to ease her pain, but the babe struggles to be born. It is with God."

The midwife took out a small mortar and pestle and mixed water with some herbs that she carried in packets in her goatskin bag. Athaliah lifted Marah's head and they put the strange mixture to her lips.

"Drink this, it will ease your pain, Daughter-in-law."

Marah's screams tore the silence, and once or twice she heard Hannah's voice, speaking low with comforting words in her ear. As she bore down, they held her over the birthing stool, for she could not stand on her own. Her legs would not hold her up, and she felt her bones wrench as this great thing that was lodged within her body struggled to be free of her. Her body was drenched in perspiration as the wrenching pains came and went. From time to time they would lay her down again on her pallet to rest. She heard Hannah's voice again.

"It goes badly for her. Will she be able to bear the child?"

"She has lost much blood. If she does not have the child soon, we may lose both of them. Perhaps God will be merciful, but she cannot take much more." The midwife sighed.

"I have done my best," she said softly. "It is in the hands of God."

Marah was so tired. Was she going to die? She was ready to welcome death if only to escape the pain. Then, in her delirium, she thought she felt a man's hand on her forehead, stroking her hair. Men were not allowed in at the birthing time. Was it Zibeon? It did not seem like Zibeon. A man's voice whispered in her ear, "You shall not die." The voice was gentle, yet with authority and in spite of the pain she felt a peace come over her.

Then they were lifting her, compelling her to push and push again. There was one final wave of pain and tearing its way, the babe slid free of her body. The midwife caught the child and Hannah laid Marah down again on her pallet.

Athaliah's cry of triumph died in her throat. There was a terrible silence as Hannah stroked Marah's head.

"Have I a son?" Marah murmured, exhausted, yet anxious over the child.

"It was a boy," Shelomith said slowly.

"Was?" With a cry, Marah tried to sit up. "What has happened to my baby?" she cried.

The midwife looked down at the still form in her hands.

"The cord of life was wrapped around his neck. In the birthing, it must have choked him. He is dead."

Athaliah put her hands to her face and began to weep softly.

Shelomith turned to Hannah. "The father must be told and the burying of the child seen to."

Hannah started toward the doorway. "I will tell him."

Just then Athaliah stopped weeping. Her head came up and she stepped forward, putting her clawlike hand on Hannah's arm.

"No. I will tell my son."

10

Shelomith saw to Marah's needs, for the babe had done a great deal of damage in his passing. She gave Marah other herbs to stop the bleeding. The midwife then sprinkled something in a cup and they put it to her lips. It was bitter, and Marah nearly gagged, but Hannah insisted that she drink it. Within moments she sank into exhausted slumber. All night her body struggled for life.

At last, near morning, Shelomith began to gather her potions and herbs and pack her goatskin bag. The time of danger seemed past and word had come that she was needed elsewhere in the village. Marah was barely aware of familiar voices.

"She will live. She will bear again. Return to your husband, Hannah. I will watch over my daughter-in-law."

There was grief in Athaliah's face but strength also. They gripped each other's arms briefly, and Hannah left.

Marah awoke again, later in the morning to find Athaliah dozing beside her pallet. She tried to move but her body would not respond. She lay quietly, pondering the events of the night before. God had not willed that her child should live. Deep in her chest, an ache pressed like the weight of a stone. Silent tears rolled down her cheeks and she yearned for the babe they had not even allowed her to hold. She had waited for Zibeon to come to her, for a word, anything, to share the pain of the loss of their son. But Zibeon did not come.

Athaliah woke suddenly and looked down on Marah. For a long moment she did not speak, and then, "The grief will pass, but you will not forget," she said slowly. "You are young, you will bear other children, yet always, you will remember the first."

Marah looked at her mother-in-law through her tears. She was puzzled by Athaliah's words. Almost in answer to Marah's unspoken question, Athaliah stood up, looking off into the distance of a time past. "Zibeon was not my first child," she murmured. "I lost two before he was born, a son and a daughter. Both came to the birthing and both were stillborn."

"I . . . I am sorry," Marah whispered, feeling a rush of compassion for the old woman. Their eyes met, and a look of understanding passed between them.

During the days of her travail, Zibeon had been waiting with neighbors in the courtyard. At night he went to the shop to sleep. A woman standing near the doorway had turned excitedly to Zibeon to say that the child was born.

"Do I have a son?" he had asked roughly, but the woman looked at him blankly.

"Find out!" he had bellowed as the woman hurried back into the house. Those in the courtyard listened for a baby's cry but there was silence. Then Athaliah had come slowly from the house. Her arms were empty. She faced Zibeon. "The child did not live, my son." She put her hand on his arm and shook her head sadly.

Not knowing what he would do, the men of the village backed away. Zibeon had at first looked at his mother in unbelief. With a groan, Zibeon turned away from her and beat on his great chest with one fist. Finally, "Was it a boy?"

"Yes, my son. It was a boy."

"Bring him to me." For Zibeon, the request was gentle.

Athaliah nodded and returned to the house. She and

Hannah wound the small body with cloth and burial spices. Then Athaliah walked slowly back out to the courtyard and gently placed him in Zibeon's arms. For one long terrible moment, he had held the child, looking down at the still face.

"He shall be called Benoni, child of sorrow," Zibeon said softly. Then as if in a trance, Zibeon had walked slowly away to bury his firstborn son.

After the burial, Zibeon shut himself up in the shop and vented his grief. Shimei heard the sound of things being broken and thrown around, yet he dared not try to enter the shop when Zibeon was like this. Athaliah tried to bring him some food, and he shouted for her to go away and leave him alone. On the third day, while Marah slept, he had come home. Haggard and bleary-eyed, he ate briefly and then came in and stared down at Marah. When she did not awake, he finally nodded his head curtly and left the room. He returned to the shop, working long hours. On the fifth day he returned home with a bloody cloth wrapped around his left forearm. Athaliah had been alarmed, and clicking her tongue, she sought to unwrap the arm. Zibeon had jerked his arm away.

"The awl slipped. It is nothing, old woman, a mere scratch. Stop your wearisome prattling," he had bellowed. "I can take care of it myself."

It was at this point that Marah awakened to the commotion. *Zibeon.* Forcing herself to rise, she stood for a moment, swaying with dizziness. Willing it to pass, she slowly made her way to the outer room. Taking in the situation, she had carefully seated herself down by him and taking his arm gently, murmured, "My husband, let me tend your wound lest it become worse and cause you more pain."

Zibeon opened his mouth to bellow at her and almost as abruptly closed it again. He did not pull his arm away from her. Studying her face for a moment his shoulders sagged.

He shrugged. "If you must, woman, I can see I shall have no peace until it is tended to."

Athaliah raised her eyes heavenward. She knew, as Marah did, that because Marah had given birth, she was unclean. Yet Zibeon's wound must be tended to, and if he would not let Athaliah care for him, Marah must do it. Athaliah stood by, wringing her hands, as Marah began to clean the wound. It was deep where the awl had pierced the skin, and the surrounding flesh was reddened. Marah did her best to clean the wound thoroughly and then wrapped the arm with a clean cloth. Zibeon's eyes were bright as he watched her ministrations. Perspiration ran down his face.

"I am sorry for the loss of our son," she whispered. "I grieve for him also."

Zibeon stood up suddenly and pulled his arm away from her. His softened face became a thundercloud. He grabbed the wineskin from the peg and strode out into the darkness.

"I didn't mean—" She turned to her mother-in-law, bewildered. "I only meant to comfort him."

"It is the way of a man." Athaliah sighed. She began to gather the bloody rags. "It will pass in time, Daughter."

Exhausted, Marah returned to her pallet and sank down again. Zibeon did not return that evening and all the next day. When evening came again, Athaliah sent Shimei to find him.

Shimei returned to the house a short time later. "He is in the shop, but he would not let me in. He was mumbling. He must be drunk," Shimei told them with a shrug of his shoulders. "Leave him alone. He will sleep it off."

The next morning Athaliah went to the shop to take Zibeon some food. When she returned, Marah could see she was beside herself with worry. "There was no sound and the door was bolted from within. He did not even shout at me. I am sure he is hurt. What can I do?" She began to wring her hands and sob.

Marah looked beseechingly at Shimei. He shrugged and, shaking his head in protest, reluctantly went to the shop.

When Shimei came back to the house, he and three other

men of the village were carrying Zibeon. He was unconscious.

"We had to break down the door. We found him on the floor. He tried to speak to us but couldn't open his mouth." Shimei shrugged apologetically.

"He may wake soon, but he is feverish. It is a good thing he is unconscious, I wouldn't venture to get near him if he was awake," said Joab, a craftsman whose shop was near Zibeon's.

They laid him on a pallet in the main room and turned to leave. When the men heard sounds coming from Zibeon, they bumped into one another in their haste to get out the door. Athaliah flung her hand at them in exasperation and rushed to Zibeon's side.

Marah, due to her condition, had remained as inconspicuous as possible. Now, she moved forward to join Athaliah.

"God be praised, we can change the dressing," Athaliah cried. She unwound the filthy rags and gasped at the sight. Ugly red streaks ran up his arm. The wound had putrefied and was oozing. Marah and Athaliah looked at one another in horror. Frantically Athaliah cleaned and probed the wound, trying to clear away all of the pus. Zibeon did not waken, but moaned as she worked.

Shelomith was called and the midwife came again with her herbs and potions, for she also tended the sick of the village. She examined Zibeon's arm and looked at Athaliah, shaking her head.

"It is as God wills." She pointed to the red streaks going up his arm. "The poison has spread into his body. I have seen this before." With a sigh, she stood up and began to gather up her things. "There is nothing more we can do."

As Athaliah grasped her meaning, her eyes widened. "Nooo . . . No!" she cried out.

Marah went to her and put her arms around her mother-in-law. Drawing what little strength she had left, she comforted Athaliah as one would comfort a small child. Was there no end to this? How could she bear more? How could either of them bear any more?

Athaliah would not eat or rest. She tended Zibeon constantly and would not let anyone else near, even Marah. She cooled his brow with wet cloths and, with his head in her lap, crooned to him as he tossed about in his delirium. Hannah, who had come to help, managed the food that the neighboring women had been bringing to the house after the death of the child. She went about her tasks and brought chicken broth for Marah to sip slowly as she sat nearby watching Zibeon.

Zibeon had one rational moment, but it was not his mother he sought. With great effort he lifted a hand and beckoned to Marah to come closer.

When Marah hesitated, Athaliah bent her head down near his and nodded. "He calls for you." Athaliah closed her eyes and bowed her head, tears running unchecked down her wrinkled cheeks. She stood and reluctantly moved away as Marah knelt by Zibeon's side.

"Little bird," he hissed through clenched teeth, "you shall yet escape the snare." Marah remained silent, puzzled by his words. He took a few labored breaths and forced himself to speak again. The words were slurred through his teeth since he could not open his mouth and she leaned closer to understand him better.

"I waited for you . . . for you alone. I hoped one day . . ." He lifted his head slightly and Marah took his hand into her own. It was hot. Perspiration continued to roll down Zibeon's face, and his clothes were moist and clung to his body. The dark eyes that had frightened her so many times were now bright with fever. Now they looked up at Marah pleading for her to understand what he could not say.

Anguish and compassion filled her heart as she leaned down and put her hand on his shoulder. She gave him the only comfort she knew in his last moments. "Zibeon, I too care for you."

It took all of what was left of Zibeon's great strength to reach up and touch her cheek tenderly.

Then his body shuddered and his hand fell lifeless to the pallet.

Marah cried out and bowed her head as Athaliah flung herself upon the body of her son. Her cries of anguish brought neighbors to the courtyard to join those who had gathered earlier out of curiosity. Shimei stared at Zibeon's body in disbelief. He watched Athaliah weep for the son she had loved. For a moment he started to reach out his hand to her, but then shook his head and the hand dropped back to his side. Shoulders drooping, he opened the door and slipped outside.

Exhausted with her efforts on Zibeon's behalf and overcome with weakness, Marah struggled, weeping, to her pallet. Her strength was spent. She could not even help Athaliah prepare Zibeon for burial.

Athaliah slowly and tenderly did what needed to be done for her son. She refused the midwife's offer to help. Shelomith shrugged her shoulders, gathered her pouches, and departed. Hannah quickly went home to gather spices and bring them for the preparation of Zibeon's body. Other women who lived nearby did the same. When they returned, Athaliah finally let Hannah help prepare Zibeon for burial. She tenderly washed the body and rubbed it with olive oil. She took long strips of linen and wound them around packing spices between the cloth and the flesh, for the smell of death already began to permeate the room. She carefully placed a candle at his head and at his feet. A great wailing went up from the crowd.

At last, when Athaliah could do no more, six men carried the bier with Zibeon's body to the place of burial. As they began the procession, Athaliah wept with loud cries, tearing her clothes in anguish. She gathered dust and flung it into the air as did the other women with her. As the procession wound its way, neighbors and other villagers joined the mournful group. They made their way to a cave on the eastern side of the town where the prevailing winds blew from the west. Zibeon was placed on a ledge inside the cave, and the entrance to the cave was closed again with a large stone. Athaliah remained outside the cave, weeping and moaning. She resisted the efforts of several of the women to lead her home. At last, three or four stayed with her, adding their cries to her grief.

With Marah still in her days of purification, Hannah washed the things Marah had touched and swept the house. Marah thought about Zibeon and knew Hannah witnessed his actions in his last moments.

Marah raised herself up. "Hannah?"

"Yes child, what is it?" Hannah hurried to her side.

"Did Zibeon come and lay his hand on my brow when I was in labor?"

Hannah shook her head. "No man came in, child. It is a time of women. Perhaps you were dreaming."

Marah considered her words, and at last, she fell into a troubled sleep. The man in her dream returned, smiling at her and reaching out his hand. With all her heart she longed to approach him, but the vision faded into darkness.

She opened her eyes again, aware of Hannah bending over her, a puzzled expression on her face as she lifted the cooling compress from Marah's brow that was no longer feverish. The heaviness that had pressed down on her lifted, and she was able to give her friend a tentative smile before she drifted back into a deep and peaceful slumber.

Her body would begin to heal from the trauma she'd endured these past days. In the course of a single year, Marah had married, lost her first child, and become a widow. She was fourteen years old.

PART III

Shimei

11

When she had completed her fortieth day following the birth of her son, Marah went to the temple to have the priest perform her rite of purification. To her surprise, Shimei went with her. Athaliah was not well. They were reluctant to leave her alone for very long and grateful that a neighbor offered to stay with her.

Marah brought two pigeons for the offering. They cooed and fluttered in the covered basket. While she understood the laws of purification, part of her regretted seeing the birds killed. They were beautiful white birds. Death had claimed so much from her. Keeping her eyes properly downcast, at least she didn't have to watch. She waited patiently as the priest performed the rituals and pronounced her clean. As she and Shimei were turning to go, the priest murmured his regrets in the death of her husband and son. His simple words brought back her pain. Then the priest looked closely at Shimei.

"You are the brother of Zibeon, the sandal maker?"

Shimei nodded but didn't speak. The priest's eyes narrowed as he looked Shimei up and down. He stroked his beard thoughtfully. Then he turned abruptly and left them standing there.

"Let us return to Athaliah," Shimei whispered urgently.

Marah took his uneasiness as concern for his mother, for

Athaliah had begun to murmur strange things. She would pause in the middle of a task and stare off into the distance for long moments. She would hurry to prepare the evening meal as though Zibeon were coming any moment. She would look strangely at Shimei and murmur, "Zibeon? Are you finally here, my son? You have been gone a long time." Once Athaliah had called Shimei, Josiah, his father's name; at other times she seemed like her old self. She checked every task Marah performed, advising her on how to do it better as she had in the beginning. Marah and Shimei would breathe a sigh of relief that perhaps the time of her madness had passed.

Then one day, during the evening meal, Athaliah put down her food and looked sternly at Shimei. "It is your duty, my son." Her hand gripped his shoulder with surprising strength. "You must raise up a son for your brother."

Shimei looked as though the end of the world had come. He paused with a bite of food in midair and stared at her, stricken.

"You thought I had forgotten the law, didn't you?" Athaliah said with a sly look at Shimei. "You think I'm mad," she hissed, her dark eyes snapping at them. "But I know the law. Yes, Shimei, you must marry your brother's widow and raise up a son for Zibeon."

Shimei finally found his voice. "Marah is in mourning . . . for . . . her husband, Mother. Perhaps this is not the time to speak of such things." Then, "The law says that if a man marries his brother's widow, it is a sin. They shall remain childless." Shimei spread his hands and shrugged.

"You cannot get off so easily!" Athaliah's eyes narrowed and she put her face next to his. "It is also said in the law that if a man's brother dies *without a son*, his widow must not marry outside the family; instead, her husband's brother *must* marry her. The first son she bears to him shall be counted as the *son of the dead brother*, so that his name will not be forgotten. But . . ." and Athaliah poked a bony finger in Shimei's chest, emphasizing her words, "if the dead man's brother *refuses* to do his duty in this matter, refusing to marry the widow, then she shall go to the city elders. She shall say to them, 'My husband's brother will not do the part of kinsman redeemer for me. He refuses to marry me.' The elders shall speak with him and if he still refuses, then"—and Athaliah looked slyly at Marah— "the widow shall walk over to him in the presence of the elders, pull off his sandal from his foot and *spit in his face*!"

Athaliah gripped his shoulder like a vise. "You will marry your brother's widow. My shame shall be wiped away. I will be able to hold my head up in the village again," she stated firmly. "I *will* have my grandchild!"

Shimei awkwardly tried to pat her shoulder. Just as suddenly as it had come, the storm spent itself, and Athaliah looked bewildered. She stood up slowly, looking around her as if seeing the house for the first time. Marah and Shimei both gently urged her to rest. As Shimei led her to her pallet, Athaliah suddenly clutched his hand, putting it to her cheek. Her voice took on a pitiful tone. "You will give me my grandson, Shimei? You will not refuse the law?" She had tears in her eyes as she looked up beseechingly at him. He was overcome with emotion and it was a moment before he could answer her.

"No, Mother, I shall not refuse the law."

Marah knew Shimei had watched his mother slip close to the edge of madness in the last weeks. He seemed anxious to soothe her, yet there was something that seemed to trouble him. Marah stood with mixed emotions also. She had forgotten the Levirate law. Must she marry Shimei, a strange, quiet man given to disappearing at odd moments? She looked at his long, angular face and deep-set eyes. He was obviously not anxious to marry her. If he refused, Athaliah would force her to go to the elders. Marah could not see herself spitting in Shimei's face. Over the last months Shimei had been kind to her, in his way. He did not appear to have a temper like Zibeon. Reviewing Shimei's good qualities, she reasoned that to marry him might be difficult, but not impossible. A child for Zibeon? She considered Shimei's appearance again. The child would not look like Zibeon. Then as she thought of a child, the grief unexpectedly welled up in her. The tears pooled in her eyes and slipped down her cheeks. She felt weak.

Athaliah was watching her. "You weep at obeying the law?" she demanded. "My son is not acceptable to you?"

Marah shook her head sadly. "It is not that, I think of my . . . son."

Athaliah's face softened and she patted Marah's hand absent-mindedly. "You grieve, child. You have your time of mourning. *Then* you shall marry Shimei." It was so matter of fact, as though it would solve all her problems. Athaliah let them ease her to her pallet and sighed contentedly. She had settled the matter.

"Yes, of course, you were so wise to remember." Shimei continued to speak softly in his whispery voice as weariness of body and mind drew Athaliah into its fold. In a few moments she slept.

Shimei stood looking down at her. He was like a great crane standing hunched over a nest as he stood awkwardly clenching and unclenching his fists.

At last he turned to Marah and grabbing her arm he pulled her toward the doorway. "I must speak with you."

Marah felt alarm at his tight grip. He pulled her outside, away from Athaliah. He looked around warily lest anyone be near who could hear their conversation.

"You do not want to marry me," he whispered harshly. It was a statement, not a question.

"But, Shimei, the law, we are bound by the law. Do you not wish to be my kinsman redeemer?"

He sighed heavily and looked down at the ground. "Marah, haven't you wondered why I've never married?"

She shrugged. While she sensed that she knew, she was not sure she was ready to have Shimei tell her the truth. Hannah had told her of rumors in the village. "Perhaps because you have not found the right maiden to marry?" she answered hopefully.

"You must know it is more than that. I do not do well with women." He sought for the right words. "I am more, ah, comfortable with those who share my feelings."

Marah continued to look at him expectantly.

He struggled to finish. "They are . . . not . . . women."

There it was before them, like a shadow that had sprung from the darkness. Marah felt the shadow spread its cloak around them both and spread heaviness in her chest. What could she say to him? What were they to do? At last she looked up at Shimei. His shoulders drooped with the weight of the secret he had revealed. Stripped of his mask, his face was stark and vulnerable before her. He knew she could go to the elders with what he had told her. It would mean his death. How could she do that?

Suddenly she felt pity and compassion for Shimei, for his life and all that had brought him to this terrible dilemma. Taking a deep breath, she reached out and touched his arm. "You have been kind to me, Shimei," she said again. "Would Athaliah have to know that . . . all was not as . . . man and wife between us? I would welcome a time to . . . not be a wife." She looked earnestly at Shimei, wanting him to understand.

The import of her words astonished him. "You would be my wife in name only?" Shimei said slowly. "You would not require . . ." He could not meet her eyes.

"Yes, Shimei, I would do that. Would it not protect you? I in turn would not be required to marry a distant kinsman I do not know."

Shimei had tears in his eyes and could not speak. If they were found out—if Athaliah should suspect and go to the elders, it could mean punishment for them both . . . and death. Yet he had promised Athaliah he would marry his brother's widow. He groped for the words to convey his gratitude. "I am sorry for the death of your . . . son," he murmured finally.

Marah nodded slowly. "It is now a year since Zibeon's death.

Knowing Athaliah, she will announce our betrothal to the village as soon as possible. She will want the marriage to take place soon. What else can we do?"

Shimei moved his head up and down slowly. Marah knew it was more than he had hoped for.

Athaliah cried out in her sleep. Shimei looked back at the house and gripping Marah's arm briefly, he slipped out the gate, disappearing into the night.

Marah stood in the middle of the courtyard. She felt as though the whole scene that had just occurred here was not real. For a moment she wished she were a child again. She longed to run to the comfort of Hannah's arms. She couldn't tell anyone, especially Hannah. She was not a child anymore. She had shared the bed of a husband and borne a son. She must put away childish fantasies.

As Marah returned to the house, a hymn came to her mind that her father had taught her.

> There is nothing like Him or as He is,
> There is neither likeness or body.
> None know who He is but He Himself,
> None is His creator nor His fellow.
> He fills the whole world
> Yet there is no chancing on Him.
> He appears from every side and quarter,
> But no place contains Him.
> Hidden yet withal manifest, He sees
> And knows everything hidden.
> Hidden nor appearing to sight,
> Nothing is before Him and after Him nothing.

She thought of the words "He knows everything hidden," and felt a shudder go through her body. He is the "God Who Sees Me." He knew what they planned. Would He weigh it against what she had been through? What terrible penalty would she and Shimei pay for their bargain?

92

12

The next day brought unexpected callers. As Marah went about her morning tasks, she looked up to see three men enter the courtyard. It was the shammash and two of the village elders. The shammash ministered in the temple along with his brother, the high priest, and was an imposing figure. He had a straight, high forehead, full brow, and large, almond-shaped eyes. His aquiline nose and sharp chin along with his height and lofty bearing gave him a regal appearance. His countenance was stern as Marah bowed her head in respect and welcomed him to their humble home.

Marah's mind raced. Why had they come? Something was wrong. Had the night wind whispered its secrets already?

The shammash addressed himself to Athaliah who was sitting in the sun with some sewing in her lap. "We have come to speak with your son."

Athaliah looked at him curiously. "My son is dead, but he will return. He will return soon," she crooned.

The shammash looked startled and turned to Marah who spoke up quickly in Athaliah's defense. "My lord, she took the death of my husband quite hard. He was her older son. Forgive her, my lord, she has not been herself."

The two elders whispered among themselves and Marah heard the word "demented."

The shammash waved an impatient hand, silencing them. "It is the second son we have come to see. Certain knowledge has come to me and we wish to question him." He glanced around the courtyard as though Shimei were hiding in the shadows.

"Truly, my lord, he is not here. He has gone to the next village on business. We are to marry when he returns." She looked up at the shammash, trying to hide her fear.

"You are young. Perhaps there are things you are not aware of. All is not always as it seems. Before a marriage is to take place, we must speak with this one." His face was a thundercloud. Marah felt he could hear her heart pounding within her.

"You have not consummated this union?" It was more a statement than a question. For a long moment his eyes bored into hers. She shook her head and looked quickly down at the ground again.

Apparently satisfied that she was telling the truth, the shammash moved toward the gate and beckoned the others to follow. He strode a few steps and then turned back to Marah. "He is to come to the temple, the *Bit Allah*, the House of God, when he returns. We will decide on this matter then."

Marah watched them go, her heart still pounding. They knew. She was not the only one to share Shimei's secret after all. The rumors in the village had reached the ears of the council of elders and the high priest. What was she to do? She did not know how to reach Shimei or when he would return. She prayed that he would return under cover of darkness. She would watch for him and warn him of the danger.

Three more days passed before Shimei's return. Marah had watched diligently each day and listened for him each night before she fell asleep. Her thoughts were troubled. In the Book of the Law, given to them by Moses, the agreement she had made with Shimei was against God's commandments. She knew she had done wrong, and the guilt lay heavy on her spirit. It had seemed the only thing she could do. Marah

94

made sure that Athaliah was sleeping and quietly crept up to the roof where she could ponder the situation.

She could not knowingly hurt Shimei. Then again she did not want to marry a strange relative of Zibeon's, should there be one who was able to perform the duties of kinsman redeemer for her. Shimei would have had to publicly renounce his place as kinsman. She thought of pulling off his sandal and spitting in Shimei's face. She could not do that. Then there would be the question of why. Did the whole village know about Shimei? Did they only want to put the rumors to rest? Her head swam with anxious thoughts until finally she sat down on the matting and wrapped her arms around her knees in the cool air. Then, putting her head down on her arms, her heart cried out to the God of the universe.

Lost in her own agony, she was startled by a village dog barking. She stood up and peered over the parapet to see a shadowy figure entering the courtyard. At first she was afraid, concerned it was a robber or worse, but as the figure stood in the moonlight, she recognized him. It was Shimei!

With a stifled cry of relief, she hurried down the steps to the courtyard. Shimei seemed surprised to see her at that hour of the night. Marah looked around quickly.

"Come inside the house. There is news I must tell you. I have been watching for your return." When he hesitated, she took his arm and urged him to come quickly.

To their relief, Athaliah was sleeping soundly. They moved quietly so as not to disturb the animals below them and wake her. Marah lit a small oil lamp.

"Shimei, the shammash was here. The elders wish to speak with you when you return. I am to tell you to come to the *Bit Allah* for questioning by the elders and the high priest."

Shimei did not seem to be startled or surprised. He sighed. "Word came to me from a friend concerning this. I have known for two days, but there were things I had to do. I thank you for what you tried to do, but it would not have worked.

It is too late for that now. I must leave Shechem tonight and I cannot return."

He knew? "But then why . . . ?" Marah whispered.

"Why did I return?" Shimei pulled a rolled parchment from his cloak. "We are betrothed, Marah, under the Levirate law you are as my wife, and the only way you can be free of me is . . . a bill of divorcement." Seeing the shock on her face, he tucked the parchment on a ledge and put his hand on her shoulder.

"You are divorcing me?" Marah stared at him, bewildered.

"It is best. The truth is known and I am in danger of stoning. You should be free to have a better life, Marah, to marry a man who can give you children . . . who can make you happy. I cannot be such a man, in spite of my mother's wishes. You will also be free of the Levirate law to marry a kinsman. It was the only way."

He had thought of everything. Marah nodded dumbly, her mind reeling with the shock and anguish over the terrible import of his words.

Shimei glanced over at Athaliah who was now snoring softly. His face softened for a moment. He turned back to Marah. Taking out a small pouch, he placed it in her hands. It was heavy with coins. "Listen carefully, Marah, I haven't much time. Even the shadows have eyes in the night. There are things you must know." He spoke in an urgent whisper. "Will you take care of my mother?"

Marah nodded. She was fond of the old woman and knew she couldn't leave her alone in her present state of mind. Then she also feared Athaliah's reaction when she found out what Shimei had done. Yet if she was divorced . . . ?

Shimei continued, "This is a portion of the money from the sale of the sandal shop to a man in the next village." He shrugged sheepishly. "I have no wish to make sandals."

Marah smiled ruefully at this.

"The man who bought the shop is coming with his family as soon as he is able. The house is Athaliah's with the bill of divorcement, but you do not have to show that to the elders yet." He had known what she was thinking. "When the time comes, go to your friend. She will know what to do. I have spoken to her."

Marah marveled at Shimei's resourcefulness. He had spoken to Hannah.

Shimei continued in an urgent whisper, "I have sent for a kinswoman, who will take care of my mother. I do not know how long it will take for her to come. As you are no longer my betrothed, you cannot remain after she comes. It is better this way. You understand what I have done?"

Marah nodded again. "I understand, Shimei. I . . . am sorry it turned out this way." She felt like she had lived a lifetime in the last few months.

She looked at the strange man before her, at the sharp nose and sallow face. He had aged also in the last few months. His long arms hung down at his sides.

Shimei turned and watched Athaliah quietly. "She will not be sorry I have gone," he murmured almost to himself. "I wonder if there was a time she ever really knew I was here."

"Let me get you something for your journey," Marah whispered, as he turned to go.

She sought to do something for him, before he was gone from them forever. She quickly and quietly gathered up some cheese and what was left of the day's bread. She gathered some dates and a pomegranate. Wrapping them in a cloth, she gave them to him.

"May God be merciful to you, Shimei," she said softly.

"And you, Marah." He patted her shoulder awkwardly, and slipped out into the night.

Marah stood still for a long moment after he had gone. She was still reeling from the import of what Shimei had done. Perhaps it was best, considering the circumstances. She looked up at the small scroll of parchment on the ledge—a bill of divorcement. She dreaded facing the women of the village. Then there was Athaliah. What would happen when she broke the news to her mother-in-law? Slowly she reached for the scroll and unrolled it, looking at the strange marks that had been written. She did not understand them. She must take Shimei's word for what it said. Then she rolled up the scroll and placed it back up on the ledge, time enough to deal with that in the morning. She put the small bag of coins under her pallet and turned to lie down. With a start she looked at her mother-in-law. Athaliah's eyes were open and staring at her. A shudder passed through Marah as though the face of a stranger confronted her.

"Has Zibeon returned?" Athaliah quavered.

13

Marah awoke early and felt as though she hardly slept at all. She had comforted Athaliah and told her that Zibeon would return. When at last her mother-in-law began to snore softly again, Marah sank to her pallet in exhausted sleep filled with strange dreams. She was running across the desert, stumbling in the deep sand, pursued by dark clouds like faceless hunters in great, swirling black robes who mocked her as she ran. Her feet were like lead as she struggled on, weeping. Then the swirling black clouds disappeared and the sky cleared. She stood alone, waiting for something. Suddenly the stranger from her previous dreams appeared before her. There were no words, yet she felt no more fear, only peace. At that moment she awoke.

As her eyes traveled slowly around the familiar room, she saw the small scroll on the ledge. What would she do if Athaliah awoke and also saw the scroll? Her small, bright eyes missed nothing, even in her madness. As Marah started to rise to get the scroll, she heard Athaliah's voice.

"Good. You are awake early. We have much to do today, Daughter. My son returns soon and there are preparations to be made."

Marah sighed inwardly. Athaliah was herself this morning, or so it appeared. It was going to be a difficult day. How long could she pretend she did not know about Shimei? When a reasonable time had passed, she knew the shammash would return. She could not lie to the shammash, for she knew he would know. He would see the fear on her face. How could she hide it? She did not look up at the scroll for fear Athaliah would follow her eyes and see it too.

As the day progressed Marah could not help glancing from time to time toward the entrance to the courtyard. She did not realize how many times until Athaliah patted her on the shoulder.

"You are anxious for my son's return also, Daughter. That is a good sign. All will be well, you will see." Athaliah nodded her head, smiling to herself.

Athaliah began to tick off on her fingers the various things they would need. "Shimei can bring more wine. He always knows what to get. We will need to prepare the raisin and date cakes. Now where is Shimei? He is never here when I need him. There is so much to do. Ah . . . it will be a feast to remember."

Marah felt the hair on the nape of her neck rise. She looked at Athaliah closely. Where were Athaliah's thoughts now? She nodded dumbly as she went on sweeping the courtyard. How could she let Athaliah do all those things in preparation? It would only make things worse when word of Shimei's desertion was known. If the shammash came again, he might reveal that Shimei had gone. It was said that the high priest had spies everywhere.

Over and over she turned the thoughts in her mind as one would turn over shells along the shore of the sea, examining each one carefully and discarding it. She felt the scroll was safe. It was still on the ledge and Athaliah had not seen it. When her mother-in-law was busy letting the animals out, Marah had pushed the small scroll back farther on the shelf so it was concealed by the shadows.

While she worked, Marah sought for some way to gently tell Athaliah what Shimei had done. *There is no gentle way to tell her*, Marah reasoned, *no matter how I say it.* What kind of a reaction would Athaliah have? Would it push her over into the world of madness forever? She must do as she had promised Shimei, but there was no way to make it easy. *Oh Yahweh, God Who Sees Me*, she prayed silently, *help me.*

Athaliah watched her move about the small house, setting out bread and fruit for their morning meal. Marah poured goat's milk from the stone jar that was kept in the corner of the house where it was hidden from the heat of the day. Athaliah was silent, waiting.

"You did not sleep well, Daughter?" she finally inquired.

"No, Mother-in-law," Marah confessed slowly, "there were many things on my mind."

"What things? Have you had word from Shimei on his return?" The enemy attacked head-on. Today Athaliah seemed in her right mind and was inquiring about Shimei! There was no way out left for Marah.

"Yes, Mother-in-law, I . . . have heard from Shimei. It is not . . . good news." She took a deep breath. "He has gone."

"Of course he has gone, child. He shall return soon and you will be married." Athaliah patted her hand.

"He . . . he has gone . . . forever." Marah held her breath, watching Athaliah's face.

"Gone forever?" Athaliah clutched at her arm, a puzzled look on her face. "He is not dead?"

"No. He is not dead. He has sold the sandal shop to a man in the next village."

"Sold the sandal shop? But why? He will need a trade. It was good enough for my husband and his brother. Why is it not good enough for Shimei?" Athaliah stamped her foot in consternation.

"Because he has gone away." This was going to be difficult. Did Athaliah understand? "The man who bought the sandal shop is coming here to live with his family."

"Here to this house?"

"No, here to the village."

"I do not understand. Why would Shimei do this?" Athaliah began to wring her hands. "Where is Shimei? Where is he?"

"He has gone. He will not be coming back. There will be no marriage. He . . . he had to go away . . . forever."

The old woman's face crumbled and her whole body sagged. Marah reached out and put her hand gently on Athaliah's arm. "I am sorry. I did not know until last night. He could not marry me."

An anguished cry wrenched itself from Athaliah's being, and she fell to her knees, rocking back and forth, keening, "The shame of it, how could he do this?" over and over.

Marah tried to quiet her cries and, dropping to her knees, put her arms around her mother-in-law.

Suddenly Athaliah stopped her moaning and her voice was low and heavy with anguish. "Always he has mocked the law. Because he was my son, I sought to protect him." Athaliah's eyes became bright pools in her wrinkled face. "Now he must answer to God. I can protect him no longer." She began to weep softly, letting the tears fall on her hands. Then she looked up, and Marah saw again the face of a stranger and shuddered.

Athaliah's eyes narrowed and her tone of voice took on the strange crooning of her madness. "We will find a kinsman, Daughter. We will find a husband for you and I shall have my grandchild. Zibeon might return any day now. He would not run away as Shimei has done. He will return soon."

Seeing that Athaliah was past reason at the moment, Marah nodded silently in her agony. What was she to do now? *Lahai Roi . . . God Who Sees Me, show me what to do.*

Just then Marah heard young Dibri calling her from the courtyard. He had come to gather their few sheep to take to the shepherd. Quickly she opened the lower door of the house and let the sheep move out. She thought of the boy's soft voice calling the sheep and their trust in him as they followed him out of the courtyard. Her father's words, "Does

102

the God of the whole earth not know His way?" came back to her mind. Once again she was comforted. God knew her way. Her life was in His hands. She turned back to Athaliah who sat motionless, staring vacantly ahead of her. From time to time a tear slipped down her wrinkled cheeks. The depth of Athaliah's pain nearly broke Marah's heart. There was no way Marah could shield her from the loss and the shame of what Shimei had done. There would be no grandchild now and both of her sons were gone, one through death, and the other by desertion.

Her own pain was mingled with fear as she thought of the events of the past days and sought for answers. She watched the gateway, expecting the shammash and the elders to return at any moment. Did they also know about the bill of divorcement? If they came, would she have to leave? Shimei had said to go to her friend. How she longed to talk with Hannah! Just then a neighbor's child passed the gate. On impulse, Marah ran to catch him.

"Do you know the house of Hannah and Simon?" she whispered.

The boy nodded warily, his eyes on Athaliah who had begun to rock back and forth moaning softly.

"Tell Hannah that her friend needs her and to come quickly."

"Is she ill?" the boy inquired cautiously, looking again at Athaliah.

"Yes, she is ill." Marah nodded quickly, relieved she didn't have to explain more. She took the boy's arm. "Will you go? I cannot leave her as you can see."

The boy smiled and nodded. With the energy of small children, he took off at a dead run.

Marah turned back to Athaliah. She put her arms around the old woman and laid her cheek against the leathery skin, wet with tears. "Come and rest, Mother-in-law. Come inside and rest and you will feel better."

Athaliah did not answer but allowed herself to be led slowly into the house to her pallet. Marah spoke softly, gently, as to a child as she covered Athaliah. Stroking the wrinkled forehead, she waited with the older woman until at last she slept. Marah walked slowly, wearily, to the doorway and her heart lifted as she saw Hannah hurry into the courtyard with her basket of healing herbs.

"Hannah, I am so glad you have come."

"Athaliah is ill, child?" Hannah hurried toward her and then stopped suddenly, looking at Marah's face. "There is more?"

"Oh Hannah," Marah cried, and couldn't speak. She was gathered into the comfort of Hannah's arms and the two women stood for a long moment in the center of the court-yard.

"I don't know where to start . . . ," Marah began.

"It is always best to start at the beginning." Hannah nod-ded encouragingly.

They found a place of shade, and as it was nearing the time of afternoon rest, the village became quiet as shop-keepers closed their shops for the noon meal and returned to their homes. Composing herself, Marah began with the confrontation between Shimei and Athaliah at the evening meal and told her friend all that had happened up until Shimei had given her the scroll and disappeared into the night.

"Has the shammash come back with the elders?"

"No, but I expect him any moment. What shall I say to him? What shall I do?"

"You must not add a lie to the deception that has already taken place, child. Tell him of the bill of divorcement. It will free you. I do not believe he will object to your caring for Athaliah until the kinswoman arrives. He has already seen that she is not herself and cannot be left alone."

"But what about Shimei?"

"That is not for you to trouble yourself over, Marah. He is in the hands of God and you can do nothing more for him. You do not need to tell an untruth, yet I would not recommend that you tell the shammash all." Hannah gave Marah a knowing look.

Marah sighed. It was as if a large burden had been lifted from her shoulders. "Yes, I see that you are right, as usual." She gave Hannah a wan smile.

Hannah patted her arm. "And when the kinswoman comes, you must come to Simon and me. Shimei came to us and we talked. He is indeed a strange man, but he wanted us to know about the bill of divorcement. Even if he had not suggested it first, we would have had you come to us as soon as we knew your circumstances."

"Oh Hannah, I don't want to be a burden on you and Simon."

Hannah drew herself up. "Did you think we are poor friends who cannot help someone we love in her time of need? What must you think of us?"

Marah lowered her eyes in embarrassment. "You are two very dear, kind friends. What would I do without you?" Then she looked earnestly up at her friend. "Oh Hannah, I feel so lost. First I am a widow and now I am a divorced woman. The house and all are Athaliah's and then a kinsman's after she is gone."

"It is well that it is so, Marah. This house and strange family are not for you. You must have a new life. Shimei knew. He wanted you to be free. Whatever he is in his life, he showed you kindness. He took a chance returning to the village. There. You see? It is settled. When you are relieved of Athaliah's care, you come to us." Hannah raised her eyebrows in question.

Marah smiled. She had someplace to go when Athaliah's relatives came. She would be with friends. She looked at Hannah and nodded.

"I must return home." She reached into her basket and handed Marah a small pouch of herbs. "This will help Athaliah sleep, if you need her to." She looked meaningfully at Marah. "If you need us for anything, send for us. Such a day. You will be all right, child. Peace be with you."

"And with you, Hannah. And . . . thank you." The two women embraced.

"Ach, it is nothing." With a wave of her hand, Hannah hurried home.

The bag of coins! Marah moved quickly into the house to check on Athaliah. To her relief, her mother-in-law still lay on her pallet. Her eyes were closed but her lids moved and Marah knew she was awake. Marah heated some water and ground the herbs into a powder with a small stone. She put the powder in a cup and poured the hot water over the herbs to let it steep, keeping a wary eye on Athaliah.

"Mother?" she ventured cautiously, kneeling down beside the old woman.

Athaliah turned her face toward Marah and opened her eyes slowly, trying to focus on Marah's face. There was no sign of recognition.

"Wh-who are you?"

"I am Marah, your daughter-in-law, wife of your son Zibeon."

"Zibeon?" Athaliah pondered the word. "Yes, Zibeon, a fine boy, big and lusty. His father will be proud."

Then she tried to rise. "Where is my son? I do not hear his cries. Have you hid him from me? He will be hungry." She clutched at Marah's arm. "What have you done with my son?"

Terrified, Marah looked into the twisted face of her mother-in-law, and felt like she was looking into the demented recesses of a soul.

"Zibeon is, ah, with his father. They will be back soon. You must rest. You must save your strength." Marah prayed silently with all her being. She took the cup, and lifting Athaliah's head, she gave her a few sips of the liquid.

Athaliah drank and sank back on her pallet. "Yes, I must rest so I can care for my son." She peered at Marah. "You are the midwife then?"

"I am just here to help you," Marah said softly.

Athaliah nodded and closed her eyes.

14

The days passed slowly as Marah cared for Athaliah who now lived in the shadows of the past. She was the young bride and talked to Marah as she would to her husband. Sometimes she was the young mother and longed for Marah to bring her son for her to nurse. She slept a great deal, and when one of the neighboring women came in to stay with Athaliah, Marah went for food and water. Marah used the coins sparingly from the small pouch. She did not know how long they would have to last. Hannah came when she could. Today they sat quietly in the fading warmth of the afternoon.

"Is there word from the kinswoman?"

"No, but she should be here soon. It has been weeks since Shimei left and told me he sent her word. I didn't think to ask him where they were traveling from."

Hannah patted her arm. "Who could think of everything?"

Marah looked wistfully across the courtyard, thinking back. The shammash had returned as she feared. But he had come by himself.

"I came to see the mother of Zibeon." The words were kindly said. Marah obediently led him to see Athaliah. His sharp eyes took in the clean house and noted that Athaliah was well cared for. He also noted her frail body and hands that were bones barely covered with flesh. Athaliah did not awaken. The shammash nodded his head and stroked his chin thoughtfully and then stepped back out into the courtyard.

"The kinswoman has not arrived." It was more a statement than a question, and Marah shook her head. It seemed that he did know everything. He paused as if waiting for something. Marah thought of the scroll.

"My lord, there is something I must show you." She hastily entered the house and took the small scroll down from the ledge. Her heart pounded. She took a deep breath and returned to the shammash, handing him the scroll.

His dark eyes studied her face and the slight nod of his chin told her she had been right not to try to conceal the scroll. He knew. Every sound seemed louder than usual, and Marah waited again, feeling the depth of her weariness. Perspiration ran down her back.

"I have only the word of Shimei for what it contains, my lord. Please advise your servant of what to do." She looked humbly at the ground.

The shammash opened the scroll and studied its contents for a few moments. "You know that you are free to leave this house?"

"Yes, my lord, but I could not leave my mother-in-law. Not until her kinswoman comes to care for her. If it is permitted . . . I . . . I would like to stay."

"You are a good daughter. It is permitted. You must stay until the kinswoman comes." His face became stern. "None of the land or house shall be yours. You may not marry a kinsman of this family. You will leave the house of Zibeon with only your dowry returned to you. Do you understand?"

Marah nodded. She could not speak.

His tone softened. "Do you have a place to go? It has come to my attention that you have no other family . . . ?"

Encouraged, Marah looked up at him. "Yes, my lord, I will go to the house of Simon and Hannah."

He studied her a long moment and then handed her the

scroll. "Keep this with you. It is sufficient that I have seen it." For a moment he appeared to want to say something else but apparently thought better of it. Turning suddenly, he strode purposefully out of the courtyard.

Marah stared after him. She had forgotten the dowry. Of course, she was entitled to take back her dowry. Her mother's candlesticks, and four of the sheep, the goat, some of the chickens, and the wedding coins that had been placed in an alcove in the wall. They were hers! She would not come to Hannah and Simon with empty hands. With a sigh of thankfulness, she wrapped her arms around herself and looked up into the blue sky. God truly had seen her need.

That afternoon Hannah came again, bringing some fresh cheese. They sat in the courtyard, and Marah drew the shawl closer around her shoulders. There was a chill in the air.

"The air grows cold. Do you think there is a storm coming, Hannah?"

"The rains of the month of Tevet begin soon. I do not think that Dibri will take the sheep out tomorrow. You will need to look to your animals. They will be restless."

Marah nodded thoughtfully. She was weary. Athaliah could wake at any time of the day or night and need her, and she slept fitfully, listening to the old woman moaning in her sleep.

"The day comes to a close. I must return home. You are all right?"

"Yes, Hannah, I will be all right. I will make sure the animals are in their pens early tonight."

Hannah rose to go, wrapping her own shawl tighter around her as the wind began to come up suddenly. She shuddered. "This is not to be a good night. I feel it in my bones. Keep your door bolted." Then she turned back and looked closely at Marah. "You are weary, child. Do you wish me to stay with you? Simon will not mind."

"No, thank you. I will be all right. Athaliah is no trouble and the house is sturdy. Greet Simon for me."

"Peace be with you, Marah."

"And with you."

The leaves began to swirl in small patterns in the courtyard as the afternoon shadows grew long. Marah penned up the chickens and brought in the goat. Then she rounded up their few sheep and spoke gently to them, calling each by name as they meekly followed her.

After checking the courtyard for anything that should be put away, Marah barred the gate and hurried into the house. The animals moved restlessly in their pens. For once Marah was glad the animals were nearby. They gave her a sense of company on the lonely nights. She checked Athaliah who had been sitting listlessly in a corner rolling a ball of yarn that Marah had spun the day before. In the way of the aged and infirm, her chin dropped to her chest and she dozed. This had happened many times in the middle of a conversation. Then, Marah thought of the times when a spirit of madness lashed out . . .

"Aiee, they come again," Athaliah screeched one day, throwing a pottery bowl at something only she could see. She swung wildly with the broom at the shadows of the courtyard. Marah wrestled the broom away from her as one of Athaliah's wildly flailing arms struck her on the side of the head.

Athaliah would talk for hours of her girlhood, her marriage, her sons, or casually ask about the newest gossip. The strain of anticipating Athaliah's actions was taking its toll, yet always Marah was gentle with her, soothing her when she was upset and listening patiently as the old woman talked on and on. This night Marah prayed for strength and that Athaliah would be calm.

Marah built a fire in the small, portable clay stove used indoors during cold or inclement weather. She added a few twigs and blew gently on the small flame. Then she added a few herbs and an onion to the stew they'd had for two nights and broke the bread from the morning baking into small chunks.

Smelling the savory stew, Athaliah put down her yarn and

moved with slow, hesitating steps as Marah took her arm and gently led her to the low table. Athaliah sat down heavily on the cushions and Marah brought a small bowl of water to wash her hands. Dipping her chunk of bread into the stew, Marah watched her mother-in-law out of the corner of her eye. Athaliah licked her fingers and ate greedily.

Marah had used the herbs Hannah brought sparingly. She was thankful to have them, especially the previous night when Athaliah had been restless and had cried out several times. At least there had been no sign of the madness for three days, and Marah relaxed. Finishing her meager supper, she looked forward to a better night's sleep.

"The wind blows, Daughter," Athaliah observed, pausing suddenly with a sop in midair. She cocked her head to one side and suddenly began to rock slowly from side to side. Apprehension made a tightness in Marah's chest, but outwardly she tried to remain calm.

"It is only the first rains of Tivet, Mother-in-law. We need the rain. The air has been so heavy. It will be good to smell the fresh earth again." Marah tried to speak casually, hoping to soothe Athaliah.

As the first drops of water began to be heard on the roof, Marah got up and checked the large wooden bar across the door. She glanced down at the animal pens and was assured that they would be all right for the night. As she moved about the house, she was aware that Athaliah watched her closely, the dark eyes gleaming in the light of the oil lamp. There was a smug look about Athaliah. Marah cleared up the bowl and wooden plates. Her heart began to pound as Athaliah watched her slyly. She began to wish she had taken Hannah's offer to stay with her tonight. She shuddered as if in the presence of evil. Was she in danger from Athaliah? She remembered the times she had awakened in the middle of the night to find Athaliah standing above her pallet, staring at her, the wrinkled face gaunt and macabre in the moonlight. Athaliah had been docile enough as Marah spoke gently and led the old woman back to her own pallet. While Athaliah's soft snores soon filled the room, Marah lay awake, her eyes open, listening.

This night, Marah took the herbs Hannah had brought and once again ground them to a powder to mix with warm water.

"Here, Mother-in-law, this will help you rest. You wish to be strong for the morning. We will need to begin making cheese tomorrow." She handed the small cup to Athaliah to drink.

"Yes . . . child, of course," Athaliah crooned. "Oh! Do I hear something?" She put her hand to her ear. "Is the door bolted? You must check it again."

"I have checked it. All is well."

"You must check it again." Athaliah began to weep. "Do you not care if a robber comes upon us in such a storm?"

"Do not upset yourself," Marah told her hastily. If it would make Athaliah feel better, she would go again and check the door.

When she returned, Athaliah smiled sweetly up at her and handed her the empty cup. "I will rest now," she said, went to her pallet and promptly lay down, closing her eyes.

Relieved, Marah blew out the candle. It would take all day tomorrow after the bread was done to make the cheese. She hoped that Athaliah would be a help to her. She glanced over at the old woman who appeared to be sleeping quietly. With a sigh of relief, Marah lay down and gave herself to sleep.

Later Marah could not tell what awakened her. The brush of the wind across her face, a sound in the night, but something was wrong. She rubbed her eyes and yawned, looking over at Athaliah's pallet. It was empty. Suddenly wide awake, Marah sat up and again felt the coolness of the wind, damp with the rain. The door was wide open! Somehow Athaliah had lifted the heavy wooden bar without awaking Marah and she was gone.

Quickly wrapping her cloak around her, she rushed to the doorway. There was no sign of Athaliah in the courtyard and the gate was open. She hurried back into the house, terrified.

What was she to do? She quickly lit the lamp and sought her sandals in the shadows. In the soft light she stepped in something wet by Athaliah's pallet. She held up the lamp and looked down. There was a small circle of dampness on the clay floor. Traces of herbs could be seen. The cup. Athaliah must have poured it out when Marah went to check the door. She had planned it all along, but why?

Marah hurried out into the courtyard, calling Athaliah's name over and over. It took all her courage to go into the dark street. As she peered up one direction and down another, seeking which way to go, a thought came to her mind. *Go to the sandal shop.*

The clouds opened for a brief moment and in the starlight Marah sped to the shop of Zibeon that had been closed up since Shimei had gone, waiting for the new owner. The rain began to fall softly again as she approached the shop, and there against the door, in a small heap, lay Athaliah. She was barely breathing when Marah knelt, taking the old woman's head in her lap. Marah rocked her slowly, her tears mingling with the rain.

Athaliah slowly opened her eyes, but there was no brightness or madness in them now. The dark shadows gathered about the tired body. She looked up at Marah.

"I thought I'd find Zibeon. He was not here. I called and called. Then I knew. He is dead." Athaliah looked up at Marah. "You have been a good daughter. You have done all things . . . well." She closed her eyes and with a sigh was gone.

Overcome with emotion at the unexpected praise, and the fact that Athaliah was gone, Marah continued to rock the old woman in her arms. She looked at Athaliah's face, at last peaceful in death. Then a dog barked, and suddenly the shadows seemed alive around them.

"Help, someone!" Marah cried, looking around her. Eyes seemed to be glowing in the darkness, and Marah feared the village dogs. She knew she could not lift Athaliah nor could she leave her alone in the rain. "Someone . . . please help us!" she cried again.

"Who is there?" called a gruff voice out of the night. A man approached her with a lamp held high. It was Joel, the silversmith, who lived nearby behind his shop. He saw Marah's anguished face and Athaliah lying still. Setting his lantern down, he gently lifted Athaliah in his strong arms.

"Dorcas, you are needed," he called out.

His wife came to the doorway and, pulling her mantle over her head, hurried to his side. She led Marah home as Joel followed, carrying Athaliah. He laid the frail body on her pallet.

"Will you tell Hannah and Simon?"

Joel nodded. He looked at Athaliah's still form. This was the work of women. "I will go."

Dorcas and Marah removed Athaliah's wet clothes and dressed her for burial. When the women had done what they could for her, Dorcas put her hand gently on Marah's shoulder.

"There is nothing more we can do until it is light. I will remain with you."

"Thank you both for your kindness . . ."

They sat down, each with their own thoughts, and waited for dawn.

15

The eaves of the house dripped from the rain, and the day dawned bleak and gray. Dorcas needed to return to her house to gather some spices.

"You will be all right until I return?"

"I will be all right. I must see to the animals and I know Hannah will be here soon."

Dorcas nodded and left quickly.

Marah let the animals out into the courtyard. Dibri would be here for the sheep if the rain was light. The chickens scratched for worms in the damp earth and the goat let Marah know she needed to be milked.

There was a commotion at the gate. It was opened suddenly and a strange man and woman entered the courtyard. They looked like travelers who had been journeying for a long time. With a start, Marah suddenly knew who they were. Athaliah had mentioned her sister Adah, married to a man by the name of Zerah. She hurried to close the gate before the sheep wandered out and then turned to them respectfully.

"I am Marah, wife of Zibeon, Athaliah's daughter-in-law."

The woman did not smile, but looked around the courtyard with an appraising eye.

"I wish to see my sister Athaliah. Does she still sleep? Surely she knew we were coming soon." She looked around as if Marah were hiding Athaliah behind her.

Marah took a deep breath and drew back a step.

"It is well you have come," she said hesitantly. "My mother-in-law . . . your sister, died last night. Friends are coming with spices for her burial. Follow me, I will take you to her."

With her hand to her breast and crying, the woman rushed past Marah into the house. The man eyed Marah suspiciously.

"It was our . . . impression that you would not be here," he said unkindly. "My nephew told us he had . . . given you a bill of divorcement."

Taken aback, Marah stared at him for a moment until she found her voice. "I had permission from the shammash to remain. My mother-in-law had times of madness and I . . . promised Shimei I would care for her until you came."

"You did not hasten her death with neglect?" he inquired cruelly.

Marah stared at him aghast. What sort of people were these? "I loved my mother-in-law and cared for her to the very best of my ability. The events of these past few months were too much for her. She never recovered from Zibeon's death." She looked into his face, her eyes blazing with righteous indignation.

The man stepped back, clearing his throat uncomfortably. Then, hearing his wife wailing, he turned and hurried into the house.

Dibri came then to take the sheep.

"Dibri," she called softly, "when you return to the village tonight, take the four sheep with the black markings to the pens of Hannah and Simon. Do you understand?"

The boy looked puzzled for a moment and then shrugged and nodded his head. Closing the gate behind him, she stood for a moment trying to sort out the situation. What was she to do now? Reluctantly she went into the house.

Athaliah's sister was no longer moaning. She stood in the

middle of the room talking with her husband. In her hand she had the scroll from the ledge.

"I believe that is mine," Marah said quietly but firmly. "I need to take that with me now." She held out her hand.

Adah's eyes narrowed as she reluctantly handed Marah the scroll. She waved her hand imperiously. "There is nothing more you can do here. You may go now."

Marah looked from one to the other. "I would like to bury my mother-in-law. Then I will take my things and go."

"You are no longer a daughter of the house. There is no need. I will see to my sister. As for taking your things, we do not know what things belong to you and what things belong to the house of my sister."

"Can we be of help?"

The words were said quietly, but there was a note that Marah had not heard in Simon's voice before. Marah turned gratefully to her friends, thankful for their timely presence.

"Who are you?" Adah demanded.

"I am Simon and this is my wife, Hannah. We are friends of the family." Marah smiled inwardly at the emphasis on the word "family." Simon had appraised the situation quickly and no doubt he and Hannah had heard Adah's harsh words.

Adah hesitated. "Well . . . we, my husband, Zerah, and I . . . we thank you for your help. We are unfamiliar with your burial place. I . . . did not expect my sister's untimely death." She looked at Marah as though she were solely responsible for Athaliah's sudden demise.

"You have been most fortunate that Marah has been here to care for her," Simon continued politely. "Your sister was in a demented state. It was a difficult situation. Marah showed her mother-in-law every kindness."

Adah looked at Hannah and Simon and then her husband.

"We are, ah, most grateful for her help. It is to our sorrow that we were not able to arrive in time for my wife to see her sister before her death." Zerah eyed his wife who put her hand to her breast again and began to weep loudly.

"Oh my sister . . ."

Hannah stepped forward and motioned to Marah to help as she began to pull the spices out of her bag. As they began to tend Athaliah, Adah moaned pitifully and they ignored her. Finally, with a small huff, she came to help them.

Joel brought other men from the village and they carried Athaliah to the burial cave. The women moaned and tore their hair, weeping as they walked behind the bier. Marah walked quietly beside Hannah, her head covered respectfully and her eyes downcast. Large tears rolled down her face and she did not attempt to wipe them away.

"See how she loved her," the women murmured as they passed. Adah also heard their comments and moaned louder as she followed the bier.

When Athaliah had been laid to rest in the burial cave, Hannah and Marah returned to the house. Marah had no doubt but that Adah would be close behind them. Acquiring more property evidently was more important than mourning for a lost sister, she thought grimly.

Adah and Zerah were indeed close behind them as they entered the house. Marah was glad for Hannah and Simon's presence as she went to the small crevice in the wall and removed the headband with her wedding coins.

"What is that you are taking?" Zerah asked.

"They are my wedding coins, my dowry. The shammash told me that my dowry may return with me." She waited patiently as he looked at the coins and nodded.

Marah went to her pallet and retrieved the small bag with a few coins in it, handing it to Adah.

"What is this? They are not part of your headband." Adah looked puzzled.

"They were given to me by Shimei from the sale of the sandal shop. They were to provide for Athaliah and me, to be used to care for her."

Adah glanced at her husband. "Yes, you no longer need them to care for my sister."

Adah tucked the small pouch into her girdle.

Hannah went to the table. "You will want your mother's candlesticks." The look on her face dared Adah to comment.

"I will get the animals, Marah." Simon turned to go out the door.

Zerah looked up. "What animals are hers? How do we know which ones belonged to my wife's sister?"

Simon couldn't contain his irritation. "Anyone in the village can tell you exactly how many chickens, goats, and sheep Marah brought to Zibeon's pens with her marriage. Every woman in the village counted them. Do you wish me to call in the neighbors to verify Marah's animals?"

"That will not be necessary . . . will it, Zerah?" Adah nodded meaningfully at her husband. "We only wish to do the right thing by my sister and my nephew."

Simon glared at Zerah. "It is hoped that the rest of your business in our village can be completed in a friendlier manner." He turned to Hannah. "Come, Wife, you and Marah can assist me. We are not needed here."

Marah picked up her small bag of belongings that contained the bill of divorcement and dropped in the necklace of coins. She took a last look at what had been her home for almost two years. Carrying the candlesticks, Hannah put an arm around her shoulders and led her from the house as Zerah and Adah watched.

Simon led the remaining goat and Hannah and Marah each carried a basket of chickens. Neighbors had gathered in the courtyard, some in sympathy with Marah and some out of curiosity. It was a sad procession that left the courtyard and wound its way to the house of Simon and Hannah.

PART IV

Jesse

16

Simon patiently pushed on the roller to smooth out a portion of the clay roof that had been damaged by the recent rain. Marah and Hannah wove small branches to repair the shelter that protected Marah's pallet. They worked quickly for the barley was rich and ripe for harvest and soon they would be busy in the golden fields.

For several days Simon noted the weather and the crops. Each farmer wanted to choose the most favorable time to harvest.

"It should begin after this Sabbath," Simon said, studying the sky.

"My lord, is it not too early? What if we have more rain?" Hannah asked.

"Better two days early, than two days late," Simon responded in his practical way, quoting a well-known proverb.

Hannah shrugged. Marah shook her head slowly and smiled at her. The two years had passed quickly since Marah had come to live with her friends, yet with each month that passed, she became increasingly aware that she needed to consider the direction of her life. She could not live with Hannah and Simon forever, yet what should she do?

Marah thought of the strange family that Shimei's bill of divorcement had released her from. Zibeon with his temper; poor Shimei and his sad face; Athaliah and her madness . . .

then there had been Athaliah's sister and brother-in-law. How they had tried everyone's patience.

Adah complained to anyone who would listen. The neighbors, who dutifully brought in food for the week of mourning when the law forbade cooking, ignored her remarks.

There was no other relative to step forward and buy the property, Shimei would not return, Marah no longer held any claim, and Zerah had no wish to remain in Shechem. They disposed of what they could and sold the house to a man in the village. Simon witnessed the signing of the deed and the exchange of money, which was carefully counted out in the presence of the witnesses. He came home shaking his head. It was always a sad day when property that had been held in a family for generations passed into the hands of others.

Marah knew she should marry again, but whom? Marah laughed to herself when she thought of the two unacceptable suitors who had courted her. The son of the shammash accosted her one day when she was leading the sheep to the shepherd. She had noticed Shelah eyeing her furtively as she went about her tasks. He appeared wherever she went and twice she found him hanging around the courtyard gate. He finally asked for her in marriage, and was turned down by Simon with Marah's prompting. Crestfallen and lovesick, Shelah followed her around the village. The more she ignored him, the more determined he became. Then, one day when she came by with the sheep, he suddenly jumped from behind a rock where he had been watching for her. As he grabbed her, they struggled. The heavy staff fell to the ground. Shelah tried to kiss her and press her to the ground. She pulled herself free and instead of running away, she snatched up the staff that she had dropped and in a fury began to beat him with it. He was so surprised he covered his head from the blows with his arms and ran back to the village. When word got back to the shammash, Shelah was quickly sent to relatives in another village to avoid the shame and gossip. Marah felt sorry for him, and for a time feared the shammash. Yet when he passed her in the marketplace he did not look at her and she lowered her eyes respectfully.

Hannah was outraged by the incident. "Simon, what is a young woman to do if she cannot walk near our village without fear for her own safety? If the son of the shammash tries to accost her, then who else will it be?"

Simon listened quietly and then turned to Marah. "From now on Dibri must come for the sheep each day."

Marah felt she would be all right, but there was a note of authority in Simon's voice and Marah nodded respectfully. Secretly she was thankful for their concern and protection.

One evening when Simon returned from his field, there was a knock at the door.

Peninnah the matchmaker stood smiling on their doorstep.

"I would like to speak with Simon," she said, brushing by Hannah when she held the door open. "Oh, and peace be with this household," she added hastily.

"Peace to you, Peninnah."

Peninnah hurried over to Simon. "There you are," she gushed, as though just discovering him, "I have a proposition for you."

"You have a proposition for me?" Simon looked at her patiently as Hannah pursed her lips and waited.

"It concerns the young woman you have so generously taken into your home, out of the kindness of your heart. Poor girl, with all she has been through, but now I have the solution to your problem." She beamed at them all.

Simon cleared his throat. "Our problem?" He turned to Hannah. "She has a solution to our, ah, problem."

"An offer of," and Peninnah paused for effect, "marriage!"

Simon turned solemnly to Marah. "She has an offer of marriage for you." He turned back to Peninnah. "Do you wish to speak to Marah? She can speak for herself in this matter."

Peninnah seemed uncomfortable. "Well, it is just that I am used to, well, to speaking with the parents of the bride-to-be. Of course, yes, there have been some occasions when I have been most helpful in bringing others, in Marah's position, into a very suitable marriage."

Marah nodded and waited.

"Very well, I present an offer of marriage and a home from a most eligible man, a widower. A fine man, in need of a wife most urgently. He has chosen Marah." The last was stated with a flourish of her hand.

"Does he have a family?" Marah inquired. "A mother, father, children?"

"No parents to care for, God be praised, but less for you to do. Children? Yes, lovely children who need a woman of compassion to care for the home."

"How many children?" Marah was prompted by Hannah's mouthed urging behind Peninnah.

"Praise God, it is so wonderful. He has four, a family already, for a poor woman who has none of her own."

"Four?" Marah kept her voice even and rolled her eyes at Hannah when Peninnah turned for a moment. "How old are they?"

"The oldest is eleven, a fine boy, then a girl, eight, another little girl, five, and a dear baby boy, just a year old. Just think, with no children of your own, praise God, a lovely family."

"Could this be the family of Korah the potter?" Hannah had opened her eyes wide at the description of the children.

"You know him?" Peninnah had whirled around. "The very same. What could be better? Korah needs a wife, and Marah needs a husband." She beamed at them again. "Now," she began briskly, "shall we settle the arrangements?"

Marah thought quickly. She did not wish to offend the matchmaker who carried tales all over the village. Marah knew of Korah, as did everyone in the village. His children were dirty and whined a great deal. He did not rule his own house as the Book of the Law commanded. He did not take the laws of cleanliness as seriously as he should and was sometimes avoided by the other men on the Sabbath. She shuddered inwardly.

"You are most kind to come with such an offer, Peninnah," Marah said, choosing her words carefully. "I will consider this matter carefully."

Peninnah sniffed. "Beggars cannot be choosers. You need a husband. He needs a wife. You cannot expect to burden yourself on others forever."

Simon gently but firmly took the matchmaker's arm and guided her outside the doorway.

"We will discuss your most generous offer. If Marah agrees to accept, we will let you know at once. May God bless and keep you."

As he was closing the door, Peninnah called over his shoulder, "Don't wait too long. Another woman may take this opportunity and it will be too late. This may be your last chance." Peninnah took herself off down the street like a ship in full sail.

Marah stood quietly, feeling wretched. "Perhaps she is right, Hannah. I cannot stay here forever. Sooner or later I must marry again. There aren't that many eligible men left in Shechem."

Hannah took her by the shoulders. "You have spent too much time today in the sun. Simon, tell her she is welcome. Tell her she can wait to make a right choice. Tell her she doesn't have to marry a man like Korah, with those four horrible children!"

Simon waited patiently through his wife's tirade. He shrugged. "So I am telling you, Marah, wait."

"Tell her she is like family."

"You are like—" Simon stopped and looked at Hannah. "You have already told her. She is not deaf. She knows this." He turned to Marah, putting a fatherly hand on her arm. "You know this?"

Marah nodded, tears welling up in her eyes. They would not press her or urge her to leave. She was not a burden to them. In time, she knew she would marry, but it would be in her own time. With a grateful heart, Marah turned to help Hannah with the evening meal.

17

Word came that Dibri was ill and could not come for the sheep. Hannah was busy with the washing and Simon was repairing a sickle. The harvest would begin tomorrow. There was no one else to take their few sheep to the shepherd, so Marah put on her shawl and reached for the heavy staff she had used before.

"I don't feel right about you taking the sheep alone."

Marah laughed. "I'll be all right, Hannah, it's a fair day and I'll take a stout staff to drive off any animals." The emphasis on the last word was not missed by Hannah.

Hannah was still anxious. "Should I send Simon to walk back with you when he returns?"

"Oh Hannah, if I am not back within a reasonable time, send Simon, but really, I shall enjoy the walk this morning." Marah smiled and began to speak softly to the sheep. They knew her voice and willingly followed her down the path.

The warm sun felt good on her back as she led the small flock toward the hills where the shepherd would oversee them for the day. *What could happen to me on such a day?* she mused as she walked.

The sheep were suddenly restless, milling around and bleating. Looking around for some sign of danger, Marah saw a young child sitting in the dirt in the road in front of her. He held a small stick and great tears rolled down his cheeks. He looked up at her hopefully, but as she approached, his face fell. Obviously she was not the one he had hoped to see.

There was a low growl and she looked on the hillside to her right. A fierce-looking wild dog was eyeing the boy and the sheep. When he saw her, he bared his teeth. Though her heart pounded with fear, Marah quickly picked up a good rock and bravely hurled it at the dog, striking its soft muzzle. She shook her staff menacingly at him and shouted loudly. The dog hesitated a moment and then, with another growl, loped away. Marah let her breath out slowly. When she was sure the dog was gone, she turned to the little boy.

"Are you lost?" she inquired, gathering the small child in her strong arms to comfort him.

"I want my papa," he cried between large sobs. "I don't like the bad dog."

"Hush, little one," Marah crooned, "the bad dog is gone. You are safe now."

The little boy lifted his head.

"Papa!" he cried joyously over her shoulder.

She turned and stopped, staring at the familiar figure walking quickly toward her.

"Caleb. I have looked everywhere for you." He walked anxiously, his eyes on the child. "Are you all right?" Stooping down, he hugged him in relief. "I saw what you did, thank you for caring for my son." In his concern for the boy, he had not looked up at her.

"He is your son, Jesse?" Marah felt her heart begin to beat erratically. She stood staring down at the top of his head in astonishment.

At the sound of her voice, Jesse suddenly looked up at her. "Marah?" He stood up and looked from his son to her face. "It is you that saved him?" He stared back at her for a moment. "It is good to see you again." A slow smile spread across his face.

"It is also good to see you, Jesse." The silence was an eternity.

Then Jesse recovered himself. "Ah, thank you again. I will trouble you no longer." The warmth that radiated from his eyes disappeared and his face became an unreadable mask. He picked up his son, turned away, and headed back toward the village with long strides.

Marah stared after him dumbly. What was Jesse doing in the village? The bleating of the sheep interrupted her thoughts, and she hurried them on to the shepherd. When they were safely delivered into his care, she walked quickly back toward the village. She thought of Tirzah. How fortunate she was. She had a son and Jesse. Considering all that she had been through, Marah felt sad, uneasy, and jealous.

She sought Hannah as soon as she returned to their house.

"Hannah, the strangest thing happened." She related the events of the morning to her and Hannah listened in alarm.

"You were brave to drive off the dog. He could have killed the child or a sheep. I knew I should not have let you take them alone to the shepherd."

"Hannah, the sheep are fine. The child is fine. Did you hear what I said? He is *Jesse's* son. Jesse and Tirzah have returned to Shechem." Marah spread her hands and searched Hannah's face, waiting impatiently for a response.

Hannah stopped fussing and stared at her, puzzled. "It was Jesse, you say? I wonder what he is doing in Shechem?" She looked toward the village and pursed her lips.

Marah looked up at the sky and rolled her eyes in exasperation. "That is what I want to know. There must be a reason for their return. Do you know of any way I—"

Hannah was reaching for her basket. "I have some things to get in the marketplace. Perhaps you can take care of the washing?" She raised her eyebrows and gave Marah a conspiring wink.

Marah laughed. "Hannah, you are just as curious as I am.

So, go." She pushed on her friend's ample shoulders. "Go quickly and tell me *everything* you find out."

She stood pensively and watched Hannah hurry off. Events of the past crowded into her mind . . . she and Jesse cutting wild mustard on the hillside, the little flute . . . She felt a sudden lump in her throat. Perhaps she did not want to hear the news of Jesse and Tirzah after all.

She took the wet clothes up to the roof and carefully spread them out to dry. Trying to occupy her thoughts with other things, she checked their herb supply. There was plenty of dried dill and coriander, but she noted that the jar of mustard oil was only half full. They had a small bag of salt left and a small clay jar of cumin. She went to the vegetable garden and looked at what remained that could be used for their supper. She picked a cucumber and a leek and a few beans. The onions and garlic had already been pulled and now hung from the rafters in the house, giving it a pungent aroma. Noting that the plants seemed to droop a little, she took a small container and dipped water from the water jar. Carrying it carefully to the garden, she poured the precious water around the remaining plants. Turning to get more water, she was startled to find Hannah standing in the middle of the courtyard with a smug look on her face.

Marah hurried over to her friend. "You are back so soon."

Hannah took her time setting the basket down and Marah thought she would die of impatience. Settling herself, Hannah took a deep breath and then, with an air of conspiracy, poured out her news, watching Marah's face as she did so.

"Jesse is a widower. His wife died in childbirth. He has returned to Shechem because his parents are old and not well, and need his help. He will be setting up a carpenter shop here in Shechem to take care of them." Hannah took another breath and paused to see what effect her words had.

"You found all that out in such a short time?" Marah paused to consider the information. Then she had a terrible thought. "You didn't go to Jesse and ask him, did you?"

Hannah snorted. "Do you take me for a foolish woman? When I appeared at the marketplace, the gossips were only too anxious to share their news. I didn't even have to ask a single question. So now, what will you do, eh?" She looked slyly at Marah, her eyes dancing.

Marah had been thinking of Jesse, losing his wife in childbirth. Remembering her own pain and the midwife's hushed tones, she knew she had almost died in childbirth herself. Her heart went out to Jesse.

"Well?"

"What do you mean, 'What will I do?'"

Hannah feigned surprise. "Oh that I should have such a thick-headed friend. What can you do with my news? Has it been so long since a shepherd and a young girl were friends, talked—"

Marah blushed. "Oh Hannah, that seems like so long ago. So much has happened. I don't know how I feel anymore. I am dead inside. Perhaps Jesse feels the same way I do. It has been too long and too much has happened to us."

"You are so dead inside you blush? He is a man. You are a woman. You like each other. Can anything be plainer? Of course much has happened, but don't you see? You are both free now to marry. He is no longer a boy, he is a man, a widower, and you . . . you are free to choose the man you wish at last. What could be so bad, hmm?" Hannah spread her hands and shrugged.

Marah felt tears come to her eyes as she looked away. "I am not sure about anything anymore. I don't know how Jesse feels now. He turned away so abruptly as if he didn't want anything to do with me."

"So . . . how could he know you were a widow? That Zibeon was dead? Had he not just arrived in the village and then had to spend his time searching for his lost son? Did he not care enough to protect you? God be merciful. He was not going to give Zibeon any reason to trouble you."

She considered Hannah's words. "Yes, perhaps you are right. Maybe that is why Jesse turned away like he did."

She hesitated, biting her lip. "What should I do?"

Hannah laughed. "I don't think you will have to do anything. When he finds out what has happened and that you are free, he will not rest until *he* has done something. You can be sure of that." She gave a sharp nod of her head to emphasize her words.

"I wish I could be as sure of that as you are, Hannah."

"God be patient that I have such a stubborn friend." Hannah rolled her eyes and headed for the house. "Come, there is supper to prepare. Busy yourself and you will have less time for thinking!"

Marah smiled then, and the two women, out of long practice, began to work companionably together.

18

In a steady rhythm the reapers grabbed and swung, grabbed and swung, as the harvest finally began. Every available man and woman in the village helped in some way. They gathered the cut grain and bound the loose bundles into sheaves. When the gatherers had left a portion of the field, gleaners were called in to gather the remains. These were the poor of the village, widows and those who did not own land. The gleaners were not allowed to touch the sheaves that were loaded onto donkeys or wagons and taken to the community threshing floor. Here, by beating the stalks, the edible grains would be loosened.

The women of the village called out greetings to one another and gossiped as they worked. They started in the fields at sunup and many times did not head homeward until after dark. The women poured the barley into large pottery jars. Some of the jars were set aside for the tax collector who watched the proceedings with sharp eyes, lest he miss any profit. Simon's portion was loaded on a donkey and taken to their house to be stored.

Each evening when Simon, Hannah, and Marah returned to the house, there seemed barely time to prepare a quick meal and tend to a few household duties, before falling exhausted to their beds to be ready for the next day's work.

Marah sat mending a garment and Simon and Hannah were engaged in animated conversation concerning the taxes soon due on their small property.

"A half a shekel again. They will bleed us dry. What do they think we can live on when they take most of what we have?" Simon muttered. There was a firm knock at the door.

"Simon, someone has heard you," Hannah whispered urgently. She looked in fear toward the door as Simon opened it. Jesse stood on their doorstep holding his small son.

"I've come to thank Marah for her kindness in saving my son from a wild dog. He wandered away while I was unloading our things. I can't tell you how anxious I was until I found him. I would have come sooner, but I have been working my father's field." He stood looking hopefully at Simon.

With a hint of a smile, Simon stepped aside. "Enter our humble home. Peace be with you."

"And with you," Jesse returned.

Gratefully he bent his tall frame and entered, standing quietly in the center of the room. On hearing his voice in the doorway, Marah rose suddenly and stood with her sewing in her hand.

"You are well, Marah?"

She nodded, then looked down and smiled at the little boy, Caleb, who was looking at her curiously.

"Hello, Caleb. Have you been a good boy and stayed by your papa's side?"

Caleb nodded with large and solemn eyes. Jesse put him down and Caleb clung to his father's leg, peering up at Marah.

"Caleb, this is the woman who saved you from the big dog. Would you like to thank her?"

Marah knelt down and the little boy shyly put out his hand. Marah could not resist and gave him a warm hug. He smiled up at her and sighed deeply.

"It is a wonderful evening, Wife," Marah heard Simon say pleasantly. "Perhaps you would like some fresh air up on the roof?"

Hannah had been visibly relieved to find Jesse at their front door instead of one of the Roman soldiers. She looked at Simon and then Jesse, nodding reluctantly. For a moment Jesse and Marah were alone. They looked awkwardly at one another and each waited for the other to speak.

"It is good to see you again, Marah," Jesse said at last, his eyes on her face. "You are happy here?"

"Yes . . . I am happy, Jesse. Simon and Hannah are kind to me."

"I heard what happened to you from my parents."

"Zibeon?"

"About Zibeon, and the child. All you have been through, your kindness in caring for your mother-in-law."

"I could not leave her."

Jesse moved closer. Marah could smell the scent of new wood and the fields.

"Marah, I am sorry for the loss of your son."

She caught her breath. Time had tempered the pain at the mention of her son, but the sorrow remained. "It is kind of you to say so. They were a strange family, but things were not as bad as I had thought they would be."

Jesse nodded. "I am glad. I lost Tirzah the night Caleb was born. She was not strong. It was difficult, but there were other members of her family to help care for him. When I heard from my parents that they needed me, her family reluctantly let me go. My wife had a brother and two sisters to care for her parents, and well, as you know, I am an only son. I came for their sakes, but was dreading seeing you with Zibeon. Then, when I found out . . ." His voice trailed off as he stared at her in the lamplight.

"You are still so beautiful. Surely in Shechem there are many who have wished to marry such a maiden."

Marah laughed softly. "I am no longer a maiden, Jesse. And yes, there were those who offered marriage, but I could not choose them, at least not at this time."

"I am glad to hear that. Not for your misfortunes, but that

you are not married again." He was smiling down at her in such a way that her legs felt weak. Her heart was beating loudly in her chest, and she felt herself swaying slightly toward him. He caught her shoulders with his strong hands. "Marah," he breathed softly.

The moment was interrupted by a small but audible yawn from Caleb, who had been sitting quietly on the floor. He rubbed his eyes. Jesse stepped back reluctantly and dropped his hands. With a grin he picked up his son.

"I think my son needs to go to sleep. I should go. Tomorrow will be another long day." He touched the tip of his finger to her chin. "You can be sure I will come again, soon. You wouldn't mind?"

She nodded. "I wouldn't mind, I would like that. But go, your son needs his bed."

The little boy could hardly keep his eyes open. He waved shyly to Marah as they left. Jesse looked at her and smiled before heading through the gate in the evening shadows. It was as if all the moonlight had been captured in his face.

Hannah and Simon nodded "good night" as he passed them. They looked expectantly at Marah.

"Well? So what did he say?"

"He would like to come again, to talk. I told him he was welcome. Is that all right?" She looked anxiously at Simon and Hannah who had exchanged a smile between them.

"Yes, it is fine. He is going to come just to talk?" Simon queried with a twinkle in his eyes. "I do hope he does not want to just talk until the rains come. It could get cold up on the roof."

Simon checked the animals to be sure they were settled, and blew out the lamp. Marah lay awake for a long time in the darkness, listening first to the soft voices of Simon and Hannah below and to her own thoughts. She loved Jesse. She knew that with all her heart. And Jesse still cared for her. Suddenly the future seemed full of promise.

19

Tucking their tunics into their girdles to free their legs, Hannah and Marah took their turn at the village mill. They pushed the wooden arms of the grinding stone as they moved steadily around and around grinding the grain to flour. Both of them were strong women, and since Marah found so much to talk about these days, the time passed quickly.

"Will Jesse take supper with us again soon?" Hannah inquired. He was a frequent visitor, sometimes with his small son, and sometimes alone. He didn't stay long, for he was constantly concerned about his parents, especially his mother, Abigail. When he came alone, Hannah and Simon stayed nearby, apparently occupied with handwork, yet Marah knew Hannah hung on every word.

It was not proper for a man to speak to a woman in public, even his own wife. They longed to be alone, and had finally conspired to meet secretly. When she took the sheep to the shepherd, early in the morning, Jesse slipped out and joined her on the path. The trees hid them from the view of prying eyes. Her heart quickened as she thought of their meeting this very morning.

"Marah, I have only a moment today, but there is something I must say to you." He looked so earnest as he took her hand

and looked tenderly down at her. "I have given this much thought and feel that now would be the right time."

"Are you going to go away again?" She searched his face.

He grinned. "Far from that." Then he became serious. "I would like us to marry." He searched her face and waited.

Joy flooded her soul. "Oh Jesse, yes, I would like to marry you." She thought of the little boy. "I hope that Caleb will be happy to have me."

"You would make a wonderful mother to Caleb, beloved, but I was thinking more of a wife for me." His eyes shone brightly as he looked at her.

She looked at his earnest face and met his eyes. "I long to be your wife, Jesse."

"Then it is settled." Slowly he leaned forward to brush her lips with a gentle kiss. As she put her arms around his neck and pressed against him, the gentle kiss deepened into passion. With great effort, Jesse broke away and with his hands on her shoulders, stepped back. "Truly, beloved, if we do not marry soon, I shall not be able to think at all."

She took a deep breath. "Will you speak to Simon? They have watched over me for so long."

"I will speak to Simon. It would be right." He gave her a glorious smile that made her catch her breath. "And it shall be soon, lest I not be able to work either." He headed for his shop in the village.

Marah stood looking after him and thought her heart would burst with happiness. Now, lost in her own reverie, she only heard Hannah when she felt a poke in her ribs.

"If you do not keep your mind on your work, we shall never finish." Hannah laughed. "And you didn't answer my question."

"Question?"

Hannah sighed patiently and looked heavenward for support. "I was asking you if Jesse will be sharing supper with us again soon?"

"Supper? Oh yes, he is coming to share our meal after the

Sabbath." She lowered her voice and looked around to be sure no one overheard. "He wishes to speak to Simon," she whispered, her voice heavy with meaning.

"At last!" Hannah breathed and, at Marah's admonishment, also lowered her voice to a whisper. "I should be an old woman, the time he has taken. We thought he would never get around to it. Such looks Penninah gives me when I pass her in the marketplace. I hear Korah has found a wife in another village. God be praised. Jesse is such a fine young man. It will be a good marriage for you, Marah."

Marah smiled happily and nodded.

The last of the grain was ground and they gathered their flour. As they were preparing to leave, two other women came to take their turn at the mill. They eyed Marah and Hannah with raised eyebrows.

"Have you heard any news?" Leah looked deliberately at both of them and smiled saucily.

"Nothing new," Hannah said, her face all innocence.

"You are sure? And Marah, how do things go with you? There is word that a young man comes to call at the house of Simon and Hannah. He is an old friend?"

Marah refused to be baited. When all the arrangements had been made and it was settled, there would be time enough for all the gossips to wag their tongues.

"Hmm? Yes, an old friend of the family," Hannah murmured as she scooped flour into one of the bags Marah held open.

Leah and Dorcas did not look convinced. Leah cocked one eyebrow in disbelief. Marah and Hannah gathered their bags of flour. They knew the women of the village had been gossiping for weeks. With straight faces, Marah and Hannah walked quickly away from the mill. When they had gone down the street and turned a corner, they burst into laughter. They hurried home to inform Simon of Jesse's impending visit. As Marah urgently let Simon know her wishes, he nodded sagely, his mouth twitching.

It was nearing the Sabbath and Marah busied herself sweeping the courtyard.

The bread was baked as usual that morning with enough to last them for two days. Hannah refilled the oil lamps and gathered the clothes that dried on the rooftop. A vegetable stew simmered in the pot and Marah added fresh herbs. The women wanted to be sure all was in readiness. Every woman of Shechem had a fear of being caught with tasks still to do when the three sharp blasts of the *shofar*, the ram's horn, were heard, marking the beginning of Sabbath.

The first stars of the evening were appearing when the villagers were called to prayer and the Sabbath began. Simon, returning from the fields, stepped in the doorway almost as the last of the sound of the ram's horn died away.

"Good Sabbath," he said, eyeing Hannah as she handed him the bowl of water and a towel to wash for the Sabbath meal.

"Good Sabbath to you, my lord," Hannah returned, then with a fierce whisper, "You are late!"

Simon poured the wine and Hannah spoke the *kiddush* over the goblets. Marah waited quietly as Hannah said her blessing. God had indeed been kind and her heart swelled with her good fortune. Yet while she loved the Sabbath, she was impatient for tomorrow when Jesse would again join them. He would speak to Simon then, would he not? Perhaps tomorrow they would talk when the men gathered in the synagogue for Sabbath worship.

As Simon cleared his throat, Marah realized she had been staring off into space. Respectfully she bowed her head and added her prayers to the worship.

20

Hannah and Marah went to the Court of the Women, while Simon went into the synagogue with the men of Shechem. It was a joyous gathering in the *Bit Allah*, the House of God.

Marah found herself impatiently glancing through the latticework to see Jesse. She found her beloved quickly, for he was standing beneath the small circular window in the roof of the synagogue. His father Elon was at his side. Hannah was absorbed in her prayers and no one was in front of Marah to block her view of Jesse. She could modestly watch, her face hidden by her shawl. She knew that Jesse knew she was there, but as a man of the *Samarim*, he would dedicate himself to prayer. He would not look for her, to embarrass himself in the eyes of the men of Shechem.

The high priest, *Kohen ha-Gadol*, as they named him in Hebrew, was an imposing figure in white. Of the blood of Levi, he, along with the shammash, officiated during the service. The high priest removed the sacred roll of the Law of Moses from the *mucbach*, the small alcove on the altar, which was placed so the congregation faced Mount Gerizim. Marah always felt an excitement when the sacred roll was removed. The *mucbach* also contained a sacred codex that

142

the Samaritans believed was written by Abishua, the great-grandson of Aaron.

The scroll was opened to the blessing of Aaron and read aloud,

> The LORD bless thee and keep thee,
> The LORD make his face shine upon thee, and
>   be gracious unto thee;
> The LORD lift up his countenance upon thee, and
>   give thee peace.
> And they shall put my name upon the children
>   of Israel, and I will bless them.

The scroll was then reverently passed from one man to another through the congregation and each worshiper kissed the sacred passage.

The songs that had been handed down through each generation were sung, and Marah's heart lifted at the words of each one as they rose from the throats of the men and poured from within the four walls of the synagogue to spread on the wind that blew gently through the town.

> Praise ye the LORD.
> Praise, O ye servants of the LORD.
> Blessed be the name of the LORD from this time forth
>   and forevermore.
> From the rising of the sun
> Unto the going down of the same
> The LORD's name is to be praised.
> The LORD is high above all nations,
> And His glory above the heavens.
> Who is like unto the LORD our God, who dwelleth on
>   high!

As the men continued their service, the women returned to their homes to rest and pray and be prepared to serve the midday meal.

No fire could be lit on the Sabbath, so the stew that had

simmered with a wonderful fragrance the night before was put on the table cold. Marah added the bread that had been baked the day before. Wrapping her shawl closer, she caught herself wishing for a fire. Feeling guilty for her lack of respect, she looked heavenward, half expecting the God Who Sees to strike her down for her irreverence.

When Simon returned, both women looked at him expectantly. He shrugged, removed his hat, washed his hands, and sat down for the meal.

"So, you have no news?" Hannah persisted.

"I have come to enjoy my Sabbath meal. Can a man not eat in peace without being badgered?" He said the blessing, reached for the bread, and tearing off a piece, dipped it into the stew. Then, aware of both sets of eyes watching his every move, he relented.

"Jesse's father leaned heavily on his arm during the service. He had to take him home as soon as he could. Perhaps his father is not feeling well today. Jesse did not speak to me except to say, 'Good Sabbath, Simon.' Now may I eat in peace?"

Marah sighed, Hannah shrugged, and they both sat down to share the meal.

21

The day after the Sabbath, Marah was up before the sun had barely risen. She swept the courtyard and the clay floor of the house with vigor until it shone. Every movable object in the house was dusted and placed just so.

She slipped out to meet Jesse on the path, but he did not come. Perhaps he was not coming tonight. Perhaps his father was too ill. All that day as she worked, Marah thought of everything that could go wrong. When it was well into afternoon, Jesse had not sent word he wasn't coming so Marah grew hopeful. The two women prepared a special meal. Hannah killed one of the chickens in honor of the occasion and made a fine stew. They placed vegetables and fresh cheese in the center of the low table. Having washed her face and brushed her rich, auburn hair, Marah braided it carefully. Tonight she wanted to look her best.

"You would think the young man had never been here to supper," groused Simon when he found himself in the way of their vigorous activities for the fourth time. He put on his hat. "I have business in the village," he announced. When neither woman acknowledged his statement, he shrugged and left the courtyard.

Marah felt the day was as a year in its passing. Hannah

complained good-naturedly that all that energy was wearing her out.

Evening finally approached and all was in readiness. Marah sat trying to work on her loom. Her heart leaped when Simon rose to answer a knock at the door. Jesse stood on the threshold.

"Peace be with you," he said as Simon motioned for him to enter.

"And with you. It is good of you to join us for our humble meal."

Jesse came alone, dressed in his Sabbath clothes. His blond hair was carefully combed and his beard trimmed. Marah's heart nearly melted at the sight of him.

Catching Jesse's eyes several times as she served the men, they gazed at each other. Simon's words were bees buzzing softly in the background. The meal and the conversation took forever.

"The carpenter shop goes well for you?" Simon was saying.

"It is hard work, but I like creating useful things out of it. Even when I was a boy, and tended the sheep, I carved things . . ." Jesse caught Marah's look and his eyes danced.

"It is a good thing to do that which you enjoy as your daily living," Simon answered heartily.

They talked about the carpenter trade in detail and then went on to solemnly discuss Simon's crops. From their somber tones, it was as if the mundane things of every day had assumed great significance.

"You would think that the next harvest was the most important topic of conversation at this meal," Hannah whispered fiercely to Marah as they served. When at last their supper was finished, the women cleared the few wooden platters, cleaned them carefully, and placed them on a shelf. Hannah stood back, her hands clasped in front of her. Marah waited anxiously. The room became extremely quiet. Simon looked expectantly at Jesse who cleared his throat.

"It was a fine meal, a fine meal. I thank you for the honor of letting me share it with you." He smiled at them both. Marah, standing in the shadows, felt she could barely contain her impatience.

"There is something else you wish to speak about?" Simon prompted gently.

"Yes. I wish to, ah, thank you for your kindness to Marah through the events that have taken place."

Simon waited.

"It is truly God's blessing that she has good friends who have shared their home with her."

Simon smiled and nodded encouragingly.

"I have come to ask your blessing and permission. I wish to make Marah my wife."

At last the words were out and Marah discovered that she and Hannah had both been holding their breath.

Simon smiled broadly, enjoying his role. Then he became solemn. "You can support a wife and children?"

Knowing Simon, Marah knew he had already inquired tactfully in the village.

Jesse grinned and nodded. Simon was looking out well for the young woman in his charge. "I can support us, and Caleb, . . . and more children when they come."

Hannah clasped her hands to her breast and beamed.

Simon reached out and shook Jesse's hand enthusiastically. "You have our blessing . . . and for what it is worth, we are not blood relatives, you have our permission."

Jesse grew taller as he rose and stood in the lamplight, reaching out his hand to Marah. She longed to be in his arms, but modesty held her back in front of Simon and Hannah. She took Jesse's hand and returned his warm gaze. Simon cleared his throat, reminding them they were not alone.

"And when shall this wedding take place, hm?" Hannah was always the practical one, getting down to business.

"Since it is the end of the barley harvest, I felt it could be soon. My shop does not depend upon the seasons and my father's field is small, so it will not take long to harvest. Since we are both widowed, it did not seem necessary that we wait out the year of betrothal."

Simon grinned from ear to ear. "I think that a short betrothal would be best."

Hannah nodded and looked at Marah. "This is in agreement with you?"

"Yes. I want the wedding to be soon. It nears the end of the month of Nisan. Perhaps the beginning of Tammuz, after the wheat harvest?" That was three months away. It would be a short time to prepare for a wedding, but there was little dowry to discuss and it would be long enough to keep the town gossips from surmising another reason for a hasty wedding.

Simon stroked his beard thoughtfully. "Yes, I think that under the circumstances, this would be acceptable. Your time of mourning has long ended." He nodded his head. "We will announce the good news in the village tomorrow and your betrothal ceremony will be in three days."

Three days. In three days she would be betrothed to Jesse. Marah could hardly breathe for the joy that filled her.

"Wine, woman," Simon said, reaching for his goblet. "We must celebrate!"

Jesse and Simon raised their goblets. "To your wedding!" cried Simon exuberantly.

"To our wedding," Jesse echoed, and they drained their cups.

Marah thought how different it would be this time. She had been so terrified and unhappy before her marriage to Zibeon. She had taken no pleasure in their betrothal ceremony. The betrothal to Shimei was brief and what amounted to a sham. She was thankful a wedding had not taken place. She had not been able to imagine Shimei as her husband. Yet, betrothed, she was the same as his wife in the eyes of the law. So there was the shame of the bill of divorcement. Now that shame would be erased. She would be a wife, Jesse's wife.

22

The betrothal ceremony was a joyous one with a large gathering of neighbors and friends. The women could see that this was a love match. It touched their hearts as it has done with women through the ages. The good wishes were plentiful, and from the bawdy comments of the men, it was easy to see they envied Jesse his bride.

The high priest had not attended, but the shammash solemnly blessed the occasion. He did not speak to Marah again concerning the matter of Shimei, for the whole village knew he had fled and was not likely to return. The bill of divorcement had been duly noted and recorded by the scribes.

The shammash ended his long blessing and turned to Marah. "It is good that you will marry at last," he said.

"Yes, my lord," Marah had answered softly, respectfully lowering her eyes. The shammash turned and left with the elders of the village.

The time of the wheat harvest came. Marah worked closely with Hannah as they fed Simon and the men in the fields. Hannah stayed close to Marah in the fields.

Jesse also came to help in the harvest, and though Marah modestly looked down when they passed, her heart quickened. On the few occasions when Jesse caught her eye, no words were needed.

The month of Sivan passed slowly and in a week the month of Tammuz would usher in her wedding. The women of the village smiled and nodded at Marah as they gathered at the village well. Marah had not gone to Jacob's well for water since the day Reba sent her.

"Are you ready for the wedding, Marah?" asked Leah. "I'm glad you are to marry again. I thought you had not found any of our men to your liking."

Marah ignored the inference and smiled sweetly. "It is good of you to ask, Leah. Yes, I am looking forward to the wedding."

"Such a change from last time. For such a man, I would be eager for the wedding also!"

The women laughed and Marah laughed with them. They could tease her now. In her love for Jesse, nothing could bother her. She also knew the source of their lighthearted camaraderie. They did not have to fear for their husbands any longer. She was no longer a single widow, eyed by half the men of the village, but a betrothed woman. Soon she would be a married woman among them with all the duties of her own household. She would be helping Jesse to care for Caleb and his parents.

As she walked back to Hannah's with the jug of water, she smiled to herself, thinking of Caleb. He was an exuberant little boy and a handful for Jesse's aging parents, Elon and Abigail. She wanted to be Caleb's mother and of course, in time, a mother to their own children. The children who would be born of the love she and Jesse shared.

Jesse was spending all his spare time building a small room adjoining the house of his parents.

"I want us to have a place of our own," he told her earnestly one day.

He made the new room with an opening to the small courtyard as well as the main room of the house. Elon, who had felt stronger in recent days, helped his son as much as he could.

150

The mud brick was carefully placed along the lines that Jesse had laid out, and as the walls went up, Jesse applied the mud plaster to the sides. For the roof, he wove brushwood branches together and laid them on the rafters hewn from several trees. He covered these carefully with a thick layer of clay. It filled the spaces between the branches and formed a hard, smooth layer of plaster. He made a set of steps that went up the outside wall of the room so he and Marah could place their pallet on the roof in hot weather. He formed a parapet around the edges of the roof in keeping with the Book of the Law—

"When you build a new house [in this case, a room], you shall make a parapet for your roof, that you may not bring the guilt of blood upon your house, if anyone fall from it."

Marah came as often as she could to see how the work was progressing. She liked to visit with Abigail.

"Have they not made wonderful progress, Daughter?"

"Oh yes, Mother Abigail. They will be done soon." How she welcomed entering the family of this gentle woman. She always had a kind word for Marah.

Jesse's mother had difficulty with her eyes and could no longer thread a needle so Marah took garments home that were in need of mending.

Elon's field lay outside the town, as did all the fields. Income from it had been meager, but Abigail had managed through the years. Now, in their old age, when Elon could no longer work his field, a helper was hired to care for it while Jesse handled the carpentry shop. Jesse cared for his parents out of love and respect. Abigail and Elon, in turn, thanked God daily for the blessing of a fine son. Elon held up his head in the village and spoke of his son with pride.

The dry season began and the first figs ripened. Soon the grape harvest would begin and the women would be busy making wine for their households. There were figs to dry and small date and nut cakes to pack in heavy crocks, not only for the household, but especially for the wedding feast.

Marah had already decided the wedding would be simple. She would wear the traditional garland around her head and her wedding coins, but her garment would not be the dress that Reba had made for her. She would wear the simple white tunic of the Samaritans, with a full mantle that covered her feet with soft, white fringe.

The man who purchased Zibeon's sandal shop was skilled, and Simon purchased a new pair of sandals for her as a wedding gift. Hannah wove her a new girdle of beautiful rich earth colors.

When the morning of her wedding day came at last, Marah thought of Timnah. She had married an older relative in another village and there had been no word from her since. Atarah had married her potter and in three years had produced two husky children, a boy and a girl. She gained even more weight, but she'd not lost her sense of humor. Married life agreed with her.

No one had to whisper to Marah to smile at the guests. Marah beamed. Even Jesse had not waited for the late hour to come for his bride. The ceremony under the canopy was a joyous one.

Caleb had been so excited, he jumped up and down, crying happily, "I'm going to have a mama. Papa will bring Marah home and she will be my mama."

Finally, as Marah waited in the small room Jesse had added on to the home of his parents, a warmth spread through her at the thought of what God had done. Caleb's small pallet was placed near Jesse's parents for the night. This one night the bridal couple would have all the privacy the small house could afford.

Jesse entered and firmly closed the wooden door that hung on its leather hinges. He had one hand behind his back, and as he came and stood by Marah, looking down at her, his eyes were alight with the love that burned in his heart. He handed her a small bundle of lambskin and waited. Marah looked at Jesse and back to the bundle. There was a lump in her throat as she unfolded the lambskin to reveal a small, beautifully carved instrument.

"Oh Jesse," she breathed in wonder, "the little flute." They both looked at it shining in the dim lamplight. It had not weathered but looked as new as on the day Jesse had first given it to her. Marah looked into Jesse's eyes and saw herself reflected in their depths. Wordlessly she went into his arms.

23

It was early in the day, but there had to be plenty of time allowed for preparation. It was the sacred day of Passover. A time of a *hajj* or serious pilgrim-feast. The whole community would join them as they began their journey to the sacred mountain.

"Caleb, quickly, close up the chickens. It is time." Jesse was to take part in the ceremonies this year and was anxious to get to Mount Gerizim with the others.

A number of lambs were carefully chosen from those born during the previous month of Tishri. They would be sacrificed, as many as needed to feed the community. Extra lambs were also set aside to be used should one of the chosen lambs prove to be unacceptable or unclean.

As they arrived on Mount Gerizim, Jesse helped his father pitch their tent as the women put their things in order for the long wait of Passover. Jesse, now clad in a blue robe given to him for the occasion, joined several other young men as they dug the trenches for the fires.

Over one fire hung a caldron with boiling water necessary for fleecing the lambs. In the other trench, a mass of kindling was lit to make an oven for roasting the lambs. As the fires were started, several elders of the village took turns reading portions of the story of the exodus from Egypt and leading the people in the ancient Passover hymns. The people of Shechem, including the women and children, all faced the *kibla*, the top of Gerizim, as the elders read. It was toward the *kibla* that the *Samarim* prayed. They listened in reverence and awe as the high priest extolled the names of their holy mountain: *Beth-el, the House of God; the Great and Chosen Place; the Tabernacle of His angels; the place destined for sacrifices; the House of the powerful God; the Mount of Inheritance and of the Abode (Shekinah glory).* Surely nowhere in the land was there anything like their holy mountain, Gerizim.

As sunset approached, one of the young men deftly cut the throats of the lambs over a ditch. The blood was passed among the families and was touched to the faces of the men, women, and children. Marah bowed her head as Jesse touched her face with the sacred reminder of how their ancestors had been saved from the Death Angel. For the Death Angel passed over the homes of those families who had applied the blood to the doorposts of their homes as Moses had commanded. The firstborn of Egypt, from the son of Pharaoh to the lowest servant, had died. It was the final plague that would set her people free.

The high priest made a ritual inspection of the lambs, looking for blemishes. The sinews of the legs were withdrawn and the lambs were spitted on a long stick. When the lambs were prepared, they were laid over the heated oven and a thick covering of turf was laid over them to seal the oven.

Waiting was the hardest time for small children, for the roasting took three or four hours.

"Mama, when will the lambs be ready?" Caleb asked again. "I am hungry."

Marah still felt a tug at her heart to have the little boy call her mama. She brushed his hair with her hand and smiled at him. "It will be a long time, Caleb. Would you like to have me tell you some stories?"

"Oh yes. Tell me again about Moses and the angels, Mama." He snuggled up against her.

155

"Well, you know that Moses was our great leader. When he died, he entered into heaven itself, and there sat on a great white throne, while he wrote our sacred Scriptures; by the glory of the angels was he nourished, of their food he ate, at their table he sat, with their bread he satisfied his hunger, in their bath he bathed, and in their tent he dwelt. In heaven he is greater than the angels, for these sing the praises of the Lawgiver, as they call upon him to read the Law . . ." She stopped and looked down at Caleb, who had fallen asleep in the miraculous simplicity of very young children. He was a handsome little boy, the image of his father. He had inherited the blond hair from his father's line, and from his size now, Marah knew he would also be tall.

Abigail was frailer than ever, and while she had walked slowly beside her husband to the mountain, it was obvious to Marah that the elderly woman was exhausted. Abigail slept quietly and Marah also closed her eyes. Most of the village rested, waiting.

The signal was given that the lambs were cooked, and the blackened lambs were removed from the oven. The high priest spoke the familiar words of the Passover service. His words echoed down the mountain to the men of the village who had gathered, their robes tucked partly into their girdles, "girding their loins," and their staffs in their hands. Elon stood in dignified silence near Simon.

Since the commandment had been to "eat in haste," the men fell upon the meat, eating their full share before taking wooden platters to the waiting women and children who remained in the tents. Marah, Caleb, and Abigail hungrily tore off pieces and ate the warm meat that Jesse and Elon brought them.

Marah and Caleb, as well as all the other families, carefully gathered up any bones and scraps and wool that was left and threw them into the still smoldering fire. All must be consumed and reduced to ashes. The commandment was that "nothing should remain until the morrow."

Marah uncovered the small earthen jar of water she had brought, and they all performed the ceremonial washing before standing at the door of their tent for the final prayers. The voice of the high priest solemnly reverberated through the mass of people. It seemed to Marah as the voice of God speaking from their sacred mountain.

With his duties over, Jesse tucked the rolled tent under his arm and Marah helped lift the sleeping Caleb to his shoulder. Jesse's strong carpenter arms carried both easily. Marah gathered the rest of their things, and they joined their neighbors as the people made their way in the moonlight back to their homes in the village. Some carried candles and others carried small oil lamps as they walked. Simon and Hannah walked close by Elon and Abigail as she held tightly to her husband's arm.

Marah, watching her mother-in-law slowly make her way home, was filled with a sense of sadness. Abigail would probably not see another Passover.

The village dogs barked, and men looked after their families. In the late hour, no one wanted to be left alone on the mountain or be a straggler on the road home.

"You did well at the Passover, Jesse," Marah said with pride as they walked. "I saw the high priest watching you and he seemed pleased."

"He is responsible for the work of the Passover. At least he did not seem as irritable as last year." His tone of voice told Marah he was happy with her observation. Then Jesse chuckled to himself. "I thought Gera was going to fall into the oven. He almost stumbled placing the lambs."

"Perhaps he was nervous?"

"Perhaps."

Marah looked at Caleb, asleep on his father's shoulder. He was as dear to her as if she really was his mother, yet, how she longed to give Jesse a child. She had been late for the time of women this month and a hope had risen in her heart that she would bear a child for Jesse at last. Her hopes had been dashed again. Though they had been married four years, there was still no child. Her barrenness lay heavy on her heart. When she had timidly spoken of it to Jesse, he had drawn her close and kissed her.

"To have you in my arms, beloved, is enough. Don't worry. It shall happen in time. I have a son already." He meant to comfort her, but it was a reminder that his only child was by another wife.

As the months stretched into years, her desolation increased. Had the Lord shut up her womb? Had the child she had borne Zibeon damaged her in some way? Her heart cried out, *Oh God Who Sees Me, am I never to bear Jesse a child? Are You punishing me for my pact with Shimei? It was wrong in Your eyes. Surely I shall not bear the shame of that forever.* Marah kept her agreement with Shimei to herself. No one must ever know she had conspired to do such a thing. Yet God had seen and heard. Marah felt a weight on her chest. Perhaps this barrenness was her punishment forever. She had gone to Shelomith the midwife to see if there were any herbs that would help, but nothing had worked.

At last Shelomith had shaken her head sadly. "You were badly torn. The babe nearly took your life with him, so great was he. It could be that there is more damage inside that we cannot see. Only God can give life. I can do no more."

Yet while her husband was strong and lusty, she was sure she would never bear another child. She looked over at Jesse's handsome face in the moonlight, a lock of hair over one eye. How she loved him. Elon and Abigail, unlike Athaliah, never reproached her for not giving them more grandchildren. They delighted in Caleb and loved Marah like a daughter. It was a peaceful household.

She looked around at her small family. She had much to be thankful for, yet a tear slipped silently down her face. Brushing it away, she moved closer to Jesse as they neared Shechem.

PART V

Haman

24

The horse galloped wildly, its flanks wet with lather, mouth foaming at the bit as it obeyed the relentless urging of its rider.

"Faster, faster, you poor excuse for a beast!"

Haman looked back briefly over his shoulder, seeking a sign of the two men who pursued him. Two small figures appeared in the distance. Far enough. He would make the gates of Shechem.

The men at the caravansary opened the gate as he approached. The sun sank behind Mount Gerizim as he dashed through the gate and brought the heaving animal to a halt. He looked to his rear with a touch of a sneer in his smile. *I have reached Shechem*, he thought. *I am safe.*

"Perhaps it is too late to find the house of Elon," Haman considered as he narrowed his eyes and pursed his lips. He needed to rest, he thought, stretching his cramped muscles and yawning. "Tomorrow is soon enough to seek out my long-lost relatives, if they are here."

No other strangers came into the caravansary before the gates closed, but it would not be wise to go about in an unfamiliar town this night. He stretched again and turned toward the man who was obviously in charge. Perhaps what he needed would come to him. Introducing himself, he made a brief inquiry and went to the cubicle of a room he had been assigned. With disgust he noted the simple bed and table with a small lamp. It was not what he had been used to, yet under the circumstances it would have to do. In due time, there was a knock on the door, and a woman lifted the heavy curtain and entered, her bracelets tinkling in the soft light.

"You sent for me, my lord?" Removing her mantle, she moved toward him with practiced grace.

In the morning, Haman stood in the doorway. He had not given a thought to his horse. A servant had led the animal away. Well, he didn't need it now anyway. From the looks of things, he would not need it for a long time. Perhaps he would sell the beast. He patted his girdle where he had tucked the bag of coins. It would have to take care of him for some time. Frowning, he considered the events of the previous night. Traveling by himself had been his downfall, that and being foolish enough to investigate someone's cry for help. He found a drunken merchant lying dead, his murderer poised with the dripping knife still in his hand as he reached for a bag of coins on the ground. When Haman slid off his horse and took in the scene, the thief, thinking him to also be easy prey, lunged at him. Strong and agile, he sidestepped the clumsy thrust of the knife and planted his own between the thief's shoulder blades.

"Fool! Did you think to make me your next victim?" He picked up the merchant's purse that had dropped from the dead man's hand and turned to look at the merchant.

"Ah Haman, you have an interesting dilemma here. Keep the gold or go to the nearby caravan and find relatives or friends of the merchant." Perhaps there was some gain here for him. He tucked the gold into his girdle with one hand and was preparing to clean his knife.

Just then riders appeared on their camels, materializing out of the night. He stood beside the dead bodies with the knife in his hand and eyed them warily.

162

"He has killed your brother and his servant, Zadok. Kill the thief where he stands!"

"Murderer! You shall pay for your crime!"

"I didn't kill the merchant. His own servant killed him and tried to kill me. He lies beside his master."

"You lie, murderer, you shall pay!"

From the looks on their faces, this was not a time for discussion. He grabbed the reins of his horse and swung into the saddle; in a moment he was riding for his life.

The two men had stopped to take care of the dead merchant and his servant, but he knew they would pursue him. They believed he killed the brother of one of them. The Avenger of Blood would demand his life in return. His only hope was to reach Shechem. It was his good fortune that it was not only his destination but it was one of the cities of refuge, designated by God in the Book of the Law. Now, the idea of looking up these relatives appeared an even better one. He had ridden hard to make Shechem by nightfall. It was a matter of life or death.

He surveyed the compound for anyone who looked suspicious and questioned one of the camel drivers.

"Has anyone else entered the caravansary this morning?"

"No one," the man replied, shrugging his shoulders.

Haman strolled toward the gate that led from the caravansary into the city of Shechem. Now, where to find the house of Elon. A family would be extremely convenient now. He congratulated himself on his good luck. Now if he could only convince the elders of the city of his innocence, but it would be his word against the testimony of two men who had seen him with the knife in his hand. May a thousand flies descend upon their camels! Why did they have to appear just when they did? He shook his head and walked quickly toward the street of the carpenters. His head was covered, but his eyes did not miss anyone who looked too closely in his direction.

A man on the street directed him to the carpentry shop of Elon's son.

"Is this the shop of my cousin Jesse, son of Elon?" Haman asked, observing an ax and hatchet leaning against one wall and an adz for shaping wood on the work bench.

"I am Jesse." Jesse put down the plane he had been examining for sharpness and walked toward Haman. "Did you say cousin?" He appeared puzzled.

"I am Haman, son of Jemuel, your father's eldest brother."

Puzzlement turned to delight. Muscles rippled on the arm that Jesse extended. His large hand clapped Haman on the shoulder.

"Truly I had forgotten my father had an elder brother," Jesse said with a smile. "He has not spoken of him in many years. You are his son?" The brown eyes appraised Haman, in a friendly but cautious way.

Haman was a sizable man himself, but had nearly buckled under the strength of Jesse's exuberant hand. He moved away ever so slightly and nodded with a wry smile. "Your father Elon lives?"

"He lives. He is not strong but he does well. He will be glad to meet you. Come, I will close my shop and take you to him. Please make our humble home yours and share our evening meal."

"It would be my pleasure."

Jesse secured the doors to the front of his shop and with a grin beckoned Haman to follow as, with great strides, he headed homeward.

Marah watched for Jesse as she always did at the end of the day. She was surprised to see a stranger enter the courtyard with him. Caleb ran to meet his father, and Marah watched from the shadow of the doorway as Jesse introduced his son to the stranger. Caleb, now nine, was already helping his father in the carpenter shop and doing tasks usually left to older boys or apprentices. He was also taller than most boys his age.

Caleb eyed the stranger quietly but hung back when he was introduced.

Haman put a hand on Caleb's shoulder and smiled. "It is

good to meet the son of my cousin." He turned toward the house and the smile that had not reached his eyes became an ingratiating one as he gazed at Marah. She stepped out to meet them.

"Haman, my wife Marah. Marah, this is my cousin Haman, son of my father's older brother Jemuel. He has been living in Joppa and has traveled a great distance to pay us a visit."

While Jesse was making his introduction, Marah was aware of the warm, appraising eyes of Haman. She noted his beard, combed to a point. A gold earring gleamed in one ear. He was nearly as tall as Jesse, but thicker in girth. A handsome man, sure of himself . . . and his welcome.

"Welcome to our home, Haman. I didn't know my husband had any relatives in Joppa."

Haman had an easy manner. He stood by the house as if he had always belonged there.

"Peace be unto this house," he said as he stooped to enter. He looked around with frank admiration at the wooden furnishings that Jesse had made for their home. "Truly it is the blessing of God to have a husband gifted in the working of wood."

"Peace be unto you," said Elon, rising slowly to greet them. "Welcome to our home." Then, turning to Jesse, "And who is this stranger who graces us with his presence?"

Jesse put an affectionate arm around his father's frail shoulders. "Father, this is no other than Haman, the son of your elder brother Jemuel. He comes to us from Joppa."

"Jemuel?" The old man's eyes widened and became moist. "My older brother Jemuel? I had given up hope of ever hearing from him again. Tell me, he is well? What news do you bring us of him and your family?" He peered anxiously at Haman.

Haman shook his head ruefully. "Your brother, my father, died when I was just a boy. He was a merchant of sorts. I confess I can tell you little of the family. My mother . . . also died. I have fended for myself for a long time."

165

Elon's shoulders sagged as he pondered the news for a moment. Then he straightened up with dignity and regarded Haman warmly.

"But Jemuel leaves a son, a nephew I did not know I had. It is good of you to come to us. But tell me, how is it you have not come before?"

Haman shrugged his shoulders good-naturedly. "I only heard recently that my father had a brother who was living in Shechem. I determined that I would look you up when I came this way. As it turns out, I will be, ah, spending some time in Shechem."

Jesse and Marah had listened intently, and Jesse was delighted that the son of his father's long-lost brother had come while Elon still lived and could enjoy the reunion. Marah moved quickly to set out a simple meal. She brought the wineskin and poured wine for the three men. She still had a few small raisin cakes in the crock, and she placed them on the table.

"You will stay with us, of course," Elon was saying. Marah waited for Haman's answer. She was intrigued with this strange relative who had appeared out of nowhere.

"Yes," added Jesse, "our home is your home. You must tell us of life in Joppa."

"Your offer is a gracious one. You must forgive me, for it is difficult to resist." He glanced at Marah. "I have already taken quarters at the caravansary."

"The caravansary?"

"Yes. I know of a merchant by the name of Ahmal who follows the trade routes. He lives here in Shechem, when his caravan is not on route. I was told he as well as the owner of the caravansary can use someone of my, ah, skills."

Jesse nodded. "I have heard of Ahmal, the caravan master. His caravans do a brisk trade here in Shechem."

Marah listened eagerly as she went about her duties. She was eager to learn about the world of the caravans.

Haman gave them all a dazzling smile, but Marah felt

166

somehow it was for her benefit. "The son of my uncle is indeed a fortunate man to have captured the most beautiful of women for his own."

Marah felt her cheeks grow warm. She lowered her eyes quickly, for the gaze of Haman was bold as well as disconcerting. She had not missed the thoughtful look on Jesse's face as he gazed quietly at his cousin.

Caleb, who had been penning up the chickens, came in and sat down, reaching for a raisin cake. They usually just had these on special occasions.

"Did you come in a caravan?" he asked.

"No, I rode alone. I have a horse."

Caleb's eyes grew wide. "You own a horse? No one in our neighborhood owns a horse!" He looked admiringly at Haman.

"You travel at risk, to travel so far alone, cousin," said Jesse, whose face in the last few moments was unreadable.

Haman nodded ruefully. "I ran into bandits in the hills. I was able to outrun them, but I feared I would not make the city before they caught up with me. God in His mercy was with me and I entered the city gates just as they were closing for the night."

Elon looked startled. "You were indeed fortunate. The soldiers patrol the hills, but the roads are not safe for a lone traveler. Tell me, nephew, why would you not travel in the safety of a caravan?"

Marah thought she saw the briefest hint of annoyance on Haman's face, but his rich laugh covered the moment.

"True, I have a tendency to become impatient when I have set my mind to do something. I could not wait another month for the caravan to leave for Shechem. I was anxious to meet the relatives I had never seen." He gestured to include them all, but his gaze lingered for the briefest possible moment on Marah. Then he looked around the room and turned to Elon. "Your wife, my aunt, she is not with you?"

Jesse sighed. "To our sorrow my mother, Abigail, died over

two years ago." He glanced at his father who had bowed his head at the mention of his wife's name. He still missed her.

Haman put a comforting hand on Elon's arm. "I am truly sorry to have missed her, Uncle. It is clear that she was dear to you." He turned back to Jesse. "Now tell me, cousin, how does your carpenter shop go? You do well here?"

Jesse's face was thoughtful for a moment, but he smiled and leaned forward as they began to discuss his trade. Haman asked seemingly innocuous questions—a relative just gathering news of his family.

Marah listened unobtrusively as she moved about the room, refilling the wine goblets and quietly halting Caleb's hand as he reached for a third raisin cake. He sighed and with a grin reached for a dried fig. Marah smiled indulgently. It was hard to resist Caleb. He was constantly hungry, always eager to please, and an obedient boy. She loved him dearly.

There was a commotion outside and Caleb jumped up and hurried to the door. "The goat is loose again," he cried as he dashed outside. Marah and Jesse quickly followed.

Between the two of them, they caught the goat, but not before it had wreaked havoc with the plants in the courtyard.

"Did you tie him securely, Caleb?"

He hung his head. "I was excited when Cousin Haman came. I forgot."

"He is your responsibility, my son." Jesse spoke from behind Marah as he surveyed the damage. "Tomorrow you must help your mother repair what you can."

"Yes, Papa," Caleb mumbled. He adored his father and seldom did Jesse have the occasion to rebuke him. He stood silently, ashamed and forlorn.

Marah softened. "It is time for sleep, Caleb. We will work together tomorrow to put things right again."

At the gentleness of her tone, Caleb brightened. She was not angry with him. He nodded to them all and hurried into the house.

Haman came outside and observed the scene quietly.

Marah knew he did not miss the look of love that Jesse gave her as they all returned to the house.

Marah was aware of Haman walking on her other side. He smelled of leather and fragrance. It was not unpleasant.

When Haman had gone, Marah turned to Jesse thoughtfully. "What do you think of your cousin Haman?"

Jesse considered a moment, then spoke quietly. "An interesting man. A bit mysterious, perhaps a tale that is not all told."

25

Haman was a frequent visitor to their home. He stayed at the caravansary where he now worked. He seldom spoke of what he did there, but they knew he had something to do with the merchants and the caravans that came to Shechem. Somehow he didn't seem the type to work at that sort of task, but he seemed always in good spirits and did not complain. He brought occasional small gifts for Caleb and spent time talking with Elon and Jesse about Joppa.

"Joppa is called the gateway to Palestine, for it is built on a rocky knoll that projects out into the Great Sea."

"The Great Sea?" interrupted Caleb, fascinated with the stories of the caravansary and places far away.

"Its other name is the Mediterranean." Haman seemed inordinately patient with Caleb's questions. He believed Caleb to be the son of Marah and Jesse and there did not seem to be a need to tell him differently. It was as if she had always been Caleb's mother.

"Joppa has a circle of great rocks that form a harbor," Haman continued. "The cedars of Lebanon were shipped to Joppa when King Solomon was building the great temple in Jerusalem. I have seen the temple. It is magnificent."

"We believe that Mount Gerizim, our holy mountain, is the place to worship," Jesse put in. "The Jews worship in Jerusalem, but we of the Samarim do not share their views. There is none greater than our holy mountain, Gerizim."

"That is true, Cousin, but the temple is magnificent all the same. Great pillars, courts bustling with many people from many lands, moneychangers, merchants selling doves, goats, lambs for sacrifice. It is a meeting place. Many teachers and rabbis come from far and near to talk to the people who gather there."

Elon became stern when they mentioned the temple in Jerusalem. "What could they tell the people that we of the Samarim do not already know? When have you heard a Jewish rabbi with any new thoughts?" he growled.

Haman was not deterred. "As a matter of fact, there are many with new and different thoughts these days."

Jesse changed the subject. "Have you been to Caesarea, Cousin? I hear it is also a great seaport."

"Yes, an interesting port. Two giant towers mark the entrance to the harbor. Merchandise from all over the world comes into Caesarea."

"What sort of merchandise?" Caleb asked, fascinated.

"Well, there are stevedores, workmen who unload bales of wool and amphorae, or large clay storage jars used for wine or dried fruit. Much grain is shipped through there. There is also glassware from Syria, timber from Palestine, frankincense and myrrh from Arabia . . . many wonderful things. These are brought in by the ships and transferred to the caravans that take them inland, like the ones that come here to Shechem."

Caleb asked so many questions that Jesse, sensing his cousin's slight impatience, put a hand on Caleb's shoulder. Caleb realized he had spoken more than he should in the presence of his elders and was instantly silent.

It was time to finish serving the meal. Jesse and Caleb spoke quietly and Elon observed them benignly as he ate. Glancing at Haman, Marah unexpectedly met his bold stare. Instinct told her to be careful. He was too open in his admiration, and Jesse was becoming increasingly wary of Haman's casual visits, especially during the day when Jesse was at work in his shop. Haman always had a good reason for his visits, a question for Elon, a small gift for Caleb, or to tell about what was happening at the caravansary. He knew she loved to hear about the caravans, the merchants and goods being carried on the trade routes. Haman always had a tale to tell of some incident.

Jesse had been brooding ever since he learned that his father had invited Haman to join them for yet another evening meal.

"I am glad for my father. He and Caleb at least seem to enjoy the many visits of my cousin." The last word was spoken harshly. "But surely he is not as devoted a nephew as he would appear. It is plain he admires my wife!"

"Husband, you are the light of my life and the keeper of my heart. No man could take your place, ever. Perhaps that is just Haman's way." She looked earnestly into his face, her hand on his cheek, and laid her cheek on his shoulder.

He held her close. "I am a foolish, jealous husband. You are so beautiful, wife of my heart. If ever I were to lose you, it would be as though my life had ended."

"And if anything happened to you, my life would end also. Oh Jesse, may we be as one all the life that God has given to us."

"May we be as one," he whispered gently and brushed her hair with his lips.

26

When can I come to see the caravansary, Cousin Haman?" Caleb had longed to see the inside for a long while, but Marah knew, as a woman, she did not belong among the muleteers and camel drivers, even with her son as companion.

"How about tomorrow?" Haman said casually, anticipating the boy's response.

"Tomorrow? Oh Papa, tomorrow. Please, may I go with Haman? I will be very careful and not get in anyone's way? Please?" He implored his father.

"Actually I thought my uncle Elon and Marah could accompany me, as well as yourself, Cousin." The last was added hastily.

"It is no place for a woman," said Elon with a frown.

"I agree. It is no place for Marah. Take my son and my father if you will."

Haman's face was bland. "I only wished to have my friend Ahmal, the merchant, meet the family I told him about. His caravan comes into Shechem tomorrow with many goods for the marketplace. Perhaps the wife of my cousin wishes to choose something from the caravan?" He turned innocent eyes on Marah.

"You present an enticing offer, Cousin," Jesse said evenly.

"But we are a simple family, not used to purchasing trade goods from passing merchants."

Marah had been watching the two of them and felt the tension building. She raised her eyes appealingly to her father-in-law.

"I would be honored to go with you, Nephew, to meet your friend. My grandson can go with us, and I believe that my son might spare a few moments from his work to accompany us also. In the care of three," he glanced at his grandson, "or should I say four males of her household, our Marah should be safe."

Caleb had straightened his shoulders noticeably at his grandfather's words, and Marah turned away to hide a smile and her own excitement. Jesse would go if she went, and she did want to see the caravansary. Listening quietly for Jesse's answer, she waited.

"If it pleases you, Father, we will all go. It will not hurt to take a short time away from the shop, even though I do have a rather unusual order to meet. The day after tomorrow I need to select a rather large oak tree."

"Papa, may I go with you to find the tree?"

"You will be at school in the synagogue, my son. Perhaps another time." Jesse ruffled Caleb's hair affectionately.

Ordinarily Caleb would have been devastated, but with the prospect of seeing the caravansary tomorrow, he was pacified.

"Could I be of help, cousin?" Haman offered. "If the tree is of any size, an extra pair of hands could be useful." He glanced toward the town. "Have you noticed any strange men in town you haven't seen before? I was thinking of the robbers who nearly overtook me when I came to Shechem."

Jesse shrugged. "Shechem is filled with Israelites from many of the tribes as well as men from other parts of the world who pass through with the caravans. Who knows whether they have entered the town."

Marah wondered at the strange look, almost of fear, that

crossed Haman's face. He glanced again toward the town and then turned back to them, smiling again, his eyes lingering on Marah's face in open admiration. She suddenly felt uncomfortable and looked modestly at the ground, not wishing to provoke a scene.

Jesse spoke suddenly. "How well do you handle the long saw, Cousin?"

Haman looked at Jesse, his face bland. "As good as any man." He looked down at his hands, strong, but smooth, and added ruefully, "But it has been a long time. You can teach me once again, I am sure."

Jesse nodded. "Done, I leave at dawn the day after tomorrow. And cousin, the tree I seek will indeed challenge your, ah, dormant skills."

The men joined in uneasy laughter, and Marah was glad the tension that had marred the evening was broken. Yet as she listened to Haman's conversational skills and how he drew in her father-in-law and Caleb, she wondered at Jesse's words. Was Haman indeed a tale not yet told? Was there more to this cousin than appeared on the surface? She looked at the face of Elon. He was so delighted with his brother's son. It must be a good thing, she reasoned, and smiling to herself, went about setting her cooking area in order.

27

Caleb could hardly contain himself as they started toward the caravansary. Marah watched with amusement as he fairly skipped along beside his father. She had selected a mantle of heavier than usual fabric to protect her face. Jesse was pleased that she was attired as modestly as possible and had given her one of his slow smiles that tugged at her heart.

They walked slowly, gauging their pace for Elon who walked beside Haman. As they passed through the marketplace, their noses were assailed by the tang of fish, olives packed in stone jars, and perfumes. They passed stalls of linen and the soap the Samaritans were known for, as well as baskets of dates, nuts, leeks, and cucumbers. At the stall of the spice merchant, baskets of mint, dill, coriander, rue, and mustard mingled their fragrances. Marah admired the stalls of the woolen merchants, for Shechem was known for its wool. She would have liked to stop and finger some of the garments, but moved quietly on behind her husband and father-in-law. Haman was greeted by a short, fat man who had been sitting in one of the wine shops as they passed. He appeared to want to talk, but Haman brushed him aside with a meaningful look. The man shrugged and sat down again.

Marah had rarely been to this side of the city of Shechem,

for not far from the caravansary were the weavers, who were looked down upon by the other trades. While their craft was in demand, it was considered women's work. Beyond them, outside the city walls, were the tanners and copper smelters, both odious trades. She shook her head as she remembered hearing of women who had obtained a bill of divorcement simply because they learned their "intended" was one of these tradesmen and the smell would be unbearable. They could even get a bill of divorcement *after* the marriage had taken place if they found the stench of the trade not to their liking. For a brief moment she remembered Zibeon, but that was long ago. With pride she thought of Jesse's trade. Carpentry was a worthy occupation.

The men stopped at one stall at Caleb's persistence. The tradesman carved small animals out of olive wood. Caleb looked at a delicately carved camel. Jesse could probably make one for Caleb, but he had little time for carving these days.

The tradesman, seeing a possible sale, began to extol the virtues of his work, and Jesse casually examined the camel. In a few moments of bartering, Jesse produced a coin and Caleb tucked the camel in his girdle, thanking his father profusely. Jesse nodded and glanced briefly at Haman, whose face was unreadable.

They entered the narrow gate from the city that led to the caravansary. The stench of the camels gathered at the stone troughs was hard on the senses. Some were being watered and others stood or lay in groups according to the time their caravan had arrived. Piles of straw were here and there and some were feeding. They contemplated the newcomers with large indolent eyes and chewed their cud. In the corner of the large courtyard was a stone two-story building with stairs that led to the upper level where there were rooms for wealthier merchants to stay. Doorways were covered by colorful tapestries and rugs. Down below, there were large arched openings where animals could be sheltered in inclement weather—poorer travelers were obliged to share these rude lodgings with their animals.

Haman excused himself and walked over to a group of men near the center of the courtyard, which was dotted with merchants sharing information. He spoke briefly to one of them. The man nodded and returned with Haman to where the family was waiting.

The merchant was portly, but not heavy. His beard was full and his face had a pleasant expression. He walked with the air of a man who was used to being in charge, but he did not appear arrogant.

"Uncle, Cousin, may I present Ahmal, a caravan master, who has been most kind in allowing me to work for him, truly a blessing in my time of need."

Marah couldn't imagine Haman being in a time of need. He seemed too sure of himself and too self-reliant.

"Our pleasure, my lord," murmured Jesse and Elon, nodding their heads respectfully.

"Greetings. It is my pleasure indeed to meet the family of Haman."

Ahmal's eyes twinkled as he very seriously greeted Caleb. The boy was obviously beside himself with excitement.

"A fine young man you have here." The small edges of his eyes crinkled with Ahmal's ready smile. Marah decided that she liked the man.

Ahmal inquired as to how the carpentry trade was going. Marah left them to their discussion and turned away to look at the camels. When she found a couple of the camel drivers eyeing her with interest, she quickly turned back and moved closer to Jesse.

". . . carrying the wonderful soaps and woolens of Shechem," Ahmal was saying. "I bring back copper pots, linens, spices, and other goods."

"How large is your caravan, my lord?"

Ahmal's eyes appraised Jesse carefully. It was obvious that he liked what he saw, for his head nodded imperceptibly.

"Forty to fifty camels, twenty or so mules, drivers and mule-teers, and of course my own armed men. It is an unfortunate necessity, bandits still roaming the hills." He looked briefly at Haman but said no more about bandits.

Caleb could not hide his curiosity. "The camels are different."

Ahmal put his hand up to stop Jesse's apology for his son and smiled down at the boy. "That is because they have different uses. The *djemel* is the pack animal of the caravans. A bit obstinate, that one, but built to carry a full load with ease."

Caleb looked at another camel Ahmal indicated. Its broad head was tapered to a narrow muzzle with firm lips. Its large eyes with their heavy lids and long lashes observed them in-solently. "That is the fleet and elegant riding camel. They are called *mehari*. Their legs are built to insure a fast and easy gait for their riders."

All the nearby camels had a guiding ring that had pierced the right nostril. Through the rings, the reins tied the camels to posts.

Marah was fascinated. She had questions she wanted to ask, but knew it would embarrass Jesse in front of the merchant for her to speak.

Elon broke in. "My nephew Haman works for you? There would appear much to do." Elon looked around, obviously wondering exactly what his nephew did.

Ahmal broke in as Haman started to speak. "He is a factor for me. He procures goods from the merchants of Shechem, at a fair price, and prepares them for the arrival of my caravan."

Evidently Haman was not offended, for he added, "I also sell Ahmal's goods to the local merchants. It is a good trade all around. And, of course, I have my share."

That would explain why he always had money, Marah thought. They had wondered at that too. At least Jesse's cousin seemed to be engaged in an honest business.

"Where is your horse?" Caleb asked Haman, looking all around anxiously at the busy courtyard.

Haman led Caleb to one of the stalls. He reached out to stroke the muzzle, but the horse shied away from his touch. Caleb reached up to pet him also, and to the boy's delight, the horse prodded his shoulder with his nose. For some reason this seemed to annoy Haman. Aware that Marah was nearby and watching them, he spoke casually.

"A spirited animal, you had best be careful, Caleb. Perhaps he should be left alone." He led the reluctant boy away from the horse. Caleb looked back over his shoulder.

"I think he likes me. When I grow up, I shall have a horse just like this one. Can I come to see him again sometime?"

Haman nodded absentmindedly. "Yes, of course, some other time."

Marah turned back to Jesse, Elon, and the merchant Ahmal. She did not see where Caleb went until there was a commotion nearby.

Jesse strode quickly to retrieve Caleb from the hands of an angry camel driver. Caleb had come too close to one of the camels and Marah could make out the words "stubborn . . . spits" as the man waved his hands in the air.

"A thousand pardons, my friends." Ahmal nodded to them and went to say a few words to the camel driver. The man quickly fell silent and sullenly moved away from the scene. Ahmal returned.

"He is one of my men. He was concerned about the boy. That is a mean camel. He is known to spit frequently at those who bother him. If he was not such a good pack animal, he would be made into a footstool!" They all smiled, but Jesse put a firm hand on Caleb's shoulder, insuring that he would stay close by from now on.

"Do you live here in Shechem?" asked Elon.

"My travels take me many places, too many to stay in one place any length of time. Yet I confess, Shechem is the city of my birth and I think one day I will settle down when I am too old for all this traveling. In the meantime, I have a small house that belongs to my family. I have a steward who cares for it in my absence."

He spread his hands to include them all. "Would you do me the greatest honor to take supper with me this evening? The fare is simple, but to my liking."

It was settled, and Marah knew Jesse would not return to the carpenter shop this day.

From Ahmal's words, Marah expected a small house somewhere in the city. He led them through a few streets and entered a wooden gateway. They came to a small but beautiful courtyard with flowers and shrubs with a fountain in the center. With two stories, the house itself was not small by their simple standards. Tapestries hung on two of the walls and stone shelves in the walls held treasures that Ahmal had taken a liking to on his journeys. An older man, dressed in a simple tunic, came forward to greet them.

"Welcome home, good master. Your message was received and I have prepared for your guests."

"My friends, this is Eliab, my steward. Were it not for Eliab, I would have a poor welcome and sleep with the camel drivers."

Eliab smiled at Ahmal. They were master and servant, yet Marah saw they were greatly fond of one another.

"Come, dinner is prepared." Eliab bowed and indicated with his hand that they should follow him.

"We should have such a small, humble house as this," whispered Jesse with a wry grin.

The meal was delightful. Ahmal was a charming and solicitous host. He courteously inquired about the carpentry trade and the items that Jesse made. He spoke with Elon concerning his field and the problems of a farmer. He examined the small camel that Caleb showed him proudly and exclaimed over its workmanship.

Marah listened to the men's conversation and kept an eye on Caleb. The talk flowed over and around her, and with the full meal and sweet cakes for dessert, she was pleasantly full. Glancing at Elon, she saw that he was looking a little tired. It had been a long day for him.

When Haman told an exceptionally funny tale, she could not resist laughing softly. She looked up on one such moment to find Haman's eyes on her. She glanced at Jesse who was watching Haman, his eyes glittering momentarily. Then, for some reason she looked at their host. He was observing them all, his face bland and unreadable.

Jesse stood up quietly. "We wish to thank you for your generous hospitality, my lord. It has indeed been a wonderful meal. May God bless you abundantly for your kindness to my family."

Ahmal made the expected protest, extolling the early hour. When they insisted they could not presume upon his gracious hospitality further, Ahmal bowed and reluctantly bid them good night.

Marah knew that the next day her husband would have to work hard to make up for the time missed today.

28

Jesse rose early to prepare for the day's travel. He knew where to find the oak tree he needed for a merchant's recent order. He'd made a heavy cart to bring the wood back to his shop and was hitching the mule he had borrowed from a friend. Haman had not appeared. Just as Jesse thought Haman had backed out of his promise, he strolled into the courtyard obviously dressed for work. Jesse nodded at him with approval.

"Shall we be going, Cousin? The sun rises and the day will be hot."

Haman smiled. "After you, Cousin. I'm ready to work."

Marah came out and handed Jesse a leather pouch with provisions for lunch and a jug of water in a leather sling. He swung the leather pouch and leather sling over his shoulder and touched Marah's cheek briefly with his hand.

"May God keep you on your journey, Husband."

"God keep you, Wife," he said with a smile. "We shall be hungry men after this day's work. I shall probably be ready to eat for three."

"You already do, Husband." She laughed. "And our son is following in your footsteps." She turned to Haman. "It is good of you to help Jesse."

Haman waved one hand in a deprecating gesture. "What else is family for, Cousin?" His eyes looked briefly into hers and he turned away, but not before Marah had seen a gleam of something else in their depths.

Marah stepped back from them and turned quickly to Jesse. "Those bandits that plagued our cousin could still be in the hills. You will be careful . . . both of you?" She smiled but looked anxiously at his face.

"We will take the utmost care, beloved. We are two strong men; we'll be all right." He looked around the courtyard. "Where is Caleb?"

A sudden squawking of the chickens erupted almost as he spoke, and Caleb appeared, driving the chickens into the courtyard from their coop.

Jesse laughed. "You weren't getting in the way of that rooster again, were you?"

Caleb grinned. "He doesn't bother me. I told him he might end up in one of Mama's stews if he isn't careful."

"You will be late for school if you do not hurry, Caleb." Marah put an affectionate hand on his shoulder.

"Yes, Mama." He looked a little wistfully at his father. "You are sure I cannot come with you, Papa?"

"I am sure. There will be another time, Son. For now, you must learn from the Book of the Law. Your education is important. You will be of age before we know it."

Caleb nodded. "Goodbye, Papa. Goodbye, Cousin Haman. Have a good trip." He waved at them and dashed out of the courtyard.

"A fine young man, Cousin," observed Haman thoughtfully. "You must be very proud of him."

"Yes," Jesse acknowledged as he looked after Caleb. Then, impatiently, "Let us be on our way. We will be doing well if we can return by nightfall."

Elon appeared from the house and walked slowly toward them. "Ah . . . there was a day when I would have gone with you and done more than my share of the work," he lamented. Elon stopped and peered at Haman. "You are sure you can keep up with this young giant?"

It had been meant as humor, but Haman's smile was thin. "He may have trouble keeping up with me, Uncle," he replied with a smirk.

Jesse pulled on the reins and the two men followed the cart out of the courtyard and were soon out of sight. Marah stood looking after them, as a strange feeling of apprehension came over her. Why did she feel so restless this morning? In spite of his wit and camaraderie, Haman disturbed her. She didn't know why. Haman admired her, she knew that, but she had caught a glimpse of something deeper than admiration from time to time. It was there in his glance even this morning—desire.

There was much to do today, and with resolve she shook off the heavy feelings and turned to the house.

29

The two men walked in silence for a while as the mule plodded steadily along.

"We have had an unusual number of caravans this month," Haman was saying. He did not receive a response from Jesse and sensed that his cousin was preoccupied with something. He tried again. "What will you be making from this tree?"

"A chest." No more was offered and Jesse's brow was creased with a frown. Haman glanced cautiously at his cousin. Somehow Haman sensed that the thoughts that occupied Jesse's mind did not concern carpentry. Perhaps he had been a little too open in his admiration of his cousin's wife. He'd had more than his share of successes, even with the wives of other tradesmen. Marah was different. She was truly in love with her husband, and always when he came, Elon or Caleb seemed to be around. He had his comforts, but he found himself more and more occupied with thoughts of Marah. She was beautiful and he loved to watch her body as she moved about the house. He found himself obsessed with thoughts of her at night, yet he knew she would not look at another man.

"We are nearing the place I am looking for," Jesse spoke suddenly, bringing Haman back from his preoccupation.

Haman made an effort to joke lightly. "Good. We will see who is the stronger man."

Jesse stopped and looked at Haman. "Is that why you came today? You want to prove yourself to me?"

"A thousand pardons, Cousin. I came only to help. Does something disturb you?" Haman asked casually.

"Something disturbs me, Cousin. That is why I agreed to have you accompany me. We can talk more to the point when my family is not around." Jesse's eyes smoldered with resentment. "I would have you pay more attention to my father, your uncle, and less attention to my wife!" It was out in the open. Jesse waited for Haman's response.

"Cousin, Cousin, forgive me if I have offended you. I admire anything beautiful, whether it is an animal, an item of trade . . . or a woman." He shrugged casually. "It is only my way."

"Then perhaps you need to change your way in regard to Marah. Do I make myself clear, Cousin?" The last was spoken in such a way that Haman did not mistake the veiled threat.

Haman grew hot. How dare this poor tradesman tell him what he could and could not do? No man ordered Haman about, unless a purse of gold accompanied his words. He would show Jesse who was the better man, in one way or another. Yet being a man who lived by his wits, he saw no point in forcing further confrontation. He would bide his time. With a forced show of humility, Haman looked innocently into Jesse's eyes.

"Truly, Cousin, forgive me if I have caused you offense. Perhaps I have envied you your family, having not had one of my own. I shall take pains to treat your family with the utmost respect."

Jesse hesitated, but Haman's sincere plea won him over. "Then I too apologize for my jealousy. We shall forget the words were spoken."

Haman nodded. "Let us indeed forget this incident."

They walked on, climbing the slope of the mountain, and as they talked about many things, Jesse smiled at Haman's stories as usual. Yet, underneath, Haman's anger raged like a fire barely held in control.

Jesse stopped at the base of a large oak. "This is the one. It will take both of us with all our strength on the double saw to cut it down."

Sweat ran freely down their faces and bodies as they pushed and pulled the large saw. Each man gave his best effort in silent competition broken only by an occasional grunt. Haman proved more than equal to the task. At last the cut in the tree was almost sufficient for they heard a "crack" and the big tree shuddered.

"Which way will the tree fall?" Haman asked, studying the tree.

"Toward the cut. It will fall this direction." Jesse indicated with his hand. "Before we finish the cut, we must make sure nothing is in the path of the tree."

He let go of the saw and turned to glance around. There were only a few small rocks, but just then, the mule that had been grazing a distance away wandered toward them. She was right in the path of the tree. With an exclamation, Jesse strode toward the mule. He had nearly reached her when his foot caught in a hole made by a small animal, and he sprawled on the ground. "Ahhhhhh!" He drew his breath in with the pain. Haman hurried to his side.

"What happened?"

"I caught . . . my . . . foot . . . in a hole."

"Here, let me help you up." Haman reached an arm around Jesse's broad shoulders and lifted with all his might as Jesse tried to stand.

Jesse fell back to the ground and groaned with pain. "I . . . cannot. My ankle must be broken. Haman, get the mule. I can hang on to her bridle and between the three of us we can get to the cart."

"You cannot move?" He looked at Jesse, lying helpless on the ground. Just then the tree began to crack and snap. As Haman watched, frozen in place, the great tree groaned and began to fall toward them.

"Haman, the tree, help me. Pull me out of the way!" Jesse reached out toward Haman.

Haman looked quickly at his cousin. There were only seconds. If he tried to help Jesse, he might be crushed by the tree himself. If he did nothing, the tree would surely crush Jesse. He took hold of Jesse's arm and tried to drag him out of harm's way. But Jesse's size, which was usually an asset, was now a disadvantage.

"Quickly!" Jesse was screaming at him.

Haman looked up just as the tree was bearing down on them. One branch struck him heavily as he jumped back out of the way. He went down on the ground, his head spinning. From somewhere there was a scream and then, darkness.

When Haman awoke, the sun was low on the horizon. His head ached and his face was wet. He reached up to feel his head and his hand came away with blood on it. He moved his head slowly, trying to clear his mind. Then he thought of Jesse. Painfully he turned and saw Jesse lying under the main body of the tree. He stood up slowly and waited for the dizziness to pass, then he made his way to where Jesse lay. There was no sound and no sign of life. He put his hand on Jesse's face but could feel no breath. A trickle of blood had run out of Jesse's mouth. Was he dead?

Haman cursed himself for his cowardice. In all his anger, he really meant no harm. He stood for a long moment. Marah's face came before him, and knowing the anguish she would suffer, he cursed himself again. He shook his head. It was done. There was nothing more he could do for Jesse, except bring help to free him. Seeing the mule nearby, he staggered over, caught the bridle, and swung himself upon the animal. Leaning upon the mule's neck, he urged her toward Shechem.

30

It had taken a long time for the men who had gone with Haman to recover Jesse's body. The tree had to be cut into three sections to remove the part that pinned Jesse to the ground. Haman stood nearby, watching. He had offered to help but had been waved aside. His wounded head was bandaged with one of Hannah's poultices. He had a great headache, and was relieved to sit down. In spite of his wound, he had ridden furiously back to Shechem to seek help for Jesse. This put him in a favorable light with the neighboring men in Shechem who gathered at Elon's frantic summons.

Marah waited in anguish, hoping beyond hope that they would bring Jesse back to her injured, but alive. She had tended Haman and heard his terrible story of the accident, the hole, Jesse's fall; that the tree had been cut deeper than they thought. Elon listened, pain and anxiety on his wrinkled face; Caleb listened, sobbing quietly.

Marah prepared the meal, her eyes constantly glancing toward the entrance to the courtyard. Elon sat quietly on a small stool, and Caleb tended the animals, dried tears on his small, pinched face. Hannah had brought some food and helped Marah with the meal. Simon had gone with the men to help. They waited, each with their own thoughts and fears. Marah fought the sense of foreboding that filled her chest and threatened to suffocate her. Jesse, alive and strong this morning, touching her face with his hand, his look of love. How she depended on him. How she loved him. He was to be with her forever. They would raise their children and grow old together. Even if he were crippled, he would at least be alive. She couldn't bear to think of the alternative.

Through the night they waited. It was nearly dawn when the men returned, moving slowly with the cart. Anxiously she and Caleb ran to meet them. The men were dirty and tired and hung their heads at the sight of her anxious face. Only Simon looked at her and his sadness sent a jolt of fear through her. He shook his head and laid a gentle hand on her shoulder.

"I am sorry, Marah, he was dead. There was nothing we could do except to free him from the tree."

They stopped the cart and lifted the cloth that covered him. His face seemed peaceful, as though he were asleep. Caleb cried out, "Papa, no! No!" Marah tore her mantle; her cries of anguish echoing in the street as they led her home. Beside her she was vaguely aware of the sobs of a small boy.

Elon stood with dignity as they approached the gate. Then he heard Marah's cries as a small blond bundle flung himself sobbing into his grandfather's arms. They comforted one another as tears ran down the old man's wrinkled face into his beard.

Elon tried to be strong for Marah, yet she could see his heart was broken. He bore the loss of his only son as bravely as he could, setting his own grief aside to give strength to Caleb and her.

Marah was numb with pain. She felt a hand on her shoulder. It was Haman.

"I am sorry, Marah, so very sorry. I share your grief. If only there was something I could have done. I blame myself for this."

She looked up at him and saw the anguish in his face. "I am sure you did all you could, Haman, but thank you for your words." She turned away, for she couldn't speak further.

Haman stood nearby a moment and then turned and spoke with Elon. "I would give anything to erase this day. I am sorry, Uncle. We were just getting acquainted. I didn't mean to bring grief to our family."

Elon looked past him, gazing unseeing into the distance. "Thank you, Haman, I know you did your best to save my son." He nodded quietly, putting a hand on his nephew's shoulder, but in spite of Haman's best efforts at conversation, Elon sat quietly and stared at the gate. Finally Haman left him alone.

As he stood in the courtyard and watched the women come with their spices and pieces of cloth, Haman decided not to remain while they prepared Jesse's body for burial. He turned and headed for the caravansary with heavy steps.

After the burial, Caleb woodenly moved about his chores with the animals. The fun-loving, happy little boy was now a solemn child who seldom spoke except in single syllables.

Elon seemed to fade away almost in front of their eyes. He ate little and slept even less.

Haman came as often as he could with a word for Elon, comfort for Marah, and his usual small gifts for Caleb. Caleb had been raised to be courteous to adults and he responded politely to the gifts. After Haman had gone, Caleb would toss the gift in a small basket by his pallet not to be retrieved again.

As the days moved into weeks, Marah kept herself going for Caleb's sake. Once she found him sitting in the shadows holding the little camel his father had bought him the day they went to the caravansary. Tears were running down his cheeks. She knelt beside him and wordlessly took him into her arms as they wept together. It was the one and only time he let her comfort him after his father's death. Jesse's death changed Caleb. He went about his chores in a deliberate way. He volunteered to help around the house and seemed to watch over Marah lest she do something too much for her strength. Then she realized that, with his grandfather's enfeebled condition, and his father gone, he was trying to be the man of the house. Marah watched him as he stoically strove to be all that he could.

One evening Elon spoke with Marah about their circumstances and the next morning he went into the village with Simon. When he returned, he drew Caleb aside.

"Caleb, come. There are things we must talk about." His grandfather sat down outside in the sun and Caleb sat next to him. Marah stood nearby, for Elon had told her of the results of his venture into the city.

"Caleb, you have done well. I could not have gotten through this time without you." The boy's shoulders straightened and he lifted his chin with pride at his grandfather's words. "Yet, we must consider what is now to be done."

"To be done?"

"Yes, you are a great help, but you cannot run the carpentry shop, you are too young."

"I am strong. Papa always said I could do things most boys my age can't do. I could take care of us."

"That is a comfort to me, Caleb, but the tradesmen will not let a ten-year-old boy work among them and run the shop no matter how capable you are."

Caleb looked down at the ground and shook his head. "What will we do?"

"You could be an apprentice to one of the other carpenters. You have the skill of your father. In time, when you are older, you could have your own shop, just like your father. In the meantime, we must manage." Elon tried to sound as positive as he could.

Caleb considered his words. He knew his grandfather was right.

"How would you like to choose some tools from the shop to keep?"

"I would like that," Caleb said slowly. Then a thought occurred to him. "What will happen to Papa's shop, Grandfather?"

"I will have to sell the shop, Caleb."

"Sell the shop? Can't we just keep it, for when I am ready?" His eyes pleaded with his grandfather.

Marah felt the boy's pain as Elon answered, "I wish it were so, Caleb, but we cannot just keep the shop for six to eight years until you are ready. We must live, and we have your mama to consider."

Caleb's shoulders sagged. He nodded.

"Tomorrow we shall go and you may choose a few tools. One of the other carpenters on the street, Shiva, has agreed to buy the shop. At least it will not be a stranger from another town. He has also agreed to take you as an apprentice."

"I know Shiva. My papa liked him." He paused. "I would like to be his apprentice." He looked up bravely at Elon and turned to Marah. With pride she hugged him to her. He endured her embrace for a brief moment and then struggled to be free. "I have work to do, Mama," he said, lifting his chin, and he hurried back to his chores.

Marah turned to find Haman regarding her quietly in the courtyard.

"Haman, I didn't see you." She moved toward him. He hadn't been able to do enough for them, and she knew how remorseful he felt.

Haman smiled at her. "You look as if someone has just lifted a load off your shoulders."

"Indeed. My father-in-law has arranged for Caleb to be an apprentice to one of the other carpenters, Shiva. Shiva is also going to buy Jesse's shop. It will help us a great deal."

Haman's face fell. "And here I thought I was bringing good news, myself. It appears as if I am too late."

"Too late? What do you mean?"

He took her elbow and, with an air of confidentiality, leaned closer. "I was going to tell Caleb that he has a job at the caravansary. He would be only a camel boy, but . . ." He shrugged his shoulders in regret.

"Haman, how kind of you to do this. I don't wish to have

194

him disappoint his grandfather. Perhaps if we had known sooner." She was aware that Haman was gently steering her toward the house. As they neared the doorway, Marah caught a glimpse of Caleb watching them. A jolt shot through her as she realized that the look on his face was just like Jesse.

"Marah, I wish to talk with you about another matter, a more personal one. I would give anything to bring back your husband, you must know this." He looked at her sadly. "Yet, you must also realize you need someone to look after the family, a man. I am offering myself to you. You are welcome to all that I have." He looked deep into her eyes, and in spite of herself, Marah felt part of herself responding. For a brief moment she almost let herself be held and comforted. She had missed Jesse terribly. She had missed being held and loved by a man. The nights were unbearably long and lonely.

"What are you saying to me, Haman?" She moved away slightly.

"I realize that it may be too soon. But I have come to care for you and Caleb, and I would offer myself to you, as a husband."

"Husband? Haman I . . . I cannot think of that now." Marah felt confused somehow. It was not totally unexpected, yet when she heard the words she had mixed emotions.

"Would you feel you were betraying Jesse?"

How could he know what she was thinking? She looked up with a start. "It is just that I am not ready to consider marriage again, at least not yet." Her eyes pooled with unbidden tears.

"Do not let it trouble you. I do understand. I will give you all the time you need. Just say you will consider my offer. Elon is old and Caleb needs a father to look after him while he is still young. You need a husband, in time."

She could not meet his eyes, but merely nodded. "I will consider your offer, Haman, when I am ready."

"Then I shall hope, and wait for that day." He bowed slightly and left her.

31

Hannah blushed in the warmth of the sun as she and Marah stood in the courtyard. She had brought momentous news, and for once, Marah had no words. She regarded her friend in awe and delight.

"Are you going to congratulate me on my news? I know we are getting on in years, yet the God Who Sees has taken away my shame and reproach. Blessed be the name of the Lord."

"Oh Hannah," Marah breathed, "a child. You are to have a child?"

Hannah laughed. "Simon goes around shaking his head. He is pleased to be a father at last, and is delighted at this blessing in our later years, but he still cannot believe it."

"When shall it be?"

"At the time of the olive harvest, near the month of Marcheshvan."

"Hannah. That is only six months away. How have you kept this from me for so long?" Marah looked at her friend in reproach.

"I had to be sure. There have been so many times when I thought I was in that way, and then, nothing. I had to have no doubts." Hannah's beautiful brown eyes sparkled. "Blessed be the name of the God of Abraham who has seen my tears and harkened to my cry. He has taken away my reproach among women and blessed me. Praise be to His name."

"Praise be to His name for this great gift."

The two women embraced, and Hannah sat down to rest while Marah went for the dipper of water.

Elon rejoiced with them. He had always liked Hannah and Simon and made them welcome whenever they came. Jesse and Simon had been great friends. Marah found herself with mixed feelings when Hannah had gone. She was glad for Hannah, but her head was filled with self-pity. God had shut up her own womb. She had not been able to give Jesse a child. She loved Caleb as her own, but it was not the same. Now she could never bear Jesse a child, for he was gone.

Jesse would have been happy for them, thought Marah. He loved children. She thought of Caleb. The months went by and Marah saw Caleb come home exhausted from Shiva's shop. The man was good to him but worked him hard. After he was finished in the temple school, he went to the carpenter's shop to work. Elon grew weaker by the day and she feared for him also. Haman was considerate and helpful in every way, yet she sensed he was growing impatient for an answer from her. Finally, one day, she went to Elon.

"Father Elon, there is something I must speak with you about." She sat down next to him in the courtyard.

He turned kindly eyes toward her and nodded.

"It concerns our cousin Haman. He wishes to marry me. He has offered to provide for you, me, and Caleb. It has been a year. I have put him off for a long time."

"I know of his intentions, daughter. He has also spoken to me. He has been good to our family. He waits for your time of mourning to end. He put a hand on her shoulder. "I would not wish to shorten your time of grief, for you still grieve, Daughter?"

"Yes." Her voice was almost a whisper. "I still grieve, but I think I will miss him the rest of my life. I do not know if I am ready to marry Haman."

"We must all live with our grief and pray that it will heal in God's time." Elon looked thoughtful. "Haman is a good man. He is of our family, the son of my own brother."

"You are saying that you would give your approval?"

Elon paused a moment, considering. "If you must marry again, I would be glad that it was a kinsman." He looked off into the distance for a moment, lost in his own thoughts. Then he turned to her again. "I would give my approval," he said at last.

She felt relieved. She had been thinking about it for some time now and felt it would be best for Caleb too. She did not have to ask the boy's approval, but she hoped he would also be agreeable.

That evening, Haman appeared for supper. Marah suspected that Elon had sent for him.

"It is always my pleasure to join you, Marah. It appears, from my uncle's message, that you have something to tell me?"

"Yes, Haman. I have thought about your proposal of marriage . . ."

"And—?" He watched her face.

"I have spoken with Elon, and have decided to accept."

Haman's eyes glittered as he took her hand and raised it to his lips. "You make me the happiest of men. I am also thankful for the approval of my esteemed uncle. You will forgive me, but I could not keep from speaking to him about what was in my heart. He did lead me to believe that in time you might consider me in a favorable light."

"You have been very kind to all of us, Haman."

He looked at her, his dark eyes bright. "I will be very good to you, Marah."

She grasped his meaning and found herself blushing.

"You still blush? My lovely Marah, you intrigue me. You are like a young virgin." He chuckled softly.

Marah served the meal quietly but found for some reason she was uneasy. She realized she was anxious for Caleb's reaction to the news. She watched the interaction of Caleb and Haman closely. Caleb was polite, but distant. Perhaps in time he would accept Haman, knowing his grandfather approved.

Elon spoke at last. "Caleb, I have some news for you. I have decided to give my permission and blessing on the marriage of your mother and our cousin Haman."

Caleb went white. He knew that in their culture a woman did not have the privilege of remaining widowed for long. A woman needed a man to provide for her if she was alone and had children. Haman was a kinsman. Yet he looked from Marah to Haman and, with a sob, got up and ran from the table. Elon tried to call him back, but it was no use.

"He will get used to it." Haman waved a hand at Elon who had sought to apologize for his grandson's behavior. "It is difficult for him, but he is only a boy. He will have to accept it in time."

"He still grieves for his father," Marah said softly.

Haman looked at her closely and opened his mouth to speak but thought better of it and remained silent, watching her.

As he took his leave of them, he drew Marah into the shadows of the courtyard. "I have waited a long time. Only a woman who has loved a man deeply could understand my difficulty in waiting so long. Let this seal our agreement." He bent his head and kissed her. It took her by surprise and yet she felt herself respond to him. Her mind grieved for Jesse, but her body betrayed her need.

She stood still in the shadows after he had gone. Time seemed to be moving so quickly and she had no power to stop it. She still felt the kiss on her lips, and as she absentmindedly touched her lips with her hand, she sensed someone nearby. Caleb stood in the courtyard.

She turned to him quickly. "Caleb. How could you treat your cousin so? He has been good to you."

"I don't want you to marry him, Mama."

"But why?"

"I still miss my papa."

She caught him to her. "Oh Caleb, I shall miss your papa till the day I die, but we must go on with life." She held him at arm's length and looked at his face. "You do not like Haman, do you?"

"No. I do not trust him."

"But why? Has he ever been unkind to you?"

Caleb squirmed. "Well, no, it is just something. It is like he isn't really who he pretends to be."

"Pretends? Oh Caleb, I am sure that in time you will feel differently. You will come to like Haman. He will take care of us all, especially your grandfather. And speaking of your grandfather, you had better go in and make peace with him."

Caleb nodded. He had never disobeyed his grandfather. Reluctantly he turned and went into the house.

Elon was stern, but out of love for the boy, he accepted his apology and forgave him. He admonished Caleb never to do such a thing in their household again and a subdued Caleb promised that he would not.

The next day, as Marah and Hannah washed the clothes of their households side by side at the spring, she shared her decision to marry.

"Do you think this is wise?" Hannah's tone was cautious.

"I have told Haman I would marry him, and Elon has given us his blessing. It is best. I must consider Caleb and his grand-father. You cannot take us all in as you did me, my friend. You will be busy with another small mouth in your household in a few months."

Hannah was silent for a moment. "You still grieve for Jesse?"

Strange, the same question Elon had asked. "I will always grieve for Jesse, but I must consider the best thing to do."

"How does Caleb feel?"

"Caleb? He is not very happy, but then he is only a child.

He still misses his father. He isn't ready to accept another man to take Jesse's place."

"That is my point. Are you ready to have another man take Jesse's place?"

Marah shook her head slowly. "No man could ever take Jesse's place. As long as I live, he will live in my heart."

"Take care that you do not make that obvious to Haman."

"Why would you say that? He understands that I loved Jesse. I will be a good wife to him, but how can he expect more than that?"

Hannah studied the ground for a moment. "Do not underestimate the man, Marah."

"I don't think I do."

Hannah gathered the wet clothes. She looked at Marah for a moment and then smiled. "I wish you well in this marriage. I just want the best for you, as I always have."

"Hannah, you and Simon have been like my own family, and I could not have a dearer friend. We'll be fine. You'll see."

"Yes, of course. I'm sure you're right. God go with you, Marah."

"And with you." They parted each to their own house. Marah walked back slowly, considering Hannah's words. Was she marrying Haman for Caleb and Elon? Marah wondered. Slowly she faced the truth. She was not marrying for a father to Caleb, or another son to Elon. She was marrying him out of her own need. Since Haman's kiss, she had lain awake many a night, crying out to God in her loneliness for Jesse and his strong body next to hers. Haman could never be Jesse and she must keep that part of her in her heart of hearts. She must try hard to be a good wife to Haman. But, could she ever love him?

32

The wedding had been simple with few guests. They were married in the home of Haman's employer, the merchant Ahmal, who had provided the food and refreshments. Marah watched Haman consume a great deal of wine and vaguely thought of Zibeon. When Caleb came up to speak with him, he had waved him off impatiently and continued his conversation with some men from the caravansary. Caleb's eyes had blazed, but he turned away and went to Elon. Hannah and Simon attended, but Hannah was becoming large with the child she carried. If it had not been Marah's wedding, she would have stayed home. As it was, she remained as unobtrusive as possible in a corner of the room.

Elon seemed happy with the wedding and kissed her gently on the cheek. He appeared to brood less over Jesse, and somehow her marriage to the son of his brother helped him. As the hour grew later, Simon felt the need to take Hannah home and Ahmal sent one of his servants to see them safely through the streets. Elon and Caleb went with them as far as their own home, for Ahmal had offered a room in his home for the night to the bridal couple and Haman had accepted.

As Marah waited, for the third time in her life, for her bridegroom to come, she felt strangely troubled. She expected to be happy and felt nothing. She saw Jesse standing in front of her, holding out the little flute. Deep anguish swept over her. She looked at the wedding couch and suddenly cried out in her heart, *Oh Jesse, what have I done?* Had she made a mistake?

Haman entered smiling and took her in his arms. As he kissed her, she forced herself to respond and closed her eyes. She yielded to Haman, but it was Jesse's face she saw and Jesse's arms that held her through the long night.

As the months went by, she tried with all she knew to be a good wife to Haman. As factor for Ahmal, Haman dealt with most of the merchants of Shechem, picking up and delivering merchandise from Ahmal's caravans. He seemed to delight in bringing her gifts, things he saw that he thought she would like.

"Oh my lord, the vase is lovely." She held it up and admired the luminescent colors.

"Several came in the last caravan." He smiled, watching her face.

"You will spoil me, my lord." Then she paused. "It is not a hardship to afford such treasures?"

Haman frowned. "Don't trouble yourself over such trifling thoughts, my heart. I can manage them."

Marah was frugal with what Haman gave her for the household. These things that Haman brought home to her were costly. She watched Haman reach for his cloak.

"You must leave again, my lord?"

He smiled engagingly. "There is work I must do. After all, it is my job. Another caravan comes in soon and I must prepare."

She nodded. She was proud that he had important work and seemed to be well known among the merchants. He was obviously looked upon with favor by the caravan master Ahmal. She watched him as he left the courtyard. Caleb, who had been taking care of the chickens, also watched him leave. He had a sullen expression on his face.

Marah had hoped that Haman and Caleb would reach more

friendly terms, but Haman mostly ignored Caleb when he was home and Caleb only spoke to Haman when he had to.

Caleb had become withdrawn and secretive. He took to disappearing for hours at a time, yet always returned in time to attend to his chores at home.

"Caleb," she asked once, "where did you go?"

"I, ah, had errands to run for Shiva, Mama," he answered, but did not look at her.

Caleb did work for Shiva in his carpentry shop. She said no more, but watched, alert for signs of trouble between Haman and the boy.

Marah went back into the house and looked at the beautiful vase. One by one she picked up and examined the many things Haman had brought her—fine cloth for a tunic, gold earrings, a small figure carved out of ivory.

"He does well, Daughter," Elon said, looking over her shoulder. He enjoyed Haman's stories as they shared a meal. Haman deferred to Elon and flattered him.

"These things belong more in the house of the caravan master Ahmal than in our humble dwelling."

"He only wishes to please you, Daughter. If he does well, should he not share with his family?"

"You're right, I am being foolish, and ungrateful."

He patted her shoulder and went outside. In a few moments he was back. "Have you seen Caleb?"

"He was tending the animals a few minutes ago, when Haman left."

"He is nowhere to be found." Elon sighed and went back outside.

Marah looked toward the courtyard gate in exasperation. Where could Caleb have gone now? It seemed that every time Haman left, Caleb disappeared. He wouldn't be with Haman, who'd made it clear he didn't want the boy along when he did business. They avoided each other. A thought came to her and she brushed it away. The thought persisted. Could Caleb be following Haman? If so, why? She shook her head. This was foolish. There was no reason for Caleb to do that. She shook her head again. She was letting her imagination go too far. Still, she looked toward the street and wondered.

A figure suddenly appeared at the gate. To her surprise it was the caravan master Ahmal. Elon rose and went to greet him.

"Peace be with you, my lord, welcome to our humble home."

"And peace to this household."

"May I offer you some refreshment?" Elon indicated the house with his hand.

Ahmal appeared a bit agitated, but smiled. "It would be my pleasure." As he entered the house, he nodded to Marah who lowered her eyes respectfully. The two men seated themselves and she brought them wine and fruit.

"You have been well, my friend?" Ahmal turned to Elon.

"Quite well, my lord, and your caravans, they are doing well?"

"My caravans do well. I have good men who work on my caravans."

Marah didn't miss the hesitation. She listened as she went about her duties.

"Your grandson, Caleb, is not here?"

"He's not here. He'll be sorry to have missed you, my lord."

"Ah . . . a fine boy. You must be proud of him."

Elon nodded and then eyed Ahmal speculatively. "He is indeed that . . . but I believe you did not come to inquire of my grandson. What can we do for you?"

Ahmal let his breath out and smiled ruefully. "Of a truth, I came seeking your nephew, Haman."

"Haman? Is he not at the caravansary?"

"We seem to . . . miss each other . . ." Ahmal's eyes rested on the beautiful vase. He glanced around casually and Marah saw that he was noting some of the things Haman had brought home.

"It appears your husband has learned to appreciate beautiful things, as I myself do." He appeared embarrassed. He finished his cup of wine and stood up. Elon rose also.

"I will tell my husband you were here, my lord."

"Thank you. I'm sure I will meet with him soon."

"He is probably preparing for the caravan that is coming in soon."

"Another caravan?"

"Do you not have a caravan coming in shortly?" Elon looked puzzled.

Marah stood quietly and waited for the answer.

"He is my factor, and he has much business with the merchants, but my caravan came in last week. I do not leave again for a while. I have matters needing my attention . . . here." Ahmal stroked his beard thoughtfully.

"Perhaps we misunderstood," Elon murmured.

"Do not trouble yourself. I am sure that is what happened. I will speak to Haman tomorrow. Thank you for your hospitality, I must be on my way. Peace be on this household."

Elon saw him to the gate as Marah considered Ahmal's words. Why would Haman speak of a caravan coming in when the caravan master's caravan had already come in a week before? Did he also work for another caravan master? He had never mentioned it. This was all so puzzling. She felt a sense of uneasiness. Elon was thoughtful when he returned to the house. He looked at Marah for a moment but said nothing.

Haman returned late but sought her comfort. She wanted to ask him about Ahmal's visit, but he wound his fingers in her hair and pulled her to him. It was not a time for questions.

The next morning Marah awoke to find Haman watching her. He appeared to be deep in thought.

"You are awake early, Haman, is there something that troubles you?"

He traced a finger down her cheek and did not answer for a moment. "You are happy with me, Marah?" he asked casually.

"You are a good husband, my lord."

"That is not what I asked you. Are you happy with me?"

She thought quickly. Without Jesse, the joy of life was gone, but she knew how hard Haman tried. And how could she explain the unease she felt. "I am happy, my lord," she said softly.

Haman stroked his beard. "I am glad to hear that. Sometimes I think you are distracted."

"Distracted?"

"You seem to have other things on your mind. You seem far away."

"I am sorry." She sought for the right words. "It is just that sometimes I think . . ."

"Of Jesse?"

"I do not mean to," she blurted, and realized her mistake.

Haman reached out and took her chin in his hand. There was an edge to his voice.

"Jesse is dead, Marah. He can never be your husband again. I thought you were ready for this marriage, but I do not wish to hold only the shell of a woman in my arms while she thinks of another."

She nodded dumbly, and he released her chin. "My love must be enough. Do you understand me?" His voice was dangerously soft. "I want all of you, Marah, all of you. I do not want to compete with a ghost."

She nodded again, her head down.

He did not move for a long moment and then rose suddenly and left the room.

She listened for a moment and then went to the door of the main room of the house and looked for him. Haman was gone. Elon was snoring softly on his pallet. She looked at Caleb's pallet. He was gone also.

It made Haman angry to ask about his business. She was afraid to ask him about Ahmal's visit. Probably he was speaking with Ahmal even now. Perhaps she was worrying over nothing.

Caleb returned later that morning and fed the chickens and then hurried to school at the synagogue. He ran in and out so fast she barely had time to give him his lunch, wrapped in a cloth.

Haman was gone for two days. His manner when he returned discouraged questions from Marah or Elon, but the older man persisted.

"Things go well at the caravansary, Nephew?"

"Yes, fine."

"The caravan master was here. You had missed each other. He found you?"

"Yes, Uncle, he found me."

Elon tried to start a conversation several times but finally finished his meal in silence, eyeing his nephew from time to time thoughtfully. Marah knew there was something wrong, but she knew Haman would only speak of it when he was ready. She would wait.

33

As the months passed, Haman became angry and occasionally abusive. He spent more time in the city, and she never knew when he would return home. She heard he was seen with one of the city's prostitutes and drank a great deal. Each time he returned, it was an ordeal for the family.

As Marah cleaned the chicken pen, she found herself glancing at the gate from time to time, starting at any sound. This time her fears were realized as Haman strode into the courtyard. He was drunk. He grabbed her arm and began to pull her toward the gate. The grip of his hand bruised the skin on her wrists.

"Haman, you are hurting me!"

"Who is the other man? Tell me!" He struck her across the face.

"Haman, there is no one. You know there is no one."

"You lie to me? I will have his name. There are ways to make sure you confess!" He began to drag her toward the gate of the courtyard.

Elon had risen as quickly as he could and tried to stop Haman. "She is a good daughter, Haman, there is no truth to this. Let her go." He put a restraining hand on Haman's arm and was pushed away roughly.

"Elon! Father. Haman, you have hurt him. He is an old man. Please, do not do this."

She glanced back to see Elon leaning on his cane. "I am all right, Daughter," he called after them. "I am all right."

Marah's face was hot with shame as Haman ruthlessly dragged her through the streets toward the *Bit Allah*. He was taking her to the synagogue? God be praised, Caleb would not be there but would be in Shiva's shop at this time. What was Haman going to do? She struggled to walk as fast as Haman so she would not fall. Then she realized. He was taking her to the high priest! Surely he would believe that she was innocent. He knew what was going on in Shechem. Wouldn't he know of Haman? Keeping her eyes down on the street, she could not look up and see the neighbors watching. All the commotion had caused heads to turn their way.

Haman entered the synagogue, and when a servant of the high priest came to inquire what they wanted, Haman flung Marah to the ground in front of him. "She is defiled. She has lain with another man and will not confess her crime," he spat angrily, his words slurring.

The servant looked at Marah with contempt. "I will call the high priest at once." He hurried away.

Marah wept with anguish. "Haman, how could you do this to me? You know there has been no one else. Please, take me home."

"Beg, yes, beg me. You care not for me . . . and there is another man. He is dead, yet you cling to him still. You give me nothing, do you hear? Nothing!" He swayed slightly and glared at her.

The high priest appeared and stood before them. His eyes narrowed as he surveyed Marah. She had been working in the chicken pen for some time when Haman had come upon her suddenly and there was a smudge of dirt on her face. Her hands were dirty and she wore only the tunic she worked in. She hung her head. She was as a street woman in his eyes.

"You have brought the offering?"

Haman reached into his girdle and produced a small bag of barley meal which he handed to the priest. The servant took the offering and handed the priest a pitcher of holy water. He also handed the priest a small bowl of dust from the floor of the synagogue. The high priest mixed the dust with the holy water. Then he reached out and pulled her mantle back from her head. Marah trembled with fear.

"Hold out your hands," he commanded her. She trembled as she held them out. He put the barley meal offering in her hands.

"If no man has lain with you, and if you have not gone aside to uncleanness with another instead of your husband, be you free from this bitter water that causes the curse: But if you have gone aside to another instead of your husband, and if you are defiled, and some man has lain with you beside your husband; then the LORD make you a curse and an oath among your people, when the LORD makes your thigh to rot and your belly to swell; and this water that causes the curse shall go into your bowels and make your belly to swell and your thigh to rot. You are to say amen."

"Amen . . . ," Marah whispered, her face burning with shame.

The servant brought out a book and the priest wrote down the curses and sprinkled the holy water mixed with the dust. Then he put the cup to Marah's lips. "Drink," he commanded, and trembling still, she obeyed. Haman looked on smugly, keeping his role of righteous indignation.

The priest took the barley meal out of Marah's hands and poured it upon the altar where it burned. He turned back to them. "It is done. God will judge according to her sin or," and he looked Marah over again, "her innocence."

Haman did not need to drag her anymore. When the high priest and the servant had gone, he pushed her aside and swaggered out of the courtyard of the temple as though she did not exist. Marah stood bewildered for a moment looking after him. Anger began to burn in her breast. *How dare he do this to me,* she fumed. *He punishes me for loving Jesse?* She understood the curse. She was innocent. Slowly she walked out of the courtyard. She would show him she was innocent. The God Who Sees knew. She would not fear the curse of the bitter water. When nothing happened to her, all would know she had done nothing wrong. She covered her head with her mantle and walked with her head high.

Hannah listened in unbelief, her eyes wide with astonishment. Then astonishment turned to fury. "He did this to you? Knowing you are innocent? May God strike him down for the terrible thing he has done."

"He was drunk, Hannah. I cannot be to him what he wants." Marah put her face in her hands. "I still love Jesse. Oh Hannah, I will love him always."

"'Vengeance is mine, says the LORD, I will repay.' Haman will pay for his actions, Marah, God will see to that." She gave Marah a bowl of water to wash her face and embraced her gently.

"I must go, Hannah. Elon may have been hurt. I . . . I just needed to come here first."

"I know. Go now, see to Elon."

Marah hurried through the streets to her home. She knew Hannah would vindicate her if the women began to speak against her. The neighborhood was quiet. There was no one about. For once she was grateful for the heat of the day and the time of rest when shops were closed.

Elon sat quietly in the shade, leaning against the house. His countenance lifted at the sight of her. "You are not hurt, Daughter?"

"No. And you . . . are you all right?"

"I only feel badly that I was no help to you." He looked down at the ground. "I am a useless old man, Daughter, of no help to anyone."

Marah knelt by his side and put her arms around his thin shoulders. "You are worth everything to me, Father Elon. You cheer me when the evenings are long. Your company means much to me in these times. Caleb and I love you dearly."

He patted her arm, somewhat mollified. "What is to become of this household, Daughter. Why would Haman do such a thing? Where did he take you?"

Marah hung her head and quietly told her father-in-law of the incident in the synagogue.

Elon was enraged. "He did that to you, child? My nephew has behaved badly." He patted her arm again. "You shall not fear the curse, Daughter."

"I don't. The God Who Sees knows that I am innocent." She looked toward the gate. "I fear Haman more. I do not know what he will do next. I fear for all of us." She shook her head as she thought of Caleb when he found out what Haman had done.

34

Marah stood in the courtyard facing the two men who had appeared suddenly at her door.

"We seek the home of Haman, factor for the caravans of Ahmal. Are you his wife?" Their manner was brusque.

"I am his wife. Why do you seek him?"

"He is here? We would speak with him."

"He is not here, he has gone with a caravan. I do not know when he will return." Marah felt apprehensive. What did they want with Haman?

One man stepped menacingly toward her. "She would protect him!"

The second man gave a warning look at his companion and spoke more kindly. "I am Manahath and this is my friend Zadok. We seek your husband on a matter concerning the death of my friend's brother. Your husband fled to this city. We had to return home to bury our dead according to our customs. Now we have come to Shechem to have him account for himself and this deed."

Marah stared at them with alarm. Haman involved in a man's death? He fled to Shechem . . . a city of refuge? Why had he left with a caravan, or for that matter, why had he risked going outside of the city to help Jesse cut a tree? This didn't make sense. She faced the men and drew herself up.

"I know nothing of this matter. My husband has not told us of these circumstances. None of his family know of this. He told me he had to leave with a short caravan on a matter for Ahmal. He left at dawn this morning."

Manahath studied her face and appeared to believe she was telling the truth. "And can you tell me which direction the caravan was headed?"

She frowned. "Possibly Jezreel." Until she knew the truth of this matter, she could not knowingly send them after Haman.

The man Zadok scowled at her but said no more.

"We will trouble you no longer. Thank you for speaking with us." Manahath turned to his companion and motioned for them to leave.

As Marah stood looking after them, wondering what all this meant, Elon called to her from inside the house.

"Daughter, what did those men want? Did you not offer them our hospitality?"

"They did not appear to wish to stay, Father Elon. They only wanted information."

Elon leaned on his staff. "What sort of information?"

"About Haman. They believe he had something to do with the death of one man's brother and they seek him. Father Elon, I believe they think Haman murdered the man and came to Shechem for refuge. I know he says he is the son of your brother Jemuel, but do we really know he is?" Marah spoke bitterly.

"The son of Jemuel a murderer? No . . . no!" Elon clutched his chest and swayed.

Marah caught him quickly. He was having one of his spells. His heart was weak. Why had she spoken so rashly? Now she eased him down to the ground and quickly handed him the dipper of water. He drank slowly and leaned against the house. His face was ashen, but slowly the color began to return.

"Are you all right? I didn't mean to upset you. We do not know if any of these men's accusations are true. I spoke foolishly." She laid a cool cloth on his forehead.

He smiled wanly at her. "You didn't mean it, Daughter." He sighed deeply. "Is there anything we can be sure of these days?"

"I am sure Haman will explain all this when he returns. Perhaps they have the wrong man."

"Yes, they must have the wrong man. I am sure it is all a mistake." Elon stared off into the distance and nodded his head firmly.

Just then Caleb returned from Shiva's shop. He helped his grandfather into the house and they washed their hands in the small basin. He sat down by his grandfather as Marah put their simple meal on the low table.

Haman had convinced Elon that he could handle the money from the sale of Jesse's shop better by investing it for them. They had not seen much of it since. With Haman gone they had little for buying extra food items. Marah had flour to bake the bread but little else. Hannah always had extra vegetables to share with them when she came by. It took all Marah's skill to prepare enough food to sustain an ailing father-in-law and a growing boy. She looked around at the gifts Haman had brought her over the past months. They would bring some money in the marketplace, yet she dared not risk Haman's anger if they were missing.

Elon mentioned the two men in spite of a warning shake of her head. She did not want to alarm Caleb.

"We will ask Haman about this matter when he returns," Elon said. He treated Caleb as if he were a man. As if he were Jesse.

Caleb looked at his grandfather and mother. "He didn't leave Shechem."

"Grandson, how do you know this?"

"I saw him. He was sitting in the wineshop on the street of the fruit merchants. He was talking with that man, Ahira."

"Are you sure it was Haman?" Marah asked, kneeling down to look at Caleb directly.

"Mama, I saw him. It was Haman, all right." Caleb was almost sullen.

Elon put down his bread and looked at Marah. "Why would he tell us he is going to be gone and then stay in the town?"

Marah caught her breath. "Do you suppose what those men said was true?"

"That could be why he does not leave the town, Daughter." Anger seemed to give Elon strength. "We will find out the truth when he comes here to the house. He will return sooner or later. I will find out who he is once and for all!" Elon pounded on the table and Caleb jumped.

After Elon had gone to his pallet for the night, Marah helped Caleb bring the animals in. She struggled with her thoughts and finally stopped Caleb outside.

"Caleb. Tell me again how you happened to see Haman."

The boy hung his head for a moment and then looked earnestly at her face. "I don't trust Haman. He is mean. I don't like it when he hurts you. Papa never hurt you like that."

"You followed him?" She was suddenly fearful.

"I was on an errand for Shiva and saw Ahira go into the wineshop. Haman was there all right. He sent Ahira to follow two men, but I don't know who they were."

Marah caught her breath. "Caleb, did he see you?"

"I don't think so, Mama."

She thought carefully. She must not alarm Caleb, but if Haman had seen the boy, he would be hard on him. She didn't want Caleb hurt and now she knew that she couldn't trust Haman. "My son, I want you to be very careful around Haman. Stay out of his way even more than you do. Something is wrong here, and until we know what it is, just be careful."

He put his arms around her. "I will be careful, Mama, and I won't let anything happen to you . . . or Grandfather." He spoke with courage.

Marah held him tight. She must not let him see her fear, but she knew that Caleb was in danger. Somehow she must protect him, but how?

"You are thin, my friend," Hannah said gently. "You must eat more and get more rest. You are working too hard." Then she made an attempt at humor. "I would gladly give you some of the pounds I have gained."

Marah smiled. Her eyes had dark shadows under them and her skin was pale. She had taken to rubbing the petals of a certain flower on her cheeks for color.

"You are well?"

"I am all right, Hannah. Perhaps I have been working too hard."

"Haman has gone again with the caravan?"

"Yes. He said he would only be going as far as Sebaste . . . a few days." She wanted to add that she was glad of a reprieve from his temper. The more he tried to reach her, the more she withdrew from him. Her heart still missed Jesse. Haman had taken out his fury on her more than once. She hid the bruises with a heavy tunic and mantle. She could never love Haman and now he knew that too. His jealousy and frustration knew no bounds.

Marah had convinced Caleb to just stay out of Haman's way. When he heard in the neighborhood of what Haman had done to his mother, he wanted to kill his stepfather. She had finally gotten through to him. "Would you have me suffer the loss of my son as well as my husband? Haman is not a man to be dealt with by a boy. God will punish him; we must leave it to Him to care for us."

Caleb had hugged her and wiped his nose on his sleeve, sniffling. He nodded in response to her plea, finally promising not to do anything that would bring him in the way of harm or cause more harm to her or his grandfather. She knew he worked at staying out of Haman's way when he was home. He was a constant reminder of Jesse, and Haman had cuffed him more than once for an imaginary disobedience. Even

Elon had seen another side of Haman but realized there was nothing he could do.

Caleb brightened. "Mama. I made a gift for Hannah's baby. I wanted to do something. They have been so nice to us. Shiva helped me. Mama, I made a cradle. It is at the shop. Can we take it to them?"

"Oh Caleb, how thoughtful of you. I'm sure Hannah and Simon will be very happy to have a cradle." She smiled fondly at him. "It must have taken you quite awhile."

His chest had visibly swelled at her words, but he tried to appear casual. "Well, it did take awhile, but I wanted it to be done well." He looked at her earnestly. "Papa always said, 'Take your time and do it well the first time.'"

That would be like Jesse. They were both silent for a moment at the memory. Marah ruffled his hair.

"I think we need to see Hannah and Simon. What do you think?"

Caleb grinned and they headed toward the street of the carpenters.

35

Across town, Haman sat in the small wineshop and brooded. It was easy to let Marah think he had gone with a caravan. It gave him time to do what he wished. He had been stupid to take a wife. He never felt he needed a wife before. They were a millstone around a man's neck, and soon there were little brats to feed and clothe. He had sworn never to place himself in that position . . . until he had seen Marah. Her face came before him in his mind and anger rose up in him again. What good did it do to hold the shell of a woman in your arms? Then the specter of Jesse's broken body rose before him and he closed his eyes, trying to shut the scene out. Could he have saved him? Over and over in his mind, he heard Jesse screaming . . . "Haman, help me!" He shook his head and willed the specter away. He thought again of Marah. Part of her would always belong to Jesse, but the man was dead and Haman could not fight a ghost to satisfy the rage that swept through his heart. She deserved what he did at the synagogue. She needed to be humbled. He tried to justify his actions to salvage his own pride, but in his heart he knew he had done more harm. She only avoided him before, now she would hate him.

No matter. What did he need with one woman when he could have the pick of others?

Lost in his own thoughts, Haman looked out absentmind-edly at the crowd of people passing by on their way to the marketplace. Suddenly he became alert and leaned back in the shadows. He recognized the two men who had come upon him the night of the merchant's murder. They were here in Shechem at last. They walked with a purpose. Were they going to the city elders? Haman cursed. This was a fine fix. He was supposed to be out of the city with a caravan. He could not return to the house and Marah. But then, he didn't want to do that. They would trace him there. He smiled to himself. That might be well. They would be told that he had left with a caravan. They would want to find him outside the walls of the town. As long as he remained in Shechem, designated in the Book of the Law as a city of refuge, he was safe.

A movement beside him caused him to jump slightly. Ahira, the man he had been waiting for, lowered his short, heavy bulk into a chair. He smiled benignly at Haman, his eyes like two small bright coals in his pudgy face. Ahira was a man of many talents, and Haman paid him to do his bidding. Ahira could serve him well at this moment.

The two men Haman had been watching stopped at a fruit stall and were eating as they appeared to casually survey the crowded marketplace. Haman motioned to Ahira. "See those two men at the fruit seller's stall?"

Ahira nodded, studying them carefully. He had an excel-lent memory.

"Follow them and tell me where they go and what business they are about."

Ahira's smile was ingratiating. His interest was piqued. He was very good at gleaning information and making use of it. He nodded and left the wine shop.

Haman watched the two men continue down the street with Ahira casually but closely following. His thoughts re-turned to Marah. Her beauty was quickly fading in his eyes. She was pale and seldom smiled. She shared his bed, if a man could call it that. If he had not been caught up in having to stay in Shechem, he could have had his way with her and gone on to a far city taking just the memory of her with him. Now he was saddled with an old man, a poor excuse for a wife, and a nuisance of a boy. He nursed his wine and wallowed in self-pity. Every time he looked at Caleb, it was Jesse all over again. He had his father's long legs and blond hair. He reminded Marah of Jesse too.

He was so deep in his thoughts that he didn't notice Ahira's return until the little man sat down quickly across from him. Haman could tell he had information.

"What did you find out?"

"My lord, it appears that they are looking for you." Ahira studied Haman's face to see how he took the news.

Haman remained calm, not allowing his alarm to show. He would give Ahira no cause to have an edge on him.

"Why are they looking for me?"

"It appears they have gone to the elders of the city in regard to a murder. They accuse you of killing the brother of one of the men. He has sworn to avenge the death with your blood, my lord.' Ahira's small eyes glittered.

"Fools! I didn't kill the man. I killed the murderer and thief who had done the task when he tried to kill me also. They came upon the scene and drew their own conclusions." He swore again. "Now I must consider what to do."

"My lord, if you are indeed innocent, you have nothing to worry about."

"Son of a jackal, how can I prove I did not kill the merchant when I stood with my knife in my hand, the blood of the thief still on it?" Haman smacked his palm with his fist. He appeared to be angry in front of Ahira, but cold fear welled up in Haman and it took all his skill to fight it down.

"I can yet be of service to you," said Ahira smoothly, ignoring Haman's outburst. He was used to Haman's temper. "They inquired as to your whereabouts and have been told by your wife that you had left on a caravan. It may be that if this is proved to be true, as far as they are concerned, they will leave to seek you in another city."

Haman smiled and his eyes narrowed. Ahira was just the one to make sure they believed he had left the town of Shechem. He reached for his bag from his girdle and counted out two gold coins. "There is double this if they believe you and leave Shechem."

Ahira's eyes glittered. He loved gold. Haman always paid well. He scooped up the coins and looking around him, left the shop quickly.

Haman stretched and thought about what his next move would be. He could not stay here and he could not go home, but there was one other place no one would look for him. He smiled to himself. Ahira would know where to look for him when he returned. He put a coin down to pay for his wine and looked around quickly before leaving. His sharp eyes spotted a young boy with blond hair, moving out of sight among the throng. Caleb. The boy was spying on him again. What had he heard? Haman swore to himself. Things were becoming complicated. He knew Ahmal was watching him closely. He thought he had been very careful in the things he had "removed" from the shipments. Things he had given to Marah, to please her. Now all was for nothing. He thought of the two men. Perhaps he needed to find a way to safely leave Shechem . . . and the sooner the better.

36

Ahira watched to see the small inn where the two men lodged. When they sat eating a simple meal, he casually wandered in and sat nearby. Waiting for an opportunity, he called the innkeeper over and inquired, in a voice just loud enough for the two men to hear.

"Innkeeper, do you know a man by the name of Haman, son of Jemuel of Joppa? A factor for one of the caravan masters?"

The innkeeper shrugged his shoulders. The town was full of strangers because of the caravan route that passed through. "I do not know this man, I'm sorry."

Ahira shook his head and stared at his wine, and waited. In a moment the man called Manahath turned to him. "You seek a man called Haman?"

Ahira smiled innocently. "You know of him? I seek to do business with him, but he is nowhere to be found."

Manahath grunted. "We were told that he left with a caravan this morning. We also seek him . . . for another matter."

Ahira's face reflected his disappointment. "I cannot wait a month or so until he returns. Do you by any chance know which direction the caravan is taking? Perhaps I can catch up to them."

Zadok joined them. "We were told it was headed for Jez-reel," he growled.

Ahira brightened. "There is safety in numbers. Perhaps we could travel together, since we seek the same man."

Manahath studied Ahira for a moment. "We travel best alone, my friend. If we should indeed catch up to him, we will tell him you seek him. What is the name we may give?"

"Ahira." He looked from one face to the other pleasantly. "I will forever be in your debt."

"We will remember your name. A thousand pardons, you will excuse us? We must leave at dawn tomorrow to catch up with the caravan."

Manahath turned away, and Ahira heard them whispering between themselves. Zadok obviously was in a mood to leave even at this moment, but Manahath was restraining him. Evidently Manahath had convinced him to wait for daylight for with a sullen nod of his head, Zadok stalked out.

Ahira waited a few moments and then paid for his meal and headed quickly to find Haman. He had earned his gold.

Pleased with himself, Ahira hurried through the narrow streets to a house he knew well. From a doorway here and there came the sounds of tinkling laughter and music. He looked carefully to his left and right, for there were others who frequented this dark street. He knocked and Hodash opened the door slowly, clearly resenting the interruption. Haman tossed her a few coins and promised to return. Mollified, she picked up the coins.

Ahira and Haman went to a small dark wineshop at the end of the street.

"You can be at peace, my lord, I have done as you asked."

"They believe I am on the caravan?"

"They leave on the morrow to seek you, on the caravan to Jezreel."

"Jezreel?"

Ahira nodded. "It is as your wife told them."

Haman stroked his beard with one hand. Marah had

protected him. He should be grateful for that, but it was only a reprieve. If they did not find him on the caravan, they would be sure to return. What was he to do now?

"You have done well." Haman tossed the two gold coins on the table, but just as Ahira was reaching for them, Haman's hand came down heavily on his. "Just to be sure, you may observe their early departure, my friend."

Ahira liked his sleep, but it would do no good to cross Haman. It would be better to stay in his good graces, unless of course there appeared another avenue, with more gold. He pocketed his money, and was gone.

Haman watched him leave. Now what would he do with the time Ahira had purchased for him? He could go to the elders and plead his case, or—and he brightened—he could go the other direction from Shechem. The particular caravan he knew of was a long distance away. A few simple arrangements, and he could leave his troubles behind.

Ahira, concentrating on counting his money, did not look up as he passed a dark passageway in the city. A voice spoke to his right and an arm propelled him into the shadows.

Ahira felt the coldness of the blade against his throat.

"We would speak again, my friend," said Manahath.

37

Marah wrapped the cheese and bread in a small cloth and handed it to Caleb. "This is all I can give you today. Pay attention to the rabbi and learn your lessons well. You must not bring shame to your grandfather, or your father." Word had come to her that Caleb was listless in the school, and the shammash had punished him severely for his inattention.

"I will try, Mama." His voice was almost a whisper.

"Caleb, we will be all right. We must all be strong. Your father would want to be proud of you."

Caleb nodded unhappily. "I will do better, Mama. I will do better for Papa."

She put her hand on his shoulder affectionately. "I know you will, Caleb."

She watched him go and stood in the doorway for a moment. It had been two years since Jesse died, yet it seemed like only yesterday that he was there beside her. In her mind he lived on. The more Haman revealed his dishonesty, the more deeply she clung to the memories of happier times with Jesse.

Caleb was now twelve. The Samarim did not have a Bar Miswa, making a boy a "child of the Law" as did the Jews, but they did question their young men's knowledge of good and evil, thus making them accountable to God. Her heart felt heavy to think that Jesse would not be there to see his son through this special time of his life.

Elon was feeble, but his mind was still strong. He patiently questioned Caleb in the same way the shammash would. Marah watched over him tenderly and prayed that God would be merciful and let him live to see his grandson come of age. Elon was the only one who really knew the truth of her life with Haman, and he was a comfort to her in the lonely evenings. Since he was a strong believer in dreams and omens, she hesitantly shared the recurring dream that stayed with her through the years, the stranger who reached his hand out to her. It came to her again last night, renewing her strength. Elon listened sagely and thought a long moment.

"I do not know the meaning of the dream, Daughter, but if it is a comfort to you in some way, then it must be from God. It is a good dream." He nodded vigorously to confirm his words.

"That is good to know, Elon. I thank you for your counsel."

Pleased that she had turned to him with a need, Elon leaned against the side of the house and dozed.

Marah shook her head. If her life was as God willed, it was full of peaks and valleys. Where would it all end? Caleb grew taller and she feared that one day he would defy Haman. She bowed her head quietly in the courtyard. The God Who Sees knew her life, was it not in His hands? She stood in the morning sun and prayed earnestly for them all.

Haman stood in the shadows of the caravansary. He watched the activities of the main courtyard carefully. It was a quiet time of the day and there were only two camel drivers in the area. He watched them check their camels and go off together. Now was his chance. He looked around furtively and then straightened his shoulders and strolled out to one

228

of the camels. He looked around again. There was no sign of the camel drivers returning. He saddled the camel and mounted, giving the command for the animal to rise. The beast stood reluctantly and Haman urged it toward the gate that led to the road outside Shechem.

Haman thought ruefully of his horse. It had been a good animal, but unfortunately Haman had sold him. Just when he was congratulating himself on the ease with which he had gotten the camel, he glanced to his right and saw Caleb standing defiantly by the gate.

Haman thought quickly. Appearing to be in no hurry, he ordered the camel to kneel and dismounted.

"You did well in your lessons today?" he asked sternly.

The boy looked startled, then stared at him resentfully. His eyes were suspicious. Haman didn't usually ask about his school or anything else he did.

"I have an errand I need you to help me with, Caleb."

"You told Mama you had gone with the caravan, but I knew you didn't go. I saw you." His tone was accusing.

"I had to change my mind and . . . return. There is a matter I needed to attend to. Come with me."

Fear showed in the boy's eyes, but he faced Haman bravely. "Shiva is expecting me in his shop. He does not like me to be late."

"I have already spoken to Shiva. He will expect you to be a little later today." Haman lied smoothly. "Come, I have something to show you."

Caleb appeared puzzled. "Are you going to join a caravan?"

"I told you I have something to show you. It has to do with your father."

"Papa? What do you want to show me?"

"You will see. Have you ever ridden on a camel, Caleb?"

Caleb eyed the camels and looked back at Haman. Clearly he was torn between suspicion and a desire to ride one of the great beasts. "Where are we going?"

"Just a short distance outside the gates. You will be back in time to give Shiva a good account of your adventure."

"Adventure?"

Haman smiled in a friendly way. "Every boy wants an adventure, does he not? I have been harsh with you . . . for my own reasons. I merely wish to make it up to you."

Caleb approached cautiously, and Haman helped him climb into the saddle. Caleb had never been on a camel before. Haman barely contained his pleasure. This was easier than he thought. He couldn't let the boy tell anyone which direction he had gone. Now he would have to do something with Caleb. Perhaps he could leave the boy somewhere. He climbed up behind Caleb and raised the animal again. As the camel raised its hindquarters, Caleb hung on for dear life and almost pitched forward over the camel's head. The camel then raised his front legs and stood arrogantly, chewing its cud.

Haman gathered the reins and they moved out the gates of the caravansary into the narrow valley.

When they had gone some distance from the town, Caleb looked back, suddenly alarmed. "I . . . I wish to go back now."

Haman ignored him, urging the camel on.

"I wish to go back now, Haman, please."

"Now that would not be very convenient for me, boy. I have gone to a lot of trouble to plan this trip. Surely you would not disappoint me by ending it so soon."

The boy's eyes grew wide with fear. He looked at Haman and then at the ground, and then before Haman could grab him, he had swung a leg over and jumped to the ground, going down on his knees. He straightened up quickly and ran as fast as he could go toward a grove of trees.

Cursing his negligence for not tying the boy to the camel when he had the chance, Haman gave chase. Finally he barked a command and waited impatiently for the camel to kneel. He dismounted quickly and ran in the direction Caleb had gone. He must catch him before he got back to the town. He cursed as he ran. This had gotten out of hand. He heard footsteps running ahead of him and then a sharp cry of pain. He caught up to Caleb who was lying on the ground, gripping his ankle.

"Well, well," he said nastily as he grabbed the boy. "It seems you and your father have an ability to fall down at the wrong time." He jerked the boy up on his feet.

Caleb winced with pain and looked at him with alarm. "What do you mean?"

"You are both clumsy fools." He took his sash and tied the boy's hands.

Caleb stared at Haman. "Did you kill my papa?" A sob escaped him. "The men were right. You are a murderer. We know all about you. They told us. They will catch you and you will be sorry." Caleb spat the words and his eyes blazed with hatred and anger as Haman half dragged him back in the direction of the camel. He had left the beast near an outcropping of rocks.

The camel was nowhere to be seen. Haman cursed loudly, nearly beside himself with anger and frustration. The animal was trained—they did not usually wander off. Someone had taken it. He cursed again at the irony of it and thought about his options. He could not take Caleb back to Shechem . . . not now that the boy knew what direction he was going. He could still try to make the caravan, but it was too far by foot and alone. He could travel faster if he returned to Shechem to the caravansary for a means of transportation.

Caleb began to sob again and Haman raised his hand to strike him. Caleb tried to pull away and free his wrists. Suddenly a voice spoke nearby.

"Would you strike down the boy as you struck down my brother, murderer?"

Haman whirled around and recognized the two men who had come upon the scene at the death of the merchant. They led his camel as they came from behind the outcropping of rocks

"You!"

"Did you think we fell for the clumsy ruse of your servant?" Zadok smirked. "It seems his reputation precedes him. Who can believe the word of the son of a camel driver? Hmmmm?" He drew his sword from its scabbard, moving slowly forward, his eyes glittering. Manahath also drew his sword and moved toward Haman's other side. Haman had let go of the sash that bound Caleb and brandished his knife as he prepared to defend himself.

Manahath moved quickly and with the tip of his sword, cut the bonds that bound Caleb. "You are from Shechem? This is a matter of honor and we have no quarrel with you. Go quickly. Tell them Zohar, the Avenger of Blood, has found justice and returned honor to his family."

Caleb backed off slowly. "He is a murderer?"

Manahath nodded. "He is a murderer. His victims will be avenged. Go, boy, return to Shechem." Caleb ran.

"Fools!" Haman cried as they closed in on him. "I didn't kill the merchant. I killed the thief who robbed him. It is he who killed your brother. You must believe me!" Haman's voice took on a pleading tone as he turned toward Zadok.

"And who took his bag of gold? You are a thief as well as a murderer," Zadok spat at him.

"You gave me no choice. You wouldn't listen to me then either!"

"If you were innocent, why did you not go to the elders of the city to plead your case? It is because guilt has kept you silent, son of a dog!"

As Caleb began to run toward Shechem, he heard Haman's bloodcurdling scream of terror and then silence. Then the only sound was the pounding of Caleb's feet on the soft earth and his gasps for breath as he ran for all he was worth.

Hoofbeats sounded behind him and Caleb looked frantically for a place to hide. He turned to see Manahath riding toward him with Haman's camel in tow.

"Stop, boy. I mean you no harm. We are not thieves. This camel is yours?"

Caleb gulped with relief. "It belongs to the caravansary in Shechem."

Manahath ordered the camel to kneel. "Mount. We will return to Shechem."

Caleb climbed gingerly onto the camel and they rode in silence to within a short distance of the city gates and the caravansary.

Manahath dropped the reins of Caleb's camel. "You can go on from here, boy?" His face was not unkind.

Caleb nodded.

The camel, smelling water and food, ambled on toward the caravansary as Caleb hung on for dear life. Men came out and took hold of the camel, bringing it into the courtyard. One of the camel drivers commanded the camel to kneel and Caleb was helped down. The camel driver looked at Caleb.

"What were you doing on this camel? We have ways to deal with camel thieves!"

"Leave the boy alone!" It was Ajah, the man who ran the caravansary. He stepped quickly to Caleb's side. "I know this boy. Let go of him." He turned to Caleb. "Tell us what happened."

Caleb blurted out the words, "Haman took the camel. He made me go with him. There were two men . . . they have killed Haman."

"Killed Haman?" The men who had gathered around began to murmur among themselves. Voices were raised in anger.

"We will overtake the murderers . . ."

"Saddle the camels . . ."

Caleb looked around at them. "No! We must not go after them. They said to say, 'Zohar, the Avenger of Blood, has wrought justice and returned honor to his family.' He said Haman killed his brother . . ." He hung his head. "I think he killed my papa."

Ajah held up his hand. "No one will go after them. Justice has been done. Haman has paid for his crimes with his life." He turned to the camel driver. "Did they not return to you the camel Haman stole? They did not harm the boy. We will return him to his family and consider the matter closed."

The men murmured their assent. Ajah was a just man and fair in his dealings. His word was enough for them.

Ajah turned to Caleb. "I will see you to your family. This is not news to be borne by a boy alone."

Marah saw Caleb coming in the gate with a strange man. From the look on the boy's face, she knew something was wrong. Caleb ran and buried his face against her.

The man bowed slightly to her. "I am Ajah of the caravansary. I'm afraid I bring sad news to you. Your husband, Haman, is dead."

Elon had come out of the house. "Haman is dead? How did this happen?"

Caleb looked up at his grandfather. "The Avenger of Blood killed him. He was a murderer, just like those men said."

Ajah nodded sadly. "He stole a camel and I believe he was going to kidnap the boy. Evidently, according to your son, the men caught up with him, set the boy free, and took their revenge for the man Haman murdered."

With a gasp, Marah held Caleb tightly to her. "Haman was going to kidnap you?"

"He saw me watching him. I think that he didn't want me to tell anyone where he was going. He told me he wanted to show me something, but I got scared and jumped off the camel. He said something about a journey, a caravan he wanted to meet. He was going to take me with him."

Slave traders! Marah looked anxiously at his face. "And he changed his mind?"

He told them of his flight to the trees, his capture, and of returning to find the camel missing. "The men were hiding behind the rocks. And Mama, he . . . he said I was clumsy, like Papa." Caleb began to weep again.

Elon smote his breast and shook his head sadly. "It was an evil day when my nephew came to Shechem."

Ajah was watching Marah. She had gasped at Caleb's words,

but stood with dignity, her eyes filled with the anguish of her soul.

Somehow in her heart, Marah had suspected but didn't want to believe it. She looked at Ajah sadly. "I thank you for your kindness in bringing my son back safely to us."

"My men have gone to recover the body. It will not be . . . pleasant. I have seen this before. Do you wish me to see to his burial?"

Elon stepped forward. "We will bury him. I owe it to my brother Jemuel." He looked at Marah and Caleb. "My family thanks you for your kindness."

Ajah gave them a look of understanding. "Peace be with you." With a slight bow he turned and strode purposefully away.

Marah gathered the trembling emotions that threatened to overwhelm her. She must not falter for the sake of Caleb and Elon. Tomorrow she would once again bury a husband. She took a deep breath.

"Caleb," she said, holding him by the shoulders, "let us see to the animals."

He looked at her a moment. He wiped his eyes and stood tall before her. "Yes, Mama," he said bravely, and began to gather the chickens. Marah untied the goat and led her to her pen. Elon turned and slowly went into the house. He had lost his wife, then his son, and now the nephew he welcomed so readily was a murderer, killed for his crime. His steps were heavy.

Marah knew it was better for Caleb to be busy after his ordeal. They must let family life get back to normal. But what was normal? At twenty-four she was a widow for the third time.

Looking up at the sky, she breathed a silent prayer. *Oh God Who Sees Me, look down upon Your servant. I do not know what to do. Help us, I pray.* She bowed her head and stood quietly for a moment as she felt peace settle about her. Haman was gone and with him the turmoil of her life. The God of all the heavens knew His way. The neighbors would know soon enough, and there would be a dead body laid out to make their household unclean. She felt sorry for Haman, to meet such an end. In his way he had loved her. She had not been able to return that love, and it had twisted his mind. She thought of him as he first came—charming, witty, full of stories. She kept that picture firmly in her mind. One day, she must forgive him. Now, all she could think of was Jesse and the fact that because of Haman she had lost her husband and almost lost their son. She raised her head, gathered her strength, and entered the house to prepare their evening meal.

PART VI

Ahmal

38

Ahmal had been on the trade routes for three months and was weary of travel. As his men took care of the animals, he looked around the compound. Where was Haman? He was sent word of their arrival. There was merchandise to distribute and sell. Impatiently, Ahmal called one of the men over.

"Where is Haman? We have work to do."

"My lord Ahmal, Haman is dead."

"Dead? He is dead? How did this happen?"

The servant related the news as he had heard it only a couple of weeks before. He had been near the gate of the village when they had brought in the body of Haman.

Ahmal listened to the tale, astonished.

"Haman a murderer? He may have been many things, but I find it hard to believe he was that."

"Master Ajah was there, my lord, he can tell you. It was the boy who told us what happened."

"A boy?"

"Yes, my lord, young Caleb, son of Jesse."

Ahmal stroked his beard. This was distressing news. He thought of Marah and her father-in-law. She was an admirable woman considering what she had endured. He knew Haman and disliked him, for he had suspected Haman of theft. He did his job well and had a way with the other merchants, and Ahmal had debated on how to approach the matter. Now it was settled for him. There was no longer the unpleasant task of confronting the man. Ahmal wondered how his widow and family were faring. He must call upon them in any case and present his regrets for their circumstances. He stood thoughtfully a few moments, and then after making sure the merchandise was being unloaded properly, he put one of his men in charge and went to refresh himself . . . and speak with Ajah.

Ajah shook his head. "A bloody business, my friend. They decapitated him and ran him through. He had only a dagger. Not much of a defense against the swords they wielded." Ajah looked out over the caravansary. "I had my men prepare the burial casket for his widow. She buried him . . . a gruesome task for the family." He turned back to Ahmal. "There have been many things of concern in your absence, Ahmal."

Ahmal nodded. "I know. I reviewed the accounts before I left. There were, shall we say, errors?"

"Was the family aware?"

He rose and sighed heavily. "I do not believe they knew. They are good people. I'll not burden them with Haman's misdeeds. It is a matter best forgotten." He looked meaningfully at Ajah.

Ajah nodded reflectively. "It is best forgotten."

Within the hour Ahmal was on his way to the house of Haman.

⁂

"Peace be upon this household."

"My lord Ahmal." Marah bowed her head respectfully and welcomed him to their home.

"I wish to extend my sympathy for what you have gone through recently." He nodded to Elon who stood leaning on his staff.

"It is a kindness that you grace our humble home," said Elon, moving toward their visitor.

Ahmal seemed to be watching Marah. "You grieve for Haman."

Marah looked into his face and saw compassion and concern. She bowed her head. "Haman was not all he seemed, my lord."

He nodded, stroking his beard. "And the boy? How is Caleb doing?"

"He is well. He will soon be of age. He is growing as tall as his father." She spoke with pride. "Soon he returns from the shop of Shiva the carpenter, where he is an apprentice."

"He follows in his father's footsteps, eh?" Ahmal smiled broadly.

"May we offer you some refreshment?" Marah thought quickly of what she could bring out for their guest. There was little in the house.

"Ah, I almost forgot. How careless of me. I have brought a few small gifts, in that your husband, Haman, worked for me. I would have sent them the week of mourning, had I but been here."

Elon waved a hand and stood proudly. "That is not necessary, my lord. You have been a friend to our family. There is no need for you to trouble yourself."

"It has brought me such pleasure in gathering these things. You would grieve me to the heart should I have to return with them intact." He looked genuinely injured.

Marah looked quickly at Elon. "Father Elon, how can we cause our friend ill feelings?"

"You are right, Daughter. We most humbly apologize. We would be most honored to accept your gift."

Ahmal smiled again and, motioning with his hand to wait, stepped outside, and spoke to a servant who had been waiting at the gate. In a moment, two servants came, bearing jars, bags of leather, goatskins, and more items, which they began to place on the low table. The items covered the table and more was placed on the floor. There were cheeses, wine, sweetbreads, meat, dates from Jericho, plums and figs from

Palestine, and truffles from Jerusalem. It was a king's bounty in the eyes of the poor family.

Marah and Elon stared at Ahmal in astonishment.

"My lord, this is too much. We can never repay you."

"Repay? My friends, one does not repay a gift. It eases my poor conscience that your family has had to suffer such grief at the hands of one who worked for me. I know he was of your family . . . but . . ."

"But there is a possibility that he was not, my lord." Marah looked at Ahmal directly.

Ahmal inclined his head sadly. "It would be better to believe that such a one could not come from one's own family . . ."

Elon spoke up. "I have thought a great deal about this. It is possible, knowing what Haman was like, that he only pretended to be part of our family for his own purposes."

Marah turned and looked at Elon. He had echoed her own thoughts, yet she had never had the courage to say these things to him. He had suspected Haman also.

Ahmal spread his hands and shrugged his shoulders. "God is merciful. We shall look forward to better times, shall we not?"

"You are a good and kind man, my lord, you have our sincere gratitude. We thank you for your gifts." Elon inclined his head respectfully toward Ahmal.

"God's peace upon this house," Ahmal said again, and turned to leave.

"God give you His blessing and protection. You are welcome at any time to our humble home." Elon stood tall before the merchant.

Ahmal touched his breast with a familiar gesture, nodded to Marah, and was gone.

Marah and Elon stood for a moment and looked at the treasure of goods in front of them. Tears came to her eyes. God had seen their need and truly sent that good man.

39

Ahmal passed through the marketplace on his way to the wool merchant to arrange for the disposal of goods he had brought in. As he walked, he was preoccupied with things not related to his caravan. Ordinarily he would have paid little attention to the affairs of women. He was a bachelor and comfortable with his life as a traveling merchant and caravan master. Yet thoughts of Marah stayed on his mind. In spite of the mishaps and the tragedy that plagued her life, she was beautiful and serene. She saw to the affairs of her small family and provided for them with her wool and weavings. An admirable woman. He allowed his thoughts to rest on her, remembering her laughter that evening when the family had joined Haman for dinner at his home.

Ahmal continued on in deep thought. He knew their family's circumstances were destitute. He brought them gifts each time he returned from a journey, always taking care that the small bounty was presented in such a way as to save their pride. Always they were gracious and grateful. They could not continue to live in this way. Sooner or later, out of desperation to put food in the mouth of that growing boy and to take care of Elon, she might turn to a trade she despised. The thought brought him grief and anger.

All day, as he continued his business in Shechem, the

thoughts of Marah and her family were seldom far from his mind. He wanted to do something, but what?

Slowly, as the day progressed, an idea began to form. He was more than concerned about her, and attracted to her from the first time she shyly greeted him in the company of that great brute of a husband, Jesse. She loved him, there was no doubt. He had observed the looks that passed between husband and wife. She was happy with him. Then there was Haman, a man who proved to be dishonest and a wretched excuse for a husband. A new thought crossed his mind. He smote his palm with his fist. By the God of Abraham, that was the answer.

That evening as he began to dress, the idea that formed began to whisper its doubts to him. Would she accept? Would she laugh at him? Would she think he felt sorry for her and only offered her his pity? She would scorn him if she suspected that. Truly he must present his idea in such a way as to preserve her dignity and yet offer a solution for the state they now found themselves in.

Eliab came in and observed Ahmal pacing the room. "Master, are you troubled about something?"

"Eliab, you are just the one. I have an idea . . . perhaps the idea of a foolish man, but I am considering marriage."

"Marriage, at this time of your life? A fine idea, but who is the woman who has won the heart of my master?" Eliab was astonished.

"Do you remember the family who joined us for dinner, with Haman?"

"Yes, Master."

"It is that woman. She is now a widow, and I would offer marriage."

"I recall the woman, Master. Has she not been through much tragedy in her life? I hear them speaking of her as I go about the marketplace."

"And what are they saying there, Eliab?"

"They say she has the 'evil eye.' Three husbands dead and

another who divorced her. She has endured a great deal of suffering, has she not? The women spurn her, saying she has powers of sorcery and bewitches the men . . . sending them to their death."

"Cackling hens! Do you believe that, Eliab?"

"I do not. I was impressed that she is a virtuous woman and upright."

"I agree. The family suffers much with trouble not of their own making."

"It is a fine family, master."

"Yes, and she has a young son by the name of Caleb, a good boy and one to be proud of."

"Ah, yes, master. A fine boy as I recall." Eliab studied his master a moment and then his eyes sparkled with understanding. "You have no heir, my master?"

"Eliab, you rascal, there is little that I can hide from you."

"Nothing, master," and they both laughed.

"My lord." Eliab's tone was politely respectful. "Will you permit your humble servant to make a suggestion?"

"You know I rely on you. What is it?"

"Let me send a servant to invite the family to our humble home for another meal. It would give the woman time to prepare herself. Such surroundings may perhaps lend themselves to a more favorable answer."

"Praise be to God, I was fortunate the day I found you. Of course, that is a much better idea . . . one I should have thought of. I cannot stumble in there and suddenly blurt my intentions. Prepare at once and I will send a message to Marah and her family to join us."

Ahmal clapped his hands and a servant was soon on his way.

40

Marah had struggled to walk to her home after another ordeal with the women at the village well. They had thrown a couple of stones this time and hissed at her. They accused her again of the "evil eye" and drew their skirts away from her.

"Any woman who has lost four husbands must be suffering the punishment of God. She has done wrong and kept her sin secret. God knows her!"

"Her husband was a murderer. Who knows what things they have done."

"She comes even now!"

She had ignored them and gotten her water, maintaining her dignity. She would not let them see how they hurt her. These were women who had been friends since she was a young girl. How could they treat her so?

With her last strength, she set the water jug down and unwound her mantle as she stumbled to her pallet. Her head was ringing as she gave in to the darkness.

"Mama!" The voice of Caleb seemed to come from a great distance away. Someone was putting cool cloths on her head.

"Mama, please open your eyes. Please. I cannot lose you also." Caleb was sobbing quietly.

Slowly Marah opened her eyes. It took so much effort. She turned her head to look at Caleb's anxious face. Next to him was Hannah. Behind her, Elon looked down at her, his craggy face drawn with worry. She tried to speak but no words came.

"God be praised. She is with us again," Elon murmured.

Hannah patted her shoulder and spoke gently, "Rest, Marah. You have suffered much. Now is the time of rest. I will take care of your household. You must gather your strength. Caleb and Elon need you. Rest, my friend." Hannah soothed her with words as she lifted Marah's head with her arm and put a cup of broth to her lips. She could only manage one swallow before putting her head back down. She was so tired.

"You will get better, Mama. You must get better." Caleb took her hand.

When Marah opened her eyes again, Elon slept nearby. She looked around the room. Her mouth was dry and she could not raise her head. Hannah was sweeping and had her back turned. She moved slowly for it was nearly time for her babe to be born.

Hannah turned and smiled. "You had a good rest?"

"You should not be doing my work and your own as well at this time."

Caleb came into the house. "I've gotten the herbs you asked for, Hannah." When he saw his mother with her eyes open, he gave a glad cry, which wakened Elon, and knelt by her side, laying his head on her shoulder. "I knew you would be all right, Mama. I knew it." His eyes pooled with tears.

"Caleb . . . ," she whispered softly, stroking his hair. She took a deep breath and held her hand out to Caleb with a smile. "Help me rise, my son, there is work to be done."

He happily took her hand and Elon moved to put an arm behind her shoulders. They helped her up. She stood wavering for only a moment and then moved toward Hannah.

"Let me help you, dear friend, for a change. Your time is soon."

"Nonsense, I am fine. You should rest longer, until you feel well."

"I believe I have been 'resting' far too long already." Marah laughed. "I will be all right. Everything just seemed so much to bear, for a time."

"God will see you through this, Marah, as He always has."

"Yes, and He gives me strength even now. Return to Simon, Hannah, with my heartfelt thanks. I can manage now."

"You are sure?"

Marah smiled at Elon and Caleb. "I have two fine men to watch over me. I shall be in good hands."

Elon and Caleb beamed.

After Hannah had gone, Marah contemplated what she had for supper. There was a knock on the door and a servant of Ahmal waited with a message.

Marah turned to Elon and Caleb. "It seems we are all invited to the home of our friend Ahmal to share the evening meal. What should we do?"

Elon stood. "He is a good man, and does not seek just your company, Daughter. He asks your father and son to come also. I see no harm in responding to his kind offer."

Marah thought of the meager meal she had begun to prepare. The choice was simple. She nodded to the servant and hurried to refresh herself and put on her best tunic and mantle. Elon and Caleb washed carefully and each combed his hair. Satisfied that they were presentable, they cautiously went through the narrow streets to the home of Ahmal. The servant carried a lamp and a stout staff as did Caleb, in the event they should meet up with one of the gaunt and hungry village dogs who plagued the town in the evening hours.

With a smile, Eliab greeted them at the door, treating them as honored guests. He had purposefully chosen a simple but elegant meal. There must not be a great show of wealth for he had sensed it would offend the woman and make her feel uncomfortable. With a bow he indicated the low table, and they seated themselves, waiting for Ahmal. In a moment he was with them, smiling and acknowledging each of them separately.

"Welcome, my friends, to my home. It is indeed a joy to my heart that you were able to keep company with a lonely man this night."

Marah smiled and watched Ahmal. He had a purpose in this dinner, for in spite of all his charm and gracious hospitality, he appeared very nervous. She felt slightly alarmed. Did he have bad news for them and had chosen this way to soften the impact? But then, what bad news could he possibly bring them at this point? She waited expectantly, as did Elon and Caleb.

She observed the patient and friendly way Ahmal conversed with Caleb. He didn't treat him as a mere boy to be ignored and for that she was grateful. Caleb respected him. Elon also was drawn carefully into the conversation, and his comments were met with a serious nod of agreement. She liked Ahmal. She didn't know what they would have done without his kindnesses. She wondered if he realized how carefully she hoarded and portioned out the gifts of food he brought to add to their simple meals. Letting her mind wander over the hum of the men's conversation, she thought of what she knew of him. He was a bachelor, and traveled a great deal as a merchant. He was well respected in Shechem by the other merchants. He controlled the men of his caravan with a firm, but honest hand. He and his servant Eliab seemed to genuinely respect and like each other. She suspected that Ahmal was still somewhat of a lonely man. Why didn't he marry, to have a wife to comfort him at the end of his journeys?

At that moment, Marah looked up from her musings to meet the eyes of Ahmal. There was appreciation and warmth there. Suddenly, she suspected why they had been summoned. Was he no different than the other men of Shechem?

"Perhaps Elon and Caleb would enjoy my small courtyard and the evening sounds," Ahmal was saying. With the promise of sweets, Caleb followed his grandfather with Eliab into the courtyard, bright with starlight. Marah, realizing that the invitation did not include her, remained where she was sitting. She knew Ahmal had something to say to her.

"Marah, I would speak with you concerning . . . a matter that has come to my mind only recently. I hesitate to even begin . . ."

Poor man, he was certainly not the smooth Haman when it came to speaking to women. She felt compassion for Ahmal. Let him ask her to share his bed, whatever, she would find a way to discourage him gently. He meant well.

"I have been concerned about your family . . . and you. I have heard what the women are saying."

"And what did you think of their charges, my lord?"

"Foolish and unfounded. You have indeed been through great trials, but I have watched how you have overcome your . . . adversities. I have admired you."

"You are most kind, my lord."

"Let me come to the point, if I may. I have admired you greatly since the first time we met in the company of your husband, Jesse. I saw that you were happy with him and wished you many years together. Perhaps I had hoped to have a woman look at me in that way one day, but alas, the years pass quickly and there has been no one."

"Ahmal . . . ," she sighed and spoke as kindly as possible. "What is it you would like to say to me?"

He looked at her face and there was no guile in his words. "I would offer you myself and my home, such as it is."

"In what way, my lord?" She drew herself up and looked back at him without coyness.

He stepped back, startled. "You misunderstand my intentions. I have noted you to be an honorable woman, a woman who looks to her hearth and home. I would ask you to share my home . . . as my wife."

Marah stood up suddenly. She was without words. Her eyes searched his face. "Marriage?"

"You have a son to raise, a fine boy, growing into manhood.

Elon is old and he is concerned with how you will live. He is ready to go as his wife has gone. I would offer you my protection, the security of a home to raise your son, and the means to live comfortably here in Shechem. As my wife, you would not be treated so . . . unkindly. I do not ask you to love me . . . for I believe a woman such as you loves only once. I would hope that in time, you would come to care for me a little, but I am prepared to accept the will of God." It was a long speech for Ahmal and he stood quietly waiting for her to speak.

"My lord, Ahmal, I am . . . overwhelmed by your offer. I had thought . . . it would be an offer of another kind. There have been many of those, too many. It is difficult to believe that you would give us that much, asking nothing in return."

He smiled gently. "Your presence in my home would be a gift in itself. After my long journeys, I would have a pleasant companion to return to, instead of empty rooms. Eliab is as a brother to me, but there are many times I have been greatly lonely." He paused, weighing his next words carefully. "And yes, in a way, there is something I wish in return. I have been well impressed with what I have seen in your son. He is a fine boy, one to be proud of. One day he shall be a man of influence. You have given him an understanding heart and respect for others. One could ask no more of a son than that. I am a bachelor. Not having a wife means I have no heir. Eliab is not a young man, and he does not wish to inherit my worldly goods. If he survives me, he wishes only to return to his own country, and I would leave him more than enough to do that and live there comfortably. I wish to make Caleb . . . my heir."

"Oh my lord . . ." Marah sat down again suddenly. She searched his face. "I do not know what to say. I must think. Would you be offended if I do not give you an answer just yet? I must speak with Caleb and Elon in this matter."

Ahmal seemed relieved to have finally said what he wanted to say. "I am honored you wish to consider my offer at all, and I admire the fact that you wish to consider your family.

You are most welcome to take your time. I do not leave on another caravan for three weeks. Will you be able to give me your answer by then?"

"Yes, my lord, I will give you my answer by then."

Sensing that there had been enough time for his master to accomplish his purpose, Eliab graciously escorted Elon and Caleb back to the room.

"We must be on our way home, Daughter, the hour grows late."

"Yes, Father." She turned to Ahmal and smiled. He nodded slightly and walked with Eliab to his patio where servants were waiting to escort them to their home.

"God be with you."

"And with you, Ahmal. We thank you for your hospitality . . . and friendship."

"Until we meet again, my friends." And with a hopeful glance at Marah, he turned back to the house.

Elon was weary from the long walk, and was soon asleep on his pallet. Caleb helped check the animals.

"He is a good man, Mama."

"Yes, Caleb. He is a good man. Do you like him?"

"Yes, I do. He treats me as if I were grown, not a boy."

"He is kind to Elon, is he not?" She tried to appear casual in her questions.

Caleb was too full of good food and excitement to look for anything else in her words. He nodded, then yawned and hastily bid her good night.

Marah sat quietly, looking up at the stars from the roof of the house. How many times had she come here to think about things that needed an answer. *Oh God Who Sees Me*, she prayed, *help me to know what to do*. She looked up at the star-filled sky, and for once felt no unrest in her spirit.

41

It was nearing the end of the Sabbath and Elon was saying his prayers. Caleb went with him to the *Bit Allah* and Marah went to the Court of the Women to pray earnestly for the right decision. She looked around and did not see Hannah or Simon. She felt a growing sense of urgency and quietly slipped out. It was becoming more difficult to go to any public place now. The women ostracized her or the men openly approached her. She knew she must speak with Elon tonight . . . and Caleb also. She had made a decision.

Hurrying to the house of Simon, she found Dorcas already there. The older woman nodded in greeting, but to Marah's relief, there was no malice in her glance.

"We have sent for Shelomith. It is her time," Dorcas said, indicating Hannah, who lay on her pallet. Beads of perspiration formed on her upper lip and forehead. Marah moved quickly to her side. There was a bowl of water and a cloth already wet, and she placed a cool cloth on Hannah's forehead. She saw fear in Hannah's eyes as she tried to handle the pains that came and went.

"I am not . . . a young woman," Hannah gasped between pains. "I pray our child will be born soon . . . and he . . . will be . . . all right."

"You shall produce a fine babe for Simon, my friend. Here, take my hand and squeeze when the pain comes. We shall face this together."

"I . . . tried . . . to call . . . for you. Too late . . . you had gone to the synagogue. God in His mercy heard my prayer and sent you."

"How long have the pains come?"

"Two hours. They are seeking Shelomith now."

"Did I hear my name spoken?" Shelomith appeared at their side with her bag of herbs. The midwife examined Hannah. "It is close. You will not be long in labor with this one."

"Where is Simon?" Hannah looked around her.

Shelomith snorted. "Where a husband should be at such a time as this . . . outside!" The women laughed and Hannah managed a smile before the next pain convulsed her.

True to the words of Shelomith, Hannah's son was born within the hour, just after the ending of the Sabbath. He was lusty, red and alive. Marah breathed a prayer of thanksgiving. Shelomith washed the baby and wrapped him in swaddling clothes. Marah presented Simon his son.

"A fine boy, Simon."

"A son? I have a son?" Tears of joy ran down Simon's cheeks as he took the baby from Marah and looked down on his small face. "I have a son," he whispered. Then, he looked up at Marah. "My Hannah . . . she is all right?"

"Yes, my friend. She is all right. You may see her soon."

Simon handed the baby back to be suckled.

Other neighbors came, and the men clapped Simon on the back. "It is a fine omen for your first child to be a boy . . . and with his parents the age of Simon and Hannah, all the more reason to celebrate."

Simon poured wine as they toasted the birth of his son. When Hannah was ready, Simon came in slowly and knelt by her bed. There were no words to say aloud, only the silent loving communion of two who know each other well.

Marah sent word to Elon and Caleb that she would be

staying with Hannah. Shelomith with her healing herbs also stayed.

"It is hard to lose a child," Shelomith said softly.

Marah had been gazing down at the baby. She was aware of the longing on her face. Now she looked up at Shelomith. It was the way the midwife had spoken that told her. "You too have lost a child?"

Shelomith nodded. "I was too young. He was stillborn. A beautiful little boy."

"Oh Shelomith. I never knew. I am so sorry."

"You have a kind heart. I don't believe the things they are saying about you. I was with you at the birth and death of your son. I know what you suffered. He was too large for you." Shelomith's normally stern face softened for a moment. She turned back to Hannah who was sleeping with the babe at her side. She watched the sleeping woman a moment and turned back to Marah.

"What will you do? There is talk that some of the women make it difficult for you?"

Dorcas quietly joined them. "I saw the care you gave Athaliah. It was a hard task, but you never complained to any of us. You just took care of her. If some of the women want to make fools of themselves, it is to their shame. I am your friend, Marah," she said, putting her hand on Marah's arm.

Marah looked at Dorcas and Shelomith and her eyes pooled with tears. How kind these two women were. She felt she had no friends but Simon and Hannah. It was good to know she was not alone.

"Thank you," she said quietly.

"So . . . what will you do?"

"I am, ah, making some decisions now." It was not the time to tell them what she contemplated. It would be wiser to talk to Elon and Caleb first and then Ahmal before he heard gossip in the town. "As soon as I know something, I'm sure it will not be long before all of Shechem knows it too." She laughed lightly.

"Well," said Dorcas, "I am sure you will make the right decision."

Marah looked down at the small cradle that Caleb had made for the baby. Such loving care had gone into it. She looked at the workmanship and saw his father's skill. Jesse had passed his talent with wood to his son. The very thought of Jesse brought a tightness in her breast and unbidden tears. She chided herself and bustled about putting Hannah's house in order. After Shelomith left, she fed Simon. Dorcas offered to stay, and Marah gladly agreed. She must talk with Elon and Caleb . . . tonight.

As Marah entered the doorway, Elon looked up anxiously. "We were concerned, Daughter, that you were not here. Hannah is all right?"

She beamed at both of them. "Hannah has a son."

"Oh Mama, then they will use the cradle I made."

"Yes, Caleb, they will use it. So now wash, we must have supper and then talk."

"Talk, Mama? About what?"

She shooed him toward the door. "First you wash, then you eat, and then, I will tell you."

Elon hurried to wash also. He was hungry.

They watched her face as she served them. When the meal was almost finished, Caleb looked at her expectantly. "What are we going to talk about?"

She sat down slowly and looked at her two men, a growing son and an aging father-in-law. She loved them both, but she wasn't sure how they would react to her decision. She took a deep breath and told them of Ahmal's proposal of marriage the night they went to his house for dinner.

"Mama, you did not say anything. Why?" Caleb did not seem to be angry, only puzzled. Elon was thinking quietly.

"This is a very important decision. We would have to leave our home and go to live in the house of Ahmal. Father, you would have a servant to wait on you, and Caleb, you would learn about the trade of merchants. You could still work for Shiva, if you wished."

256

Elon looked at her. "Once before I trusted that the one you were to marry was a good man. I didn't listen to my inner prompting about Haman. You suffered because of my foolish desire to have you marry the man I thought was the son of my brother. I grieved for my own son and watched your deep grief also. You only sought to do the right thing for your son . . . and your husband's father. I have considered that this might be what Ahmal had spoken to you about, and I have learned all I could about this man. Everything I have heard is good. He pays the merchants on time and cares well for his animals and men. He is generous in the synagogue and does not have a reputation with women. All I have learned, Daughter, is good."

"Thank you, Elon, for your wise council. And you, Caleb?"

"This time you are asking me, Mama?" He seemed pleased. "I like Ahmal. He does not pretend to be someone he is not. I think he is a good man. I have also heard others say so."

"Then you will give me your blessing, Elon?"

"Yes, Daughter. I believe this man will be good for you."

Caleb looked very serious. "Mama, you have my blessing also."

She hugged her son. "I will send word to Ahmal. He leaves in a few days on his next caravan and will be gone for a couple of months."

"You will send him on his way a happy man, Daughter. And give him reason to speed his return."

42

Ahmal indeed went on his journey a happy man. When he returned two months later, he made arrangements for the marriage, and the small family came to live in his home. Elon rented out their small house, for it was Caleb's inheritance and they would keep it for his future.

This was a time of peace for Marah unlike any she had known since her marriage to Jesse. Because Ahmal was respected in Shechem, Marah was treated well. When she walked through the marketplace with Caleb or one of the servants, the merchants presented their best goods, knowing Ahmal was wealthy.

Caleb fingered a bolt of cloth. At fourteen, he was as tall as Marah and moved with the grace of a young man, rather than an awkward boy. "You should have a tunic made of this, Mother." Already he had an eye for quality.

"Now what would I do with still another garment, Caleb?" she teased. "Between Ahmal and you, I shall have enough garments for ten women."

"And you deserve them all." Caleb grinned. He tossed a coin to the fruit merchant and walked along munching on a handful of dates.

She glanced at him affectionately. He had an insatiable curiosity about things and learned quickly. Ahmal had the necessary papers drawn up and signed in front of witnesses making Caleb his heir. Caleb was touched but, having grown up with little wealth, could not comprehend at the time the generosity of his stepfather. He was never inclined to be arrogant or boastful, and took the event in stride as he did everything else.

"Ahmal's caravan leaves soon. I wish he would let me go with him." Caleb's tone was wistful. "Why will he not let me go? I know his merchandise well and I have proven I can bargain better than Shema. I should be his factor, not Shema." Caleb pursed his lips.

"You are still young, Caleb. Not only must you be able to bargain well for Ahmal, you must also have the respect of the other merchants. You are growing quickly. Soon you will be a man able to represent Ahmal to the caravans."

Caleb was not pacified. "But I am ready now, Mother."

Shaking her head slowly, she turned back toward home. "It was good of you to accompany me, my son. I always feel better knowing you are at my side in the crowds of the marketplace."

As they entered the courtyard, they were met by Demas, a young slave whom Ahmal rescued from a cruel slave trader. Demas had been beaten badly and was half dead when Ahmal brought him home. Demas, wise enough to know when he was in good surroundings, served Ahmal's household well. Yet he too longed for places beyond Shechem, and Marah knew that, if he could, he would leave them and return to his home in Laodicea.

"Demas," Caleb asked, "has my father returned?" Marah marveled at how easily Caleb had taken the role of Ahmal's son.

Demas answered with deference and respect. "No, Master Caleb, but Eliab prepares for him. We expect him soon."

Marah observed the two young men. One, tall, broad-shouldered and blond, the other slender and dark. She knew there was a bond between them for Caleb often found excuses for Demas to accompany him on errands and they talked quietly when the work of the day was finished. Suddenly the feeling of apprehension returned. She had not been able to cast it aside. Did it have to do with Demas? She puzzled over the matter for some minutes until she heard voices. Ahmal entered the courtyard gate and with a smile, she moved to greet him.

"My husband, your day has been a successful one?"

He smiled back. "You are as a shaft of sunlight at the end of my day, my heart. If I had known how pleasant it was to be greeted by a beautiful wife when I returned home, I can assure you, I would have married long ago." He drew her arm through his and they strolled over to the fountain that sparkled with effervescent light as it splashed. "I shall miss you on this next journey."

"Your words are a comfort, Ahmal." She sensed the apprehension again. "How long will you be gone this time?"

"Alas, my love, it will be a longer journey than usual . . . perhaps four months."

"Four months? Why so long?"

"Word has come that the caravan of Marcus was set upon by bandits . . . a raiding party. Many of his men were killed or wounded. His caravan was the one to which I transferred my goods at Iconium. Until he has established a new caravan, I must take our wool and soaps farther to meet another caravan."

"Must you go, Ahmal? I have this feeling that something is going to happen." She looked up at him, full of concern.

Touched, he patted her hand. "It is a comfort to my heart that you are concerned for me. But where would merchants such as I be if they neglected their business because their wives 'had a feeling'?" He chuckled softly.

"Truly, Ahmal, I have not felt something like this since the day Jesse died. I had this same sense of danger."

"Dear one, I have a large company of well-trained, armed men who travel with me. My caravan is sizable. We are well protected from bandits. Now smile and say that you will wish me good fortune on my journey."

She pushed the shadows away and looked up into his dear face. "I do wish you good fortune and a safe journey. I shall be anxious for your return."

"That thought shall speed me home. Now, promise me there shall be no more talk of danger?"

"Yes, my lord, but I shall pray for your safety."

Ahmal nodded solemnly. "I will be glad for your prayers."

Eliab soon called them for the evening meal and went in search of Caleb and Demas who had disappeared. A properly chastised Demas soon appeared and hurried to the kitchen under the stern gaze of Eliab. Caleb looked a little sheepish and slipped down next to the table quietly.

"We were only talking of Laodicea, Father," he offered.

Ahmal nodded sagely, but with a half smile. "You and Demas are friends, my son, but he must not neglect his duties. He is a servant and has work to do."

Caleb nodded quickly and began to eat.

Marah went to the quarters of Elon. He was still frail and she marveled that he was still alive. Now Demas watched over him making sure he rested and was well fed. He had even gained a small paunch.

"You are well, Father Elon?"

"Ah, Marah. Yes, Daughter, I am well. I fear that young Demas will kill me with kindness." He waved a thin hand and chuckled. Suddenly he bent over in pain, clutching his chest.

"Demas!" she called, quickly helping him to sit down. "It is your heart, Father?"

He began to breathe easier. "It comes and goes, Daughter. Be not concerned. I shall be all right. It is the ailment of an old man."

They all came—Ahmal, Caleb, Demas, and Eliab. When Elon was resting comfortably, they left Demas to watch him and went quietly out.

"He has had these spells for years, yet each one I fear for him."

Ahmal took her hands gently. "We cannot stop life as we cannot stop the wind that blows. These spells come more frequently. One day God will call him."

Caleb turned and walked quickly away, but not before she had seen the pain in his eyes. He loved his grandfather dearly.

The morning of Ahmal's departure dawned. The wind blew slightly and there was a touch of cold in the air. Marah walked to the gate with Ahmal. She had not slept well. As she looked earnestly at his face, she thought how dear he had become to her. She did not love him as she loved Jesse, but he had won her respect, and with what love she could give, she cared for this dear and gentle man.

"I shall pray every day for your safe return."

Ahmal patted her shoulder and headed toward the caravansary.

Marah watched until his figure was lost in the crowd and then turned reluctantly back to the house. She was working on a new weaving. It would be just the thing to take her mind off foolish fears.

43

Caleb still worked at Shiva's carpenter shop from time to time. He no longer served Shiva as an apprentice. His status had changed with his mother's marriage and becoming Ahmal's heir. Many of the merchants deferred to him, not because of his status, but because he had learned well the ways of trading. He was already known in the marketplace as a shrewd bargainer. He was a likable young man, strong in what he believed and undeterred when his mind was set.

This morning Caleb came to Shiva's to finish a project, a small harp for his mother. Caleb loved trading and desired nothing more than becoming a merchant like Ahmal one day. Yet . . . he loved to work with his hands. The feel of the wood as he created small instruments and hand-carved animals was pleasant to him. The objects he made brought in a little money of his own. He did not wish to deceive his mother, but he had in mind to travel one day, and he had been secretly putting money aside for some time. He was not sure just what he would do, but one day there might be an opportunity, and he would go. Perhaps Demas might accompany him. They had talked in excited whispers when they were sure no one could overhear them.

"So when does Ahmal return?" It was Shiva interrupting his thoughts.

"He was due months ago. It must have taken longer than he thought it would."

Shiva clapped him on the shoulder. "He will send word. Your mother worries?"

Caleb nodded. "She looks for him often. She says she had a bad feeling when he left, that something terrible was going to happen. Now, she tries not to show how concerned she is, but it is hard for her."

Shiva thought a moment. There was gossip in the market-place among the merchants that no one had seen Ahmal's caravan. Many thought he had run into bandits or a band of marauders. One can speculate, but it was strange that there had been no word at all. They returned to their work, the older man glancing at the younger from time to time. He liked the boy as he had liked the father. It was not the boy's fault that his mother carried the curse of the "evil eye." Surely the merchant Ahmal had paid dearly for marrying her.

When Ahmal had been gone almost a year, a group of merchants came to the house led by Shema. Eliab spoke with them briefly and came to Marah.

"I do not wish to disturb you, mistress, but there is a group of men who insist on seeing you. They say it is a matter of business and they will not be put off."

She went out to the courtyard and faced them with dignity.

"What can I do for you?"

Shema stepped forward. "Have you had word from your husband as to when he will return?"

Marah shook her head. "I look for word every day. At least I have not received word that he is wounded . . . or dead. I trust he shall return soon."

"We do not wish to trouble you, but we cannot wait any longer. We have businesses to run and goods to pay for. Ahmal owes us money. He has always paid his debts, but he is not here," Shema said, shrugging his shoulders. The other merchants nodded their heads vigorously in agreement.

Marah felt alarm begin in her belly. "What would you have me do?"

"Surely your husband has set aside money . . . for necessary things in his absence?"

"How much does he owe you?" she asked calmly.

Shema handed her a scroll. She studied the figures for a moment and then spoke to Shema again. "Wait here, please." She turned and went to Ahmal's chambers. He had showed her where he kept his money box, just in case, and she had been touched that he had trusted her with this information. She had never touched the box, yet now, with trembling fingers, she pulled it from its hiding place and opened it.

"May I help you, mistress?" It was Eliab. "It is all right. I have known of the box for a long time. The master has trusted me also with this information." He smiled at her and took the box gently. He studied the scroll and then took a few coins from the box. "This should settle the debt, mistress." He put the box back in its hiding place, handed her the coins, and accompanied her back to the merchants. Marah had come to trust Eliab as Ahmal trusted him, so with dignity she held out her hand and gave the coins to Shema.

When they had gone, she turned to Eliab. "Thank you, Eliab, I . . . I'm afraid that I could not . . ."

"Could not read the scroll, mistress?" His eyes were kind and there was no hint of disapproval in his face. "I suspected as much the way you studied it." He shrugged. "I was a scribe in Iconium."

"Oh Eliab, I am worried. Where is Ahmal? Are there others who will come seeking to be paid? What are we to do?"

"Do not fear, mistress. I shall be at your side, for I have promised the master to care for you in his absence."

Marah laid a hand on his arm. "Eliab . . . thank you. That is a comfort to me."

When Eliab left, Marah sat down to consider the situation. Surely Ahmal would return before the coins were gone.

He did not. Marah began quietly selling things in the

house, sending Eliab to the marketplace to carefully and unobtrusively bargain away Ahmal's treasures. As over two years passed without word, the once affluent house looked barren.

Elon had left them all at last. Demas found him laboring for breath one morning and had called her. As she and Caleb knelt by his bed, he had tried to say a few last words, but the effort was too great for him. He had touched her hand briefly and had reached out to Caleb, gripping his hand. Caleb held the old man's hand tightly until it went limp and Elon was gone.

Caleb took his grandfather's death hard. He disappeared for almost a full day, and later Marah found out he had gone to walk the hills and give vent to his grief. They missed Elon's wit and wisdom in the household, and Marah felt as though Jesse were farther away from her than ever. Only Caleb, in a look, a gesture, the way he smiled, brought back her memories. She was thankful she at least had Caleb.

Little by little, Ahmal's wealth dwindled as Marah and Eliab settled debts and paid for merchandise that Ahmal had taken on his caravan to trade. One of the creditors had eyed Demas.

"I could use a strong young man in my shop," he mused, stroking his beard.

"Demas is needed here," she had replied quietly.

The man's eyes narrowed as he looked at her. "Surely a woman such as you is lonely. Your husband has been gone a long time, has he not? I could offer comfort in a more practical way, to settle the debt." He moved closer and Marah stepped back.

"It is best that you go now," she said sharply and Eliab firmly showed the merchant to the gate.

Caleb, finally realizing that he must help, had begun to share coins from his earnings. He worked in Shiva's shop as much as he could, but this time it was not for his own pleasure. There was no time to carve small animals. He built tables and chairs and made tools for the men who worked the fields.

Marah sensed that Caleb was restless and worried about Ahmal. She caught looks passing between Caleb and Demas and found them whispering together more than once. When she questioned Caleb, he gave vague answers. He began to be obsessed with the idea that if he could only go, he could find Ahmal.

"Mother, I know I could find him. I could at least find out what happened to him so we know. We cannot go on living like this forever. Don't you want to know?"

"Caleb! You must not speak foolishly. You are only a boy. You cannot go running off after Ahmal. We will have word from him in some way soon."

He paced the floor. "You have been saying that for almost two years. When will we hear? When everything in the house is gone?" he spat angrily.

She reacted as though he had slapped her and stepped back, her hand to her mouth. Caleb was instantly contrite. He never wanted to hurt her.

"Mother, I am almost seventeen. I am a man. I could ask questions, find out answers."

"And be captured by slave traders . . . or killed by bandits? Caleb, what would I do without you? I have lost your father and grandfather. Would you have me lose you also?"

Caleb did not answer, but by the set of his jaw, she knew the matter wasn't settled.

He looked at her a long moment, kissed her cheek, and quietly went to his quarters. Soon Marah heard the sound of the little flute that Jesse had made years ago. Caleb played on it when he was unhappy or thinking. At least the argument was over . . . until the next time.

Marah went up to the roof of the house and walked along the parapet. There, in the darkness, she poured out her heart to her God.

In the morning Eliab came to her. He looked older than his years and his face was stricken.

"Mistress, I fear young master Caleb is gone."

With a cry she ran past Eliab to Caleb's quarters. He had taken clothes and his few personal possessions. His leather bag was gone. Lying on his pallet was the little flute. He knew what it meant to her and left it behind. She picked it up and clutched it to her heart.

"Oh Caleb, how could you go alone on such a journey? How could you leave me alone like this?" She turned to Eliab who had followed her. "Where is Demas? He might have some idea which direction he has gone. Call Demas at once."

Eliab shook his head sadly. "I fear he has gone with the young master. His things are missing from his room also."

Marah took a deep breath and gathered her strength, then put a hand on Eliab's arm. There was no need for words. Mistress and servant looked at one another with a bond of sorrow. They would have to make the best of the situation and pray for Caleb and Demas as well as Ahmal.

The weeks went by and finally there was a word from Caleb by way of a merchant. He had followed Ahmal's trail as far as Antioch. He and Demas were all right. He sent his love. At her urgent questions, the merchant patiently stated that Caleb and his servant appeared to be in good health. She thanked him for his trouble and he went on his way.

The last creditor came to the house reluctantly. He knew of their circumstances and was not a greedy man, but he had a family to support and he had been put off too many times.

"I must be paid. Have you nothing you can give me?"

Sadly she shook her head. What else did she have that was not absolutely needed for food? The man appeared to think a moment and then reluctantly looked at Eliab who was standing nearby.

"He is old for a servant, but I can use the help. I will take him and call the debt. If your husband returns, he can redeem his servant, but until then, he will work for me for the debt."

Marah was stricken. She wanted to cry out . . . *No, he is all I have left. I will be completely alone.* She turned to Eliab and there were tears in his eyes.

"It is all right, mistress. Master Ahmal will return soon. This is the last debt." He left the room and returned in a few moments with his small bag of belongings.

Eliab followed the merchant out of the house, and Marah stood silently watching them as they went through the gate and turned down the street. A scream rose in her throat and she put her fist to her mouth to stifle it. Dropping to her knees in the middle of the room, she wrapped her arms around herself and began to rock back and forth with silent tears. Not knowing how long she had been there, she finally rose unsteadily to her feet and looked around her. Walking slowly through the silent house, she bolted the doors. In her mind she seemed to hear the echo of Caleb's laughter and Demas's voice as they talked. She heard Eliab's kind voice as he spoke of Ahmal, and saw him going about his duties. It was as if the ghosts of her family were there with her. She looked out a small window and could see one star shining brightly. She watched it a long time.

PART VII

Reuben

44

As they rode into the city, Reuben's eyes took in the sights around him. He delighted in the sounds and smells of new surroundings. One never knew what possibilities could emerge. He turned to the man on the horse behind him. "Ah, Tema, we at last come to Shechem. An interesting town, is it not?"

The other man looked about, his nose wrinkling. His master made comments to him, but seldom wished his opinion. His small, rheumy eyes darted here and there. At least no one knew them here. They barely made it out of the last city after his master had found the wife of a prosperous merchant to his liking. He hunched his thin shoulders, and the frown that seemed a permanent part of his face deepened. He merely nodded.

Reuben eyed his servant, his dark eyes twinkling. He threw back his head and laughed. "Ah, you can rest easily, Tema. We come only to call on my dear half brother, Ahmal. As his guests, we can refresh ourselves. No doubt, he can be persuaded to . . . how shall I say it . . . send us on our way with our pockets less empty?"

Tema perked up a bit. "He does well, master?"

"Very well. I hear he has a large caravan of his own. It is a good thing that our travels have brought us to Shechem where he dwells. Our resources are nearly at an end. Come, Tema, let us inquire as to where my dear half brother Ahmal can be found."

They lodged their horses at an inn and began to walk through the town. Reuben's eyes followed a woman passing through the marketplace. He smiled, his teeth white against the tan of the desert. She lowered her eyes and ignored him, continuing on toward the village well. Reuben watched her walk gracefully with the water jug on her shoulder. She moved with purpose and dignity. A merchant's wife no doubt, from her confidence. He observed with interest as she approached the village well. An argument seemed to ensue with one of the other women who murmured something and quickly moved away from the well. He caught the words "evil eye" as the women left her standing alone. This was interesting. Who was she? He turned to the merchant at the nearest stall.

"Who is the woman who stands there at the well?"

"It is the wife of the caravan master Ahmal. It is said she has the evil eye." The merchant looked her way apprehensively.

Reuben was fascinated. "How is that?"

"She has had five husbands, my friend, all dead or gone. Her last was a prosperous merchant until he married her."

"Was?" Reuben stroked his beard thoughtfully. Tema rolled his eyes. He could sense trouble.

"He left on a caravan almost three years ago and hasn't been heard from since. She does not know if he is alive or dead." The merchant beckoned Reuben closer and he leaned down. "I would think that by now he is dead . . . as with all the others!" He shook his head.

"So she is alone? She has servants?"

"All gone or sold for the merchant's debts. She had a son, but he has gone also. He took one of the young servant boys with him. Word is that he went to seek his father's whereabouts. She heard news once concerning him, but no more." The merchant suddenly stepped back, eyeing Reuben. "Do you know of the merchant, Ahmal?"

Reuben looked properly dejected. "Alas, I am his brother. My servant and I have traveled a great distance to see him. This is most distressing news." He looked furtively around him as if someone could overhear them. "My, ah . . . brother's wife, she remains . . . alone?" He shrugged and left the unspoken question hanging in the air.

The merchant nodded with understanding and also replied in a conspiratorial way. "She spurns the men, though there is a wager as to who will entice her to his bed."

"How then does she live?"

"She once sold wool yarn to the merchant Dathan, but her sheep are gone. Debts, you know. It is said she has friends here in Shechem who help her from time to time."

Reuben stepped back and drew himself up. "I had come hoping I would see my long-lost brother. It grieves me to hear this news. I will call on her. Perhaps there is something I can do to be of assistance. I can at least give his wife . . . his widow, my gravest sympathy. Thank you, my friend, for your assistance."

"Be warned. You must be careful or you may suffer the fate of your brother." The merchant nodded his head solemnly.

After inquiring as to the whereabouts of the house of Ahmal, Reuben approached it thoughtfully. The appearance of the courtyard was neat, but Reuben could see that what had at one time been a fine house was in need of repair. As he and Tema entered the courtyard, the woman he had seen in the village came out of the house. She was wary but stood quietly and watched their approach.

"You are the wife of Ahmal?"

"I am." She waited, watching them warily.

"I am Reuben, Ahmal's brother. My servant Tema and I have traveled a long way to see him."

Her mouth opened in surprise. Ahmal had never mentioned a brother. Pushing aside the thoughts, she spoke quietly. "I am sorry. Your brother is not here. He is away on a journey."

As Reuben studied her face more closely, he was struck by her beauty. She was a handsome woman still. Her hair was magnificent. This was indeed an interesting situation, yet somehow he sensed that this was no ordinary woman. He needed to move carefully.

"A thousand pardons for coming upon you at such a time. My brother and I have not seen each other in many years. You can imagine my sadness at hearing that he is not here and that there is no word of him. How long has he been gone?" He moved closer, keeping an attitude of sympathy and concern.

She sighed heavily. No doubt these men had heard all about Ahmal in the marketplace. "Three years." She looked off into the distance and then seemed to remember her duties of hospitality.

"Please, enter our humble home. I can offer only simple refreshments, such as they are, but you are welcome." She stepped aside and beckoned for them to enter.

Reuben glanced at Tema and raised his eyebrows. Tema shrugged slightly and followed him into the house.

Marah felt somewhat embarrassed. What had once been a comfortable home with artifacts from Ahmal's travels now possessed only the barest essentials. The house was clean and orderly, she saw to that, but she could not entertain her husband's brother in the manner that he had obviously expected. She glanced cautiously at him as he looked around the once lavish room. He was as tall as Jesse with dark eyes under bushy brows. His beard was as black as the night. He carried himself as a prince and his body was lean and trim. Somewhere within her a small sense of alarm grew. There was something about him that told her to be on her guard. She was bound by the laws of her land to treat him as a guest with all courtesy, to offer him her hospitality. He was her husband's brother; why then did she feel fearful? She found herself hoping they would not stay the full three days.

Reuben smiled at her. "You have had a difficult time, Marah." His gaze was disconcerting.

"Let me show you to your rooms. Forgive me that they are not as they should be."

She showed Reuben to Ahmal's quarters. At least there was a bed, some rugs, a small table, and an oil lamp. "Your servant can take the room below. It is the room of Ahmal's former steward, Eliab."

"And where is Eliab?" Reuben was finding the circumstances more to his liking every moment.

"He works for a merchant in Shechem. He was taken to pay a debt." Somehow she felt the need to add, "He comes to the house often, to see if I am all right."

"I see." Reuben stroked his beard thoughtfully. "Go, Tema, find the quarters she has indicated for you." He turned toward Marah.

She felt somewhat uncomfortable in his presence. "You must be hungry after your long journey. Let me prepare refreshment for you. I won't be long." She left the room quickly and went to see what she had on hand. There was little. She hurried out to the gate and saw a boy passing by.

"Do you know the home of Hannah and Simon, past the street of the carpenters?"

He thought for a moment and then nodded warily. Marah remembered that Hannah told her the children thought she was a sorceress.

"I have guests, the brother of my husband. Tell Hannah. Will you do that for me?"

"What will I receive if I do this?" His voice was sullen.

"She will reward you, I promise. Will you go?"

With a shrug, he nodded again and began walking quickly toward Hannah's street. Marah looked at the bread she had baked that morning. One loaf was enough to last her a day or two, but two hungry men? She hoped Hannah would understand her message and need.

Reuben strolled into the cooking area. As he glanced around, she indicated her meager supplies.

"I fear I have little on hand, but I have sent for more provisions. I will have a meal for you shortly."

She answered Reuben's casual questions, filling him in on what had happened since Ahmal had left on his journey. In her heart she was praying silently that God would send Hannah quickly.

To her immense relief, within a short time Hannah came hurrying in the courtyard, a basket on her arm. She was puffing from the exertion. "Marah, I received word that the brother of your husband has come to the house?"

With relief Marah reached for the basket. "Oh Hannah," she whispered, "thank you for coming. I knew you would know why I sent for you. I didn't have anything to serve them."

Simon and their young son, Jacob, came in the gate. Jacob moved more slowly than most little boys. He had one foot that was twisted slightly. It seemed to turn in more as he grew older. Simon rolled his eyes. "Such a woman, my wife, she must run like the wind and leave the two of us behind. We could not keep up."

Reuben, who had been inspecting the empty animal pens, now turned toward them.

Simon and his wife looked expectantly at Reuben.

"Simon, Hannah, this is Reuben, brother of my husband. My lord, these are my good friends Simon and Hannah. This is their son, Jacob."

Reuben smiled charmingly and nodded to them both. "It is truly God's gift when one is enriched with such friends." He ignored Jacob.

Tema came out of the house and Reuben nodded to him casually. "My servant, Tema."

Tema stood sullenly, eyeing the visitors.

"May I inquire as to whether there is a meal in your basket, Hannah? We have come a great distance." Reuben's tone was teasing and the women laughed self-consciously.

Reuben engaged Simon in conversation as the women put the bread and cheese on the table along with some figs and dates. Hannah had also brought some dried fish and a small goatskin bag of wine. She brought vegetables, but since there was no time to prepare them, it would give Marah some things for the next meal. With the fresh bread Marah had baked that morning, it would be enough.

Tema took his food outside and sat in the courtyard. There had only been a faint nod and gesture from Reuben, but Tema seemed to understand his master well and knew when he was being dismissed for the moment.

"You have traveled far, Reuben?" Simon went about his quiet and unobtrusive way of gathering information.

"Actually we have traveled from Ephesus . . . this journey." Marah had the feeling that Reuben knew what Simon was about, but she listened intently. She also wanted to know more about this strange brother who had appeared. Perhaps, she thought, feeling hopeful, he might know how to find Ahmal.

"Your home is then in Ephesus? That is indeed a long way from Shechem."

"Ah, I have not called any city my home in a long time. It has been my pleasure to travel to many countries and cities." Reuben gestured magnanimously. "You might say that the world is my home."

Simon nodded thoughtfully. "How is it then that you and Ahmal are brothers? Were you born in Shechem?"

Reuben regarded Simon for a moment, considering the question. "We share the same father but, it appears, not the same mother. My father was a merchant as is Ahmal. He traveled a great deal. Ahmal's mother lived here in Shechem. My mother was from Smyrna." He did not appear to mind giving Simon the information. Anticipating Simon's next question, Reuben offered, "My father told me before he died that I had a half brother living in Shechem. I heard word of him in my travels from other caravan masters. Finally, I decided to seek him out and make myself known to him."

279

"It is a sad thing that you have come so far and still are unable to meet."

Reuben stroked his beard thoughtfully. "You say there has been no word of Ahmal from the time he left, three years ago?"

"That is true and very strange. It is as if the earth opened and swallowed up his caravan. Not even the other caravan masters have any news of him."

"And the son? There is no word from him either?"

"None. Yet we have not given up hope. We pray that one day word will come and Caleb will return also."

"That is all one can do, my friend. His wife is an exceptional woman to have borne such a loss."

"We have known her since her childhood. She has suffered much, but she is as the tree, blown against by the sands of the desert. She bends but does not fall."

Reuben nodded and then skillfully turned the conversation to Simon. In a short time he knew all he needed to know about Marah's friends. They were not rich, but lived carefully on the fruit of their fields, the wool from their sheep, and the weaving that Hannah made and sold in the marketplace.

Jacob had been taken outside with his mother and Marah. While Reuben had not said as much, they sensed that he was not overly fond of children. Jacob watched the chickens scratch in the courtyard and now occupied himself with inspecting the progress of a small lizard on the wall of the courtyard. The women talked quietly with an eye on Tema.

"What will you do now?" Hannah was concerned as usual.

"Perhaps he will only stay the three days as is the custom, and with Ahmal gone, he will move on."

"Three days may be too long," Hannah said, looking directly at Marah, who rolled her eyes at the implication.

"With a man such as Reuben in your household and you a woman alone, who will believe that he has slept only on his own bed?"

"Your words echo my own thoughts, Hannah." Marah sighed. "What should I do?"

"He is the brother of your husband. What can you do, except to hope he goes on his way?"

"I am sure he will. There is nothing for him here."

"Let us hope so. That is a man who likes women. He has had no lack of them, I am sure. Be on your guard until he leaves, for I see the way he looks at you . . . with hunger."

"I will be careful. He is not the first, nor do I suspect the last, to seek my companionship in that way."

"The others were not staying under your roof."

Marah nodded and stared at the ground, her thoughts jumbled in her mind. Reuben was indeed handsome and when he looked upon her with those dark, laughing eyes, something within her shivered, and not out of fear. *Oh Ahmal. Please return to me. I feel so alone. Now it is as if the bulls of Bashan gather around me. Caleb, where are you, my son?* She had no one to protect her. No servants, no Eliab, no husband or sons. Simon and Hannah's house was not nearby. What could Simon do? If she were accosted and cried out, who would hear her within the thick walls of Ahmal's house? Who would believe that she had been unwilling?

Hannah put a hand on her arm. "I must go, my friend, but send for us if you need us. I will pray for your protection, and that your son and husband will return to your gates . . . soon."

"Thank you, Hannah. And thank you for bringing provisions for a meal. You do not have that much to spare and yet you share with me so generously."

"We can help with one or two meals, but who are we to be able to feed two hungry men for a long time?" She had been watching Jacob as he followed a small bug across the courtyard. A six-year-old boy found life fascinating indeed. She turned as Simon and Reuben came out of the house.

"What other news have you brought to us from the world outside Shechem?" Simon was asking.

Reuben thought a moment and then laughed softly. "There is interesting news of an itinerant Jewish rabbi traveling the country . . . with very different thoughts."

"A Jewish rabbi traveling the country? And just what does this rabbi have to say that is different?" Simon was interested.

"He is called Jesus, the son of a carpenter of Nazareth."

"It is well said that nothing good comes out of Nazareth!"

"Well, it appears this rabbi does miracles. He was a carpenter himself until a short time ago when he began to travel with his band of followers. A ragged group if ever I heard of one. Fishermen, a former tax collector . . ."

Simon had listened with interest but snorted. "Who would want a former tax collector in his following? He would be a thief as they all are," he added vehemently.

Reuben ignored the remark. "As I was saying, he is unusual. People are healed of all sorts of diseases, or so I was told. There was a blind man who came to Him, and his eyes were opened."

Simon waved his hand impatiently. "Who ever heard of a blind man receiving his sight again? Is he a sorcerer?"

Reuben laughed. "There is a difference of opinion on that. Some believe he is a sorcerer and others say he is a man of God."

Marah was intrigued. A rabbi who can heal a blind man's eyes? Truly this was a wondrous thing.

Reuben's voice became conspiratorial. "It is said that he angers the leaders of the Jewish Sanhedrin."

Simon was amazed. "A man who does miracles angers the Jews? How is that?"

"He speaks of having a father in heaven. And he openly speaks against the Law. He seems to feel that they follow the letter of the Law, but not the intent."

"A blasphemer!" thundered Simon, striking his fist in his palm. "Why do these Jewish leaders allow him to teach? They should get rid of him!"

"I am sure they have tried, my friend, but it is said that no man speaks like this man. Everywhere he goes, because of the miracles, the people follow Him like sheep." Reuben laughed scornfully. "I have only heard these things. Perhaps people exaggerate. He will probably fade away like all the others sooner or later."

Simon was still fuming. "We of the Samarim live by the Pentateuch. It is our Book of the Law. It is a good thing Jews have no dealings with Samaritans. He would find himself in great trouble trying to bring his blasphemy here." He looked closely at Reuben. "You do not follow him?" It was an accusation.

Reuben spread his hands and shook his head. There was a slight sneer on his handsome face. "Truly, my friend, do you take me for a fool? I have better things to do."

Simon nodded sagely. Marah listened. There were sorcerers in Samaria who did many miraculous things, but they did not teach the people about the Law. This was a strange man . . . different, a man who could open the eyes of the blind. She found herself wanting to hear more about this man, but then chided herself for her foolish thoughts. If he spoke against the Law, he would not be teaching the right things.

Simon beckoned to Hannah and Jacob. Reuben walked them to the gate as if master of the house.

"It was good to meet the brother of Ahmal," Simon was saying. "Perhaps when you come back another time, he will have returned. When will you be leaving Shechem?"

"I have business here. I may stay awhile. I find Shechem an interesting town, worth . . . investigating." He spoke to Simon, but his eyes rested on Marah.

For three days, Marah had been cautiously avoiding Reuben other than to prepare an evening meal. She had worked outside when he was inside, and had placed the heavy bar across her door at night. She was sure Reuben had heard her lower the bar in place. He appeared amused by her tactics. He disturbed her and he had seen her watching him from time to time. Hannah's words rang in her mind. *He is a man who likes women.* She would be on her guard, yet deep inside she knew she was afraid . . . of Reuben, or herself?

Tema slunk about the house and went on various errands for Reuben. She had taken an instant dislike to Tema and didn't trust him. If the house had been in its former condition with Ahmal's beautiful treasures, she would have feared to find something missing. As it was, it was a blessing. There was nothing of value left to take.

Marah adhered to her duties of hospitality, according to the customs of her people, and with relief greeted the third day. The men of the east would even entertain their worst enemy if he came as a guest, but only for three days. After that obligation, the enemy's life was in danger. She knew Reuben was waiting for something and showed no indication of leaving.

That evening, after the meal, she approached him. "My lord, do you wish me to prepare food for your journey tomorrow?" It was worth trying.

"My journey? My lovely Marah, you wound me. Would you have us leave so soon?"

"I . . . I thought . . . since my husband, your brother, is not here, that you would continue on your way."

Reuben moved closer, his eyes holding hers, and she could not move. "Surely if I left, you would be lonely again, and you are lonely, are you not, Marah?" He traced one finger slowly down the line of her cheek, and in spite of herself, she shuddered.

"You long for the touch of a man's hand, beautiful one?" He slipped one hand behind her and caught her to him. She tried to struggle, but he only chuckled. Slowly, he kissed her and she stopped struggling. In spite of all her willpower, she responded. Then with a start, she broke away.

"You must not do this, my lord . . . I am your brother's wife. Please, it would be better if you go." She backed away from him as he began to stroll purposefully toward her. She saw the look on his face and, with a cry of realization, knew his intent. She must escape, but where? Looking toward her room, she remembered the bar on the door. She ran to her room and closed the door. His footsteps did not hurry as he followed her. She reached for the bar, praying that she would get it in place in time, and to her horror it was gone. It had been removed. She looked around her, but there was nowhere to hide. Reuben pushed the door open and then closed it quietly behind him. She stood facing him, her heart pounding. He reached out and drew her to him again, kissing her eyes and her mouth until her knees nearly buckled. Still she tried to push him away.

"You are a woman made for a man like me, Marah," he whispered.

Hating herself, and Reuben for this betrayal of Ahmal, she tried to strike him, but he caught her wrist easily. He carried her to her pallet ignoring her struggles. She tried to dissuade him, but it was no use. He was far stronger than she. Finally, she had no more strength. The years of struggle had worn her down. Zibeon, Haman, Reuben, each one possessing her body and tearing a small part of her soul. He took her easily, but it was an empty conquest.

45

I t was the worst time of the day, yet she knew she must go to the well soon. The midday time of rest would be over and the merchants would return to their shops. Women and children would again be on the streets. She opened the door and the oppressive heat pushed against her. Sorrow and weariness pressed like weights upon her shoulders. She didn't want to hear the remarks of the men and greet the open hostility of the women. They no longer accused her of having the evil eye, for their whispers were now of another nature. It was as if a pot was nearing the boiling point and would erupt, spewing its contents on everything around it. When Ahmal had been home, she had been safe. She had family. Now, everyone was gone. Dear Ahmal, he had treated her as one would treat a special child in whom one delighted. *Oh Ahmal . . . where are you?* Were Caleb and Demas still alive?

She turned back to look at Reuben. His eyes were closed as he reclined back on the cushions. She regarded him pensively and then turned back toward the door. She was reaching for the water jar when his voice interrupted her thoughts.

"It is much too hot to go out," he murmured.

"We are in need of water," she answered simply.

He lay back on the cushions, studying her. His long, lean body was relaxed in the way of a man totally at ease and sure

286

of himself. Reuben was like no man she had ever known. Since that fateful evening when he had taken her, she was his at his whim. He seemed to know her very thoughts. It was as if he had cast a spell over her. Even in her shame, he made her feel she was strangely drawn to him. Absent-mindedly she ran one hand over her hip and smoothed her skirt. Reuben stroked his beard and watched her. His eyes twinkled and then became somber in a way she knew well. Her heart beat faster. She needed to get away, if only for a little while.

"You are very beautiful, Marah, very beautiful."

She felt the blood come to her face. She looked away and adjusted the soft folds of material that would protect her face from the fierce heat. "The street is quiet, it is best that I go to the well of Jacob now."

He cocked one bushy eyebrow. "Ah, the good women of Shechem are avoiding you then?"

"I go where I please. Their clacking tongues weary me."

"And it pleases you to go in the heat of midday?"

She sighed. "You are here when there is no one else. Your servant is often gone for days on your errands . . . they suspect. . . ." She shrugged her shoulders and did not look at him.

"And to think that they do not trust the brother of your dear, departed husband?" His smile was mocking. "I only pay respects to the widow of my dear, departed brother."

Marah looked at him quietly. "Respects? Your respect has continued for over a month."

He threw back his head and gave such a shout of laughter that she moved quickly to close the door.

"Please, Reuben, someone will hear you!"

In answer he rose quickly from the couch and with two strides was at her side. Clasping her around the waist, he kissed her firmly on the mouth, silencing her protests. "Let them gossip, my treasure, they have no proof."

"They do not need proof to tear me apart with their

tongues." She looked at him sadly. "You believe that Ahmal is dead?"

He gave a snort of derision. "Surely you do not think that he is still alive after all this time?"

"I do not know what to think." She felt weary.

"Do you wish him to live, Marah?" His words were dangerously soft. "Shall he return to the wife who waits so patiently, so faithfully?" This time his tone was mocking.

The last struck her like a blow and her head came up defiantly, her dark eyes flashing.

Reuben's voice became soft and soothing. "I find you most interesting when you are angry, my love." He believed his nearness was having its desired effect. She stood very still against him. She knew better than to fight him . . . even with words.

"We could leave Shechem and no one would know. You would have someone to take care of you," he said against her cheek. "Do you not want that also?"

Panic filled her. Leave Shechem? What would become of her? She stalled for time.

"I . . . I do not know what to do. I cannot think." She swayed against him, her mind racing. Gathering her courage, she pulled away, looking earnestly up at his face. She knew he didn't like her pulling away, for he scowled. How could she make him understand?

"My lord, you have taken me, yet I do not know if I am still a married wife. God will surely punish us."

He snorted. "Surely God must have more important matters to concern Himself with. All the more reason we should leave Shechem."

Marah opened her mouth to reply and promptly closed it again. Did he see only what he wanted to see? She had tried to speak to Reuben about Ahmal, to make him understand what was in her heart. He did not want to see what he had done. He had been annoyed, impatient as he was now, that she as a woman would try to speak to him about things of God.

Suddenly a strange thought came to her and she voiced it without thinking. "Reuben, do you think the Messiah will truly come?"

The change of topics caught him by surprise and he stared at her a moment. His eyes narrowed and then he gave another shout of laughter. "You are much more interesting, my love, when you don't concern yourself with matters best left to men." His hands tightened painfully on her arms.

She had gone too far. Reuben had an easy manner on the outside but liked having his way. He could be unpleasant when he was angry. She stood silently, submissively, waiting, her emotions conflicting as he turned away from her abruptly.

"Go for your water. I have matters to attend to."

"Will you be here when I return?" Perhaps he would leave at last.

"You will miss me?" There was a gleam of satisfaction as he turned back to her. He reached out and pulled her close again. "See how your heart flutters. Have I not made you happy?"

"Yes, Reuben," she whispered against his chest, relieved that the mood had passed. She would tell him what he wished to hear. It served her better. His many moods puzzled her. He changed like the wind from one moment to the next. Cold, cruel, childlike when things did not go his way, he was a man who could be dangerous.

"There is a caravan coming into Sebaste. I heard the news yesterday."

She stiffened and he murmured softly, "Perhaps the long-lost Ahmal will return?" There was a hint of sarcasm.

She tried to draw away, but his strong hands held her fast, bruising her arms. "My lord, for both of our sakes, we must know." It was almost a sob.

"Of all the caravans that have passed through Shechem, which one has brought you word that Ahmal lives and sends his love to his dear, faithful wife?"

She closed her eyes against the vehemence of his words as he continued to grip her arms tightly. "He was a good man.

JOURNEY TO THE WELL

He was kind to my family and to me." How could she wish the death of gentle Ahmal?

"And I am not kind to you, Marah?" There was no mistaking the inference in his tone as he drew her against him again and ran one finger slowly down her cheek. "I can be very kind, my love . . ." He tilted her chin up and kissed her slowly. When he released her, she swayed momentarily, staring up at him.

"You are mine, Marah. If Ahmal were to return, what would the good people of Shechem say to him about his wife and his half brother, hmmm? Even now, the women draw their skirts away from you. Where are the friends who were so anxious to help you? It is only a matter of time. I will take you with me. There are other lands, other towns to live in. You cannot remain in Shechem much longer." Then, persuasively, "Nothing holds you here . . ."

She looked up at him. Who was he, and what power did he have over her? He remained a stranger in many ways. His garments were the finest quality, but she had yet to learn the source of his recent income. He was well liked as he laughed and moved among the merchants. He had come seeking resources, and yet now he seemed to have money. Where did it come from? She watched him closely in the marketplace, and she pretended indifference, noting that the eyes of the men and women of Shechem watched them both. She had also noticed that the women watched Reuben . . . with open admiration.

"This house is all I have, Reuben, and all that is left of Ahmal's after the debts were paid. My son would return here. I pray he lives and is safe." A tiny trace of doubt brushed her thoughts . . . as though on the verge of something she could not explain. She waited for his answer.

"All this concern is foolish. Why do you not face the fact that he is gone? He has a life somewhere else in another city or country. As young as he was when he left, no doubt the slave traders found him." He shook her. "Or they are dead.

Do you not understand? Why do you persist in this tiresome game of waiting?"

A sob escaped her lips at the cruelty of his words. She could not look at him.

"I will sell the house and the last of your belongings. You need little to take with you and the proceeds from my brother's property will do us nicely."

"But . . . Ahmal is not—"

"Enough!" he bellowed at her. "What difference can it make to you now? Who is the wiser? No one really knows. We can say we have finally heard news. As his relative, his brother, I can receive his possessions and do with them as I wish. *All* of his possessions."

Marah continued to look down at the floor, hiding the turmoil within. Mistaking her silence for submission, he relaxed his grip and stepped back.

"Go for your water. I have other things to do. I will go to speak with the caravan master in Sebaste. Perhaps they bring news. Since it seems to concern you so, if my brother should return, we would do well to leave Shechem. I fear that stones would mar that lovely face, and I do not care for that end for myself."

Marah gasped. It was the first time her unspoken thoughts about that had been voiced. It was true. She and Reuben were in great danger if Ahmal should return and accuse her of adultery. She tried to picture gentle Ahmal in the role of an outraged husband. He was kind, but yet she had seen him deal with his drivers and the men who worked for him. They respected him. Respect? She could not even claim self-respect since the night that Reuben had come to her room.

Reuben was speaking again, breaking into her thoughts. ". . . will go and see what I can find out."

"When will you return?" She tried to appear casual. She must have time to think about what to do.

"I do not like to be questioned on what I do. Since you

291

must ask, as soon as I find out what I need to know . . . what we need to know to proceed."

She caught her breath sharply, her eyes wide.

"I shall return within the week. The thought of you will hasten my return."

"You will take Tema?" She did not want the man skulking about while Reuben was gone. Reuben knew she disliked his servant.

"I will take Tema. He is useful to me in many ways."

He adjusted the mantle to protect his head from the sun and gathered up his goatskin bag.

As he opened the door and nodded to Tema who had been lounging by the gate, Tema hurried away. She knew he had gone to prepare the horses. Before he left, Tema had looked at Marah and smirked. She wanted to throw something at the man.

Reuben thanked her loudly for her hospitality. He wished her good health and added, for the benefit of eavesdropping neighbors, "I will seek further word on your husband and my brother on my journey. Peace be unto you."

Marah stood in the shadow of the house watching him for a moment. Then she sighed and reached again for the water jar, lifting it to her shoulder as she had done so many times before. *When was the first time*, she mused, *that I went to draw water from the well of Jacob?* She thought of the day she and Hannah had walked together. Tears came to her eyes as she remembered that happy walk with Hannah, and then the terrible news Reba had given her when she returned. It all seemed so long ago. She sighed, closed the door, and with her sandals making a soft slapping noise on the quiet, dusty street, began her journey to the well of Jacob.

PART VIII

Jacob's Well

46

The brightness of the sun took her breath away as she walked as quickly as possible toward the well of Jacob. Even the birds were silent as her lone figure passed the date and olive trees and headed for the summit. She did not look up at Gerizim. The holy mountain seemed to loom up against her in judgment. She had not been to the synagogue since Reuben had come. She could not face the questions in the eyes of her neighbors. Hannah had told her of the gossip in the village among the women. She had not asked about the situation with Reuben, yet Marah knew that she knew. Hannah was her friend. She would not ask to bring Marah's shame into the open.

She had not seen Hannah in two weeks. She wondered what the men were saying to Simon. Had Reuben claimed the wager? Had he been tempted to brag about his conquest? She didn't know, but this morning she wondered at the sorrow that her life had become. Was there any end to it? One by one, like leaves falling from a tree, the incidents of her life fluttered past. How could she have changed their coming? Reuben raised that small prick of fear. Having lived in Shechem all her life, was she now forced to leave? If she left with Reuben, how long before another woman took his fancy? She knew what he was, a dog that roamed the streets mating with any female in heat. He would go on his way and leave her in some city, alone. What could she do? Could he persuade the elders that he was indeed Ahmal's brother and therefore had the right to Ahmal's possessions? He could claim her as a kinsman. Then where would Caleb send word if she were gone? He could return and not know where to find her. Would the elders believe her if she told them Reuben had taken her against her will? How then could she explain these last weeks? With agony, she faced the truth in her heart. Part of her had tried to remain faithful to Ahmal and part of her had responded to Reuben's touch and caresses.

Yet, how could she live with what she had become? In time, even her faithful friend Hannah must turn away. On and on, the questions probed her being, laying before her the deepest secrets of her heart. And with the revelation came choices.

Marah was so absorbed in her own thoughts that it startled her to see that there was someone else at the well, a man. What was a man doing at the well at this hour? She saw no horse or camel. Had he traveled this far on foot alone? As she drew closer, she saw by his garments that he was a Jew, and not only that, a rabbi. Jews did not journey alone through Samaria. This was strange indeed. He sat quietly on the edge of the well as if he were resting . . . and waiting for someone.

As she drew near, he turned to face her. It was an incredible face. His eyes looked deep into hers. She had the feeling that he knew her . . . that he knew her entire life. He smiled confidently at her, and she paused momentarily, unsure of what to do. Then he reached out his hand, "Will you give me a drink?"

What was familiar about that gesture? She sought in her mind, but it was hidden from her. She looked at him, puzzled.

"How is it that you, a Jew, ask a drink of me, a woman of Samaria? You Jews have no dealings with Samaritans."

He spoke again and his words were gentle, but carried authority. "If you knew the gift of God, and who it is that says to you, 'Give Me a drink,' you would have asked of Him, and He would have given you living water."

She looked around the well. Why would he ask her to give him a drink if he had water of his own? Her curiosity gave her boldness. "Sir, you have nothing to draw with and the well is deep. Where then do you have this living water?" Perhaps he was a sorcerer . . . ? "Are you greater than our father Jacob, who gave us the well and drank thereof himself and his children and also his cattle?"

He stood and faced her and his words seemed to echo in the stillness of the moment.

"Whosoever drinks of this water," he said, gesturing toward the well, "shall thirst again. But whoever drinks of the water that I shall give him shall never thirst; but the water that I shall give him shall be in him a well of water springing up into everlasting life."

She marveled. *Water that will last forever?* Even if he were a sorcerer, if he was able to give her this water, she would not have to come here again or to the village well for that matter. Encouraged and hopeful, she looked around him to the well. "Sir, give me this water, that I will not thirst nor will I have to come here to draw."

He smiled again, his eyes sparkling with tiny flecks of light. She felt as though her very being was drawn into their depths.

Then his next words caused her hopes to come crashing down. "Go, call your husband, and return here."

She hung her head. What could she say? He would do nothing unless she brought her husband. She had none . . . now. He was a rabbi. She may as well tell him the truth. "I have no husband."

He did not seem surprised, but nodded his head as if the answer was expected and he was pleased with her. "You have said well, for you have had five husbands . . . and this man that you have now is not your husband. In that you have said the truth."

How could he know these things? She had never seen him in the town of Shechem. A Jewish rabbi alone in Shechem would be noticed! There was only one way he could know these things about her.

"Sir . . . I believe that you are a prophet!" She must turn this conversation or incriminate herself. She looked up at Gerizim. "Our fathers worshiped in this mountain; and you Jews say that Jerusalem is the place where men ought to worship."

He chuckled, as though he knew what she was doing and then his face became earnest.

"Woman, believe me, the hour is coming when you shall neither in this mountain, nor even yet at Jerusalem, worship the Father."

She was confused and it must have shown in her face.

"You worship what you do not know," he said softly. "We worship what we do know, for salvation is of the Jews."

The rebuke was kind, but he spoke with that same authority. Slowly she sat down on the well to hear the rest of his words.

"The hour has come and now is at hand when the true worshipers shall worship the Father in spirit and in truth; for the Father seeks such as these to worship Him. God is a spirit; and they that worship Him must worship Him in spirit and in truth."

Suddenly Marah remembered the rabbi whom Reuben had told Simon about when he had first come to Shechem, a man with a ragged following. A man who performed miracles and healed the sick. Was he that man? She looked at him again, not even considering that at the moment she was talking with a strange man alone . . . and a Jew. There was love, not the love of the body, but love of the soul that radiated from his eyes. He seemed to know her very life, and yet she saw no condemnation in his voice or his manner. Who was he? Was he that Jesus of Nazareth? Cautiously she began . . .

"I know that the Messiah comes which is called Christ.

When He comes, He will tell us all things." She held her breath.

The rabbi smiled and there was glory on his face as he spoke softly, "I that speak to you . . . am He." He reached out his hand to her and there in the stillness came recognition: the face in her dream, the stranger who had brought peace to her heart over the years. This was the one that spoke to her in the pain of childbirth and death. His was the voice that had told her she would not die. Joy filled her being as understanding came. She knew who He was. Love poured through her very being. She felt cleansed, and as she slowly looked into His face, the words echoed in her soul, "You are forgiven of your sins."

At that moment, she heard voices and looked around to see a small group of men approaching. She looked fearfully back at the rabbi, but He seemed to know them. These men were with Him. They must be his disciples. They carried bundles—food, no doubt, purchased in Shechem. Their faces showed concern and puzzlement as they looked from their master to Marah, yet none stepped forward to ask why He was speaking to a Samaritan woman. They did not even question her, yet waited patiently, respectfully.

The rabbi looked at her, and suddenly thoughts filled her mind. She knew what she must do. The water jar was forgotten, and she nodded, as if He had spoken to her aloud. She hesitated a moment, looking at all of them, and then began to run back down the path toward Shechem.

As she entered the gate of the town, she went to the center of the marketplace. The merchants had opened their stalls and people milled about. They turned to look at her. The woman who had avoided all of them for so long stood in the marketplace with tears streaming down her face and joy radiating from her soul.

With her hand, she entreated all of them, "Come! See a man who told me all that I have ever done! I have met Him at the well of Jacob. Could this be the Christ? Come . . . come and see!"

The men began to lay down the things in their hands, and as if moved by a power beyond themselves, they followed her. As she went down the street, she called to them from shop to shop. "Come, see the Messiah. Come and see the Christ. He is at the well of Jacob. He has told me everything I have done in my life. Come!"

As sheep follow the shepherd, they poured out from Shechem and hurried after her as she laughed and gestured with her hand to follow. She could hear the voices murmuring, "Is this the woman we have known all our lives? What change was this? What has happened to her?" With curiosity they resolved to see this man she spoke about.

The rabbi stood on the hill by the well and, with a smile, watched them approach. As the group of men in the white garments of the Samarim approached, they heard Him cry out to His disciples, "Lift up your eyes and look upon the fields, for they are white and ready to harvest!"

One of the elders of Shechem, Zebulun, approached Him respectfully. "This woman testifies that You know all her life. Something has happened to her and we would hear more of Your words. Come. Stay in Shechem and teach us. We would hear what God has to say to us." He spread his hands out toward the disciples who stood cautiously in the face of the larger group of Samaritans. "Come, all of you. You are welcome."

The rabbi seemed hardly to be able to contain His pleasure and nodded to Zebulun and the other Samaritans.

"I will come." He beckoned to His disciples.

Zebulun paused, "How are you called, Rabbi?"

"I am Jesus. Jesus of Nazareth."

And they headed toward Shechem.

47

No one had ever spoken the words that this man spoke. His words held hope and life. Marah listened, and the heaviness that had bowed her spirit was gone. She felt cleansed of all that had passed before . . . as though God were giving her another chance.

He was indeed the Jesus whom Reuben had spoken of, and the people of Shechem marveled at the miracles as He healed the sick and crippled. They flocked to Him.

Jesus told them that if they turned from their sins and cried out for forgiveness, if they believed that He, Jesus, was the Messiah, they could ask forgiveness of their sins in His name and they would be forgiven. Hundreds came to hear Him speak as He stood on the steps of the synagogue. He shared their reverence for the Pentateuch. He opened the Holy Scriptures to them as they had never understood them.

Marah sat nearby, unconcerned about who was near her. The sin that bound her had been lifted. She was forgiven. He had given her hope when all hope appeared to be gone. For hours, she and the people of Shechem took in His words as He taught them. Litters with the crippled and sick were carried and placed before Him. The ears of the deaf were opened and the lame got up and walked. He healed them all and the people lifted their hands in praise to God.

As Marah listened, she longed for Ahmal and Caleb to be there with her to hear these wondrous words. If only her son could know what this Jesus, the Messiah, had done for her.

All of Shechem came to hear Jesus speak. Shiva the carpenter stood near her and spoke earnestly. "Now I believe, not because of what you told us, but because we have heard Him for ourselves. Now we know that this is indeed the Christ, the Savior of the world."

Other townspeople standing nearby nodded their heads in agreement.

Hannah stood on the other side of Marah with Simon and little Jacob. Hannah had seen the change in Marah's countenance at once and knew a miracle had happened. They had rejoiced with her and gladly listened to the wonderful teaching of Jesus. They had accepted Him as their Messiah also. Marah glanced down at Jacob's twisted foot. It had been assumed that it would straighten out as he got older, yet as the boy grew, the foot seemed to turn in even more. Jacob had developed a rolling walk to compensate for the foot. Sometimes the other children teased him, and Marah knew it pained Hannah and Simon. She looked at the foot and lifted her eyes to meet Hannah's. Then she turned and looked toward Jesus. Hannah nodded slowly. She gathered her son in her arms and, before Simon could speak, carried him to Jesus. She knelt down and gently placed her son in front of the Messiah. Her eyes beseeched Him to have mercy on her . . . and Jacob.

Jesus looked at Hannah with love in His eyes, knowing this gentle woman had always been ready to help anyone who was in need. Now she came to Him with a need she could not meet. He smiled at her as she waited expectantly before Him. Jesus smiled at Jacob, who met His gaze with the trust of a child. Jesus reached out and took hold of Jacob's foot. He bowed His head for a brief moment, and then as the people watched, the foot began to turn slowly in His hands. The leg straightened out and the foot turned into its correct position.

Jacob stared at his foot and his eyes were alight with wonder. At Jesus's urging, he stood slowly and began to take a few steps. Then he ran around his mother and jumped for joy. Tears streamed down the faces of all those who were near enough to see. Jesus laughed out loud as Jacob ran back and forth in front of Him, crying, "Look, look at my foot! It is fixed! Mama . . . Jesus fixed it!"

Hannah watched her son and turned to Jesus. She tried to speak, but no words came. His eyes told her no words were necessary. He had heard her heart.

All that day, the people scarcely moved, even to get food. Mothers tended to small children, yet even the children were silent and attentive in the presence of this man of God. He had gathered them around Him and one even sat on His lap as He spoke to the people. He taught the Scriptures, opening their understanding, and even the high priest and the shammash nodded their heads. He spoke the truth. They had listened reluctantly at first, their faces betraying skepticism. Then, as He spoke with that voice of authority, as one learned in the Law, they nodded their heads to the elders standing by. This man was a gifted teacher. They marveled that one who had not had years of learning spoke with such knowledge. They watched the miracles He performed and agreed aloud that indeed this man was the Christ, the Messiah. Only the Messiah could do the things this man had done. Such power radiated from Jesus that those in Shechem who were known to be involved in sorcery hung back on the fringes of the crowd. One man finally came boldly before Jesus and laid the tools of his sorcery at the Master's feet. He got down on his knees and bowed his head. He was set free that very hour, and he went from the presence of Jesus, rejoicing. The articles of his past occupation were burned.

Marah now walked through Shechem with her head held high. Those who had avoided her spoke kindly, for they too had found hope and change in the words of Jesus.

"Marah, please, forgive me for my unkindness . . ." Leah

303

looked beseechingly at Marah with tears running down her cheeks. "I have learned that in the eyes of God we have all committed sin. I have asked forgiveness of God . . . now I ask yours." Leah bowed her head humbly. "I did not step forth to help you when you needed help. I have been a selfish woman."

Embracing the woman whose sharp tongue had caused so much pain, Marah said softly, "As He has forgiven me, I also forgive you, Leah. We will serve Him together."

Leah looked at her, her face radiant. "Yes, we shall serve Him together." They embraced again and Leah went her way. She was only one of the neighboring women who came to share their love and acceptance. It was as if they suddenly saw her in a new light.

When evening came, the people reluctantly went to their homes. Jesus and His disciples were offered places to stay for the night for the people recognized that they were weary and needed to rest. With the promise of more teaching the next day, they departed, each to their own place.

Marah considered all that had happened to her. She knew she wanted to stay in Shechem, no matter what the consequences. The God Who Sees had shown her His mercy. She would know what His will was in time. Kneeling by her bed, she prayed with all her might for Ahmal's return and the return of her son. She prayed fervently for Reuben to stay away, for she feared his return. She would face whatever needed to be faced with Ahmal . . . should God bring him back to her.

Surely if God had forgiven her, would He not help her still? Peace and strength flowed through her. The God Who Sees had brought her this far. He would protect her from Reuben.

48

With a start, Marah awoke and realized that someone was knocking on her door. Who could it be? Had Reuben returned? He would not just knock on the door. With her hand on her heart, she approached the door cautiously.

"Who is there?"

"I seek the home of the merchant Ahmal. It is a matter of grave importance."

It was not Reuben. She breathed a sigh of relief.

"He is not here . . . at this time."

"Are you his wife? Please, I would speak with you. It will only take a moment."

She hesitated and breathed a quick prayer. An inner voice told her to open the door. She opened it a short way and peered out. An older man, well dressed, stood before her. She looked at his face and realized he was no threat to her person.

"I am Shamir, a merchant like your husband."

She bade him enter and offered him a small cup of wine and some fruit. He partook out of courtesy, noting the shabby surroundings with a glance. Then he began a strange tale, and she listened with rapt attention.

"Over two years ago I was traveling on the way to Jericho when I and my servants were set upon by thieves. They took my servants and my goods, robbing me of all we carried, and beat me, leaving me for dead beside the road. I lay there wounded, fearing that death would soon overcome me. There were those who passed me, but thinking me dead, they did not stop. Then, a man stopped and looked at me. When he saw that I was still alive, he helped me onto his own camel and took me to the nearest inn. There he poured oil on my wounds and dressed them. He watched over me through the night, and when at last he had to go on his way, he gave the innkeeper coins to pay for my care. He told the innkeeper that if more was needed, he would repay him when he came again that way. I was too ill to think to ask his name; only the innkeeper told me that by his garments he was a Samaritan. It is only recently that I learned his name, having described him to another merchant. I wish to leave a gift and my gratitude for the love of God that he showed me in my distress." Having finished his long speech, he pulled a box from his sash. As he opened it, a great luminous pearl gleamed in the light of the sunshine streaming in the window.

She stared at the beautiful jewel and bowed her head.

"How can I accept such a gift in the absence of my husband?" Then she realized he had spoken of seeing Ahmal. "My husband has been gone a long time. I fear for his life. Do you have any news at all?"

Shamir shook his head slowly. "I regret that I do not know where he is nor do I have news that would comfort you. I can only tell you when he helped me. He was also traveling alone. Let me at least leave my gift and my thanks with you. When you see him, tell him of my gratitude." He put the small box in her hand and waited.

"I will tell him," she said softly and pressed the small box to her heart.

The man beamed at her and then bowed and took his leave. She stood looking after him for a long moment. Was this a sign? Hope rose again in her heart. First, Jesus coming to their city, bringing a change in her life, and now this man who spoke of Ahmal. Surely he lived. And if he lived, he would return. She lifted her face toward the heavens. The God who sees her had surely heard her prayers. Then she thought of Tema. In the hidden place where Ahmal had kept his box of coins, she concealed the small box with the pearl. Not even Reuben knew of this hiding place and would never suspect that she had anything of value.

Washing her face quickly, she put on her shawl and hurried to the synagogue. People were already gathering and Jesus was seated on the steps where everyone could see and hear Him. He spoke to them again of the commandment to love one another.

"Upon this commandment hangs all the Law and the Prophets," He told them. "For love is the fulfillment of the Law."

Everyone marveled at His words. People who had carried on a quarrel for years with another asked forgiveness and friendships were mended. Merchants who had been known to weigh their scales in their own favor scrupulously weighed their goods in favor of their customers. There was openness in Shechem among the townspeople and visitors alike. Some who came to Shechem and scoffed at the words of Jesus had an unexplained urging to move on to another town. Those who stayed were added to the growing number of believers.

On the third day, Jesus and His disciples bade the people of Shechem goodbye. They had all urged Him to stay longer, but He had other villages to visit and others who needed to hear the words He had spoken to them. Reluctantly they bade Him farewell, and the people watched at the gate of Shechem until He and His band of followers were but specks in the distance. They had sent the group on their way with all the provisions they could carry. Shechem would never be the same again.

49

Aman stood in the gateway. He was gaunt and his clothes hung loosely on his sparse frame. At first Marah was tempted to dismiss him as a beggar. Yet compassion stirred her heart. Were they not all beggars in the sight of God? She would give him what she could spare and send him on his way. As she approached to tell him to rest himself while she prepared some food, she gave a cry and the jar of water in her hand crashed to the ground. Her hand flew to her mouth as she stared at him. He reached out his arms and she fell against him, tears of happiness streaming down her cheeks.

"Your tears and glad welcome have made my long journey worth it all, dear wife," Ahmal said gently.

"Oh Ahmal," she wept, "My prayers have been answered, for God has brought you home to me. It has been so long. Where have you been for all these years? I had almost given up until . . . oh, I will tell you of that later. Come, refresh yourself." They entered the house together and Ahmal looked sadly around his once beautiful home.

She hung her head. "There were creditors to pay. I did what I could. Please do not be angry with me."

He turned and pulled her gently against him. "I am only glad to find you still here. Possessions can be replaced, but you, my wife, are all the treasure my heart has longed for."

She could not do enough for him. She hovered over him as he ate, waiting until he was rested, and ready to tell her what was on his heart. For a long moment he sat quietly, his eyes looking off into a distance to things she could not see. At last he took her hand and, looking into her face, began to speak.

"What I have to tell you, Marah, is a strange story. You must believe that it indeed happened, or I would not be here at all."

She nodded, urging him to continue.

"I was only a couple of weeks into my journey. One evening, as I bathed myself, I noticed a strange spot on my arm. I looked over my person, and behold, there were two other areas. I realized when I touched them that the skin appeared to be numb. At first I did not want to think about what it might be, and I concealed my arms with my garments. When we entered the next village for provisions, I quietly went to see the priest. When he examined me, he told me the most terrible news. My worst fears were confirmed, for he told me I had . . . leprosy."

At the word, Marah instinctively drew back in alarm. He patted her arm. "Do not fear. It is gone now. But let me finish my story.

"For the sake of my men, who have been with me many years, I left the caravan. I only told them that I was gravely ill and must leave and that they were to go on without me. No one was to tell anyone where I had gone. They were puzzled, but obeyed and joined another caravan. They did as I asked, for I could not return to Shechem. I felt it was better that you think I was dead than watch my body begin to rot before your eyes."

She looked at him wide-eyed. "But you show no symptoms. I see no sign of the disease upon you."

Ahmal smiled. "That is the most amazing part of my story. Wife, I have met the Messiah, the Christ. But then I am getting ahead of myself. Let me see, where was I? Oh yes, I had turned back toward Samaria, joining a small colony of lepers near the village of En-gannim. There I had resolved to live out the days remaining to me. One day, as some of us begged for food along the side of the road near the entrance to the village, we heard that Jesus of Nazareth was coming with His disciples. We had heard of Him. He worked miracles and those that He touched were instantly healed. We resolved among ourselves to approach Him as He passed by us. He was our only hope. When we saw Jesus and His disciples walking along the road toward the village, we made our way toward Him and cried out, 'Jesus, Master, have mercy upon us.'"

When Marah heard that Ahmal, covered with leprosy, had been reduced to begging for his food by the side of the road, she wept again. Ahmal's face seemed to shine with an inner light as he continued. The afternoon shadows had begun to form, but she did not even think of getting the lamp, so wrapped up was she in Ahmal's story.

"Yes, yes. What did he do?" she asked anxiously.

"As I said, we approached Him crying out for God's mercy. He stopped in the road and looked at us. His gaze was almost tender, as if we were but children. He said, 'Go, show yourselves to the priests,' and then continued on the road. We stood there for a moment, not sure what to do, but my faith was kindled and I resolved at that moment to do as He had asked. I started toward the village and the others followed. As we walked, I heard gasps of amazement from the other lepers. Their lesions were healed. I looked down at my hands. The skin was as if it had never been touched by leprosy. I felt my face and the skin was whole and healthy. My heart leaped within me in gratitude, and as the others rushed on, I turned back and fell on my face at Jesus's feet. With all my heart I gave God glory and thanked Him for healing my body of the cursed disease. I realized that now, finally, I could return to my home . . . and my family." He paused, remembering, and wiped the tears that flowed freely down his cheeks.

"Jesus said almost sadly, 'Were there not ten cleansed?

Where are the other nine? Have none returned to give glory to God save this stranger?' Then He lifted me to my feet, gave me the most radiant smile, and said, 'Arise, go your way. Your faith has made you whole.'"

"You are healed? Jesus touched you and took away your leprosy? Oh my husband, this is too wonderful."

Then, her countenance fell and she felt a prompting within. She must tell Ahmal before he heard from someone else in Shechem. She'd had this moment of glorious reunion, and no matter what happened, she could rejoice that he had returned healed.

"My husband, I too have a story to tell you, and before my courage fails me, I must tell you all of what has befallen since you left." She took a deep breath and began with the creditors who came to the house and how Eliab had helped her with the money box. She told how they had doled it out carefully until it was gone. She told of Caleb and Demas who had gone to seek word of him. His countenance went from sorrow to surprise.

"Caleb and Demas left to seek me?"

"Yes, my lord. Caleb felt that somehow he could follow your trail and find you." She shook her head sadly. "I fear the worst has happened to him, for I have had news of him but once from a passing merchant and that was over a year ago."

Ahmal patted her hand. "Jesus healed me of leprosy. Surely the God who kept you in His care until my return will watch over our son and bring him safely home."

At the words "our son," Marah began to weep softly. Ahmal put a comforting arm around her. "And Eliab? There is more you wish to tell me?" he said gently.

She told him of Eliab's care of her and the last merchant who came and took Eliab away. How he came to see her as often as he could, but it had been several months since the last time. She did not know if Eliab was still in Shechem.

"I will ask at once," Ahmal vowed. "I will buy him back." He looked around their home. "We will restore our home,

Marah. I give you my word." Then he looked at her face. He realized she had more to tell.

Slowly she began to tell him of the women of the village charging her again with having the "evil eye." He clucked his tongue as she told of going to the local well each day for water and facing them.

"It is to my great shame that I must tell you this last part, my lord." She looked at his dear face and it took all the courage she had.

"I have been fortunate that my friends Simon and Hannah have shared what little they had with me. I have no more sheep to make yarn to sell. When your treasures had been sold by Eliab to pay the creditors, there was little left . . ."

Ahmal looked puzzled. "The men did not return with my caravan?"

"Not to my knowledge, my lord."

"Shumah! That scoundrel, he was my second in command, but coveted my place as caravan master. No doubt he did well for himself with the merchants' goods. God is not mocked, my heart, He shall avenge me of that thief." Ahmal pounded his fist into his palm.

"If the caravan did not return with money from the trade goods, how then did you live, Marah?"

"The small rental from the house of Jesse helped only a little. Then, when at last I was alone in the house, considering what I must do to live, a man came to the house calling himself your half brother . . ."

Ahmal interrupted her with an oath. "Reuben, that son of a camel, he came here to the house? I know he is a relative, but not one you would want near your wife. He has been here once before. I have not seen him in years, yet he has a reputation that precedes him!" At the stricken look on her face, he stopped suddenly. "Marah, did he hurt you?"

"He . . . he . . . oh Ahmal, I am so ashamed. I tried to tell him to go on his way. He could see you another time. He laughed at me. The third evening, he took hold of me and kissed me. When I understood his intention, I ran to my room to bolt the door. He had taken the bar from my door, sometime when I was not in the house. He followed me and came into my room and . . . oh Ahmal . . ." She could not go on for the tears.

"He forced himself upon you?" Ahmal's face was red with righteous indignation. He pounded his fist into his palm in anger. "I will avenge you, my heart."

"I fought him. I tried to cry out. There was no one else in the house except his servant, Tema. He would be no witness for me. I should have gone to the elders the next day to accuse him. But I was afraid they would not believe me. I had been alone a long time and Reuben is a handsome man. Why should they believe that I had not shared his bed willingly? After that night, I was at his beck and call. I was ashamed. He wanted to sell this house and what remained and have me go away with him to another town. He . . . he talked of being stoned if you returned. I did not know what to do."

She had been speaking with her head down, afraid to look Ahmal in the face. Now she hesitantly looked up, hanging back as if he would strike her. Ahmal was looking at her with a face of such love and compassion that she was overwhelmed by the depth of it.

He reached out and took both her hands in his.

"Do not be afraid, my dear one. You will not suffer anymore. Jesus healed me from a living death and forgave me for the sins of my life. As He has had compassion on me, should I not extend that forgiveness and compassion to one who has suffered far more than I? I know Reuben too well. It was not your fault. He has a way with women that is of the devil. Dear one, I have found Jesus as my Messiah. That is cause for joy." Ahmal once again embraced her, patting her shoulder as her pounding heart began to subside in the wonder of his gentle response.

Marah's face lit up and she pulled back from Ahmal to look up at him joyfully.

"Ahmal. Jesus of Nazareth came here. I met Him at Jacob's well. He forgave me . . . knowing what I had done. He gave me hope again. I too have believed on Him as the Messiah."

"Jesus was here, in Shechem?" Ahmal asked in wonder.

"Oh yes, my husband, people were healed and changed. Remember Simon and Hannah's little boy, Jacob? Jesus healed his twisted foot. He now runs and plays like the other children."

She was so full of relief and happiness she felt her heart would burst. Ahmal had not turned from her. He loved her still and had forgiven her.

Ahmal gently embraced her and kissed her forehead. He held her to him and she felt the beating of his heart. "If that evil one should return, I will deal with him, Marah. He should be whipped for the agony and sorrow he has caused everywhere he has gone. It is a wonder some woman's husband has not killed him before this. I am ashamed myself to call him a kinsman."

The tender scene was interrupted by voices in the courtyard. There was a knock at the door. The faces of their neighbors showed astonishment as Ahmal opened the door and greeted them.

"We had heard news that someone had seen you, but we didn't believe it. Now we can see for ourselves." They all began talking at once.

50

Marah sat working on her weaving. As she looked around the house of Ahmal, now restored, her heart was full of thankfulness. She thought of the moment when she brought out the beautiful pearl from its hiding place and told Ahmal of the merchant's visit.

Ahmal gasped when he saw the size of the pearl. "Marah, do you know what we have here?" He held the beautiful pearl in the palm of his hand and touched its smoothness with one finger. "Do you have any idea as to the value of this jewel?"

She shook her head. "Is it worth much, my husband?"

Ahmal chuckled. "It shall restore the house of Ahmal."

Wide-eyed, Marah looked again at the treasure. It must be worth a great deal. Ahmal was delighted and grateful.

"We must both give thanks to God for His provision. He saw our need and has gone before us."

They sank to their knees and Marah bowed her head as Ahmal lifted the pearl toward the sunshine and praised God for His mercy and care.

Ahmal sold the pearl for even more than he had hoped. There was once again food in the house, in abundance. The fountain in the courtyard was repaired. A servant swept the courtyard and once again the footsteps of Eliab sounded through the house. Ahmal had gone to Zohar and bought back his steward . . . and his friend.

Their neighbors and friends had gone to their homes the day of Ahmal's return and gathered food and wine. How they rejoiced with music and dancing. The high priest came and listened solemnly to Ahmal's story as he shared what the Messiah had done for him. The high priest had blessed the house. Believers began to gather in their home to share the things the Messiah had done for them.

Marah waited fearfully for several days for Reuben to return to the house, yet he did not come. She wondered, knowing there was money for him in the sale of Ahmal's house. Nonetheless, she was grateful to the God Who Sees for protecting her.

As she looked to her household and went about her duties, there was still a small sadness in her heart. She had so much to be thankful for, yet she still longed for word of Caleb. She prayed to see her son again.

This morning, the household was busier than usual. Ahmal had put out word and, little by little, gathered his caravan to him again. Shumah, hearing of Ahmal's return, fled to Egypt rather than face Ahmal's wrath. The men of his caravans returned, astounded as word spread of Ahmal's miraculous healing from leprosy. Ahmal left on a short journey to trade and reestablish his contacts with other merchants and caravans. Today, after nearly two months, he was due to return.

Marah thought about how hard it had been to let him go again after having him restored to her. Yet they prayed and trusted in God, and she had sent him on his way with a smile and with thanksgiving.

The town was alive with visitors, and there was almost a tangible change when the caravans came in. Village dogs barked, the hustle and bustle of the marketplace increased as merchants anticipated receipt of the goods they had ordered. Others anticipated the profit from goods they had sent to be sold or traded. It was as if the pulse of the town beat harder with the coming of the caravans. She sensed such a pulse now and she knew the caravan had arrived. She waited patiently, knowing there was merchandise to unload and business to conclude. Toward evening, Ahmal would return to his home.

She was surprised then that she heard the voice of someone in the courtyard, greeting Eliab. It was early afternoon. She hurried out, thinking to greet her husband, and saw a stranger with his back to her, talking with Eliab.

She hurried toward them, and the stranger turned around.

Jesse! She gasped and stood staring at him in unbelief. Then, reason reasserted itself. It could not be Jesse. He was dead. It was . . . Caleb.

Caleb hugged her exuberantly. "I am glad to be home, and you are here to welcome me, Mother."

She touched his face with her hand. He had grown a full beard and was as tall and strong as his father had been.

Eliab beamed. "I thought you would be glad to see this young giant."

Caleb grinned back. "Eliab, you old rascal, I'm glad to see you again too."

Watching the two of them, Marah's heart sang in gratitude. "Oh Caleb, I feared you were lost. Tell me, what happened to you? Do you know of Ahmal, that he has returned?"

"We followed Father's trail to Antioch, but going farther, it was as if he had not existed. No one had word of him, and though they knew him well, there was word his caravan had disbanded. I was told the leader of the caravan had simply disappeared. I returned to Antioch and found work in the shop of a carpenter. Each time a caravan came in, I asked for news of the merchant Ahmal. So much time had passed that I almost gave up. I was sure he was dead. This last time, I heard the amazing news that the caravan master Ahmal had once again gathered his caravan and was on the trade route. Seeking to catch up with him, I found passage with a caravan coming into Shechem. I did not know where he was, but I knew he would come home. I knew I had to come back, to see you, Mother."

"I have prayed and God has heard my prayers." She touched his face gently with her hand.

He shook his head. "I was a thoughtless fool, to leave you so unprotected. I didn't know what would happen. All Demas and I could think of was adventure and finding my father."

"You were a boy, my son, but you have returned a man. The Messiah taught us that in asking forgiveness of God we must also ask forgiveness of ourselves. You have learned by this and will be the stronger for it." She looked around. "You have returned alone?"

Caleb grinned. "Demas did not exactly like being a slave . . ."

They had been walking toward the house. Caleb stopped and turned to her again. "Mother, everywhere I went they spoke of this rabbi called Jesus of Nazareth. They called Him . . . Messiah. I heard that He was even here in Shechem. Tell me of Him."

Marah smiled. "First you must eat."

They sat at the table and she urged so much food and drink on him that Caleb began to laugh. "I shall be here tomorrow, Mother, you need not feed me for a week today."

Marah spoke to a servant and sent him for Hannah and Simon. She wanted her friends to rejoice with her once again. She could picture Hannah's face when she heard of Caleb's return.

As they waited for their friends and Ahmal to join them, Marah sat down by Caleb. "You asked me about Jesus. I can only tell you what He has done for me when I was alone. Ahmal can tell you his story himself. It is a miracle. Forgiveness is a miracle, my son. As we forgive ourselves, we open our hearts to the forgiveness of Christ. I will tell you how I met Him at the well of Jacob."

Softly, tenderly, with joy in her heart, she told Caleb her story. His face echoed the emotions of his heart as he felt remorse for all that she had gone through, her vulnerability, and her struggle to survive. Anger reflected when she told about Reuben, and she felt that had Reuben appeared at that moment, Caleb would have torn him limb from limb. Tears filled his eyes when she told of the Christ's forgiveness and love and His coming to Shechem for two days to teach the people.

"I wish I could have been here, Mother, to see and hear Him," he murmured wistfully.

Just then, there were footsteps and Ahmal entered the room. He stopped for a moment, seeing her sitting by a stranger. Caleb jumped up and, with a grin, strode toward his stepfather.

"I have learned a few lessons, but I pray I have returned stronger."

Concern was erased by joy as Ahmal and Caleb embraced. "My son . . . you have returned to us. We shall celebrate!"

Marah laughed. "I have already sent for Simon and Hannah."

"Have you eaten, my son? I could single-handedly eat a goat!"

Raising his hands in protest, Caleb laughed. "If I eat any more, I shall surely burst like an old wineskin."

As Marah served Ahmal his evening meal, Caleb leaned forward.

"Mother has told me of what the Messiah has done for her. I am amazed at her story. She said you would also tell me of this wondrous thing that has happened to you, Father."

Ahmal looked thoughtful. "I think I shall never tire of telling the wonderful things God has done for me." He turned to Marah. "Have the believers still come in my absence?"

"Yes, my lord, they have come each week to share the love of the Savior. Many new ones have come also. They will come this evening. It is indeed the Lord's timing that Caleb should return home this day."

Caleb looked from one to the other. "You have a gathering of believers in your home?"

"Yes, my son. Tonight you shall hear my story and the story of others who have been touched by Jesus of Nazareth, the Messiah. We meet to praise His name and worship together, to strengthen our faith."

"I think I would like to hear these stories." Caleb looked thoughtful.

Ahmal looked around. "Did Demas return with you?"

Caleb leaned forward, a bit chagrined. "I was telling Mother that Demas never did take to being a slave. We parted at Antioch and he returned to his home in Laodicea. He had been kidnapped from there as a boy and sold to slave traders. He desired to see his family again."

Ahmal thought for a moment and then nodded. "It is just as well. I'm sure his family rejoiced to see him once again." Then he turned to Caleb with a stern look, but a twinkle in his eyes.

"It would seem you have done me out of a servant. I will need recompense for his services. We will need to find work for you to make up his cost."

Caleb managed to look contrite. "I will gladly do that."

"Yes," Ahmal stroked his beard, "I believe I have just the job for you . . . it seems I am again in need of a factor."

Caleb sat up, surprised and delighted. "I had hoped . . . I wanted to do that."

Ahmal clasped him on the shoulder. "Then it is done, my son. Tomorrow we will begin."

Eliab interrupted to escort Simon, Hannah, and young Jacob into the room. Jacob had worshiped Caleb and had been hurt and disappointed when he had gone. Now, he ran and flung himself at Caleb with childish exuberance.

"You are here! You are home!" He grinned from ear to ear in his excitement.

"Jacob, my young friend, how are things with you?"

"The Messiah was here, Caleb. You should have seen and heard Him. He did miracles and He taught at the synagogue.

Look at my foot." Jacob stuck out his foot and laughed as he saw the amazement and wonder on Caleb's face.

"Your foot . . . it is not twisted anymore. This Jesus did that for you?"

"I saw it with my very eyes, Caleb," Hannah said. "It turned in the hands of Jesus and straightened out. He runs and plays with the other children as though it had always been normal."

Tears ran unashamedly down Caleb's face as Jacob ran and jumped for him, anxious to show what he could do.

Caleb shook his head in wonder. He had no words.

Eliab returned to the room carrying cushions that he placed about for the guests who were coming. There was a knock at the door and several neighbors were shown into the house. More people came and the room began to fill up. Some brought their own cushions or stools to sit upon. Many just sat down on the floor. There was an air of expectancy in the room. Caleb sat down with young Jacob by his side. Caleb's face was serious and thoughtful as he observed all that went on.

The people had greeted Ahmal joyfully, speaking of prayers for his safe journey and return. Many of the women embraced each other. Men and women sat down unself-consciously by one another. Marah sat down to one side of Ahmal, who was obviously going to lead the meeting.

"My friends and fellow believers in Jesus, the Messiah, I praise Him, not only for my safe return, but today the safe return of our son. Let us rejoice together and bless our God."

Many praised God out loud, and as they sang many of the hymns from Passover, Marah observed Caleb study the faces around him as joy permeated the room with its warmth.

After the singing, several people gave testimonies as to what the Messiah had done for them—healing, restoration, and forgiveness. Caleb listened intently as Marah shared the peace she had found. She felt it radiate from her like an inner glow.

At last, Ahmal was asked to tell his story once again, for the benefit of Caleb and several newcomers who were anxious to hear the tale from his own lips.

Marah watched Caleb's rapt face as Ahmal's story unfolded and she prayed earnestly that he too would become a believer.

As the tale unfolded, Caleb's face reflected his emotions as it registered surprise, wonder, and thankfulness. This Messiah had indeed wrought a wondrous change in the people of Shechem. Blind eyes opened, lame healed, devils cast out. If he did not know the people who shared these stories as those he had grown up with and known all his life, he would have been skeptical. Yet, there was Jacob's foot, as normal as any other boy's. Shiva the carpenter . . . he had worked with him and known him well. Shiva also spoke in respectful tones of the Messiah. He had become a believer.

As the guests gathered their things and began to disperse toward their own homes, Caleb went out to the courtyard, to a quiet corner by the fountain. He hugged Jacob and bade him, Simon, and Hannah goodbye. They were like family to him. Simon had always been a gentle man, but now there was an inner strength that flowed from him; from Hannah too. He stared at the fountain and contemplated all that he had seen and heard.

Marah had seen to the house after the guests left and glanced around for Caleb. Ahmal and Marah at last saw him in the courtyard and were about to turn back to the house, leaving him alone with his thoughts.

"Mother, Father, wait a moment." He walked quietly over to them and looked at each of their faces. "I want to say again, how glad I am to be home, to have my family together again."

They waited, for he had much on his heart. He looked down at the ground a moment, and when he looked up at them again, Marah saw that his face reflected the peace he had found.

"I have listened, and seen with my eyes, what the coming of Jesus to Shechem has meant. I too believe that He is the Messiah."

Marah gave a glad cry and they embraced one another.

At last, Ahmal lifted the lamp and they turned back toward the house.

"Come," he said gently. "Let us take our rest. It has been a long journey, but it is at an end, and tomorrow is a new day."

Epilogue

Reuben and his servant rode back from Sebaste. The caravan master Reuben had heard of was not Ahmal. Pleased, he spent the return trip to Shechem contemplating how he could go about selling off Ahmal's house and remaining goods. He would have to go to the elders and announce his claim as Ahmal's brother, a tiresome ordeal. There should be no problem, he reasoned. He knew Ahmal had no other relatives. He thought of Marah. Beautiful . . . yes, but there were many beautiful women, and he felt no need to retain only one. He would take her with him . . . for a time. When he was tired of her, he would leave her behind. She could make her living as women in her circumstances had done before. The men would find her desirable.

Pleased that he had resolved his problems so readily, he and Tema dismounted at an inn, where they would lodge the horses. Tema took the bridles and arranged for their care, then the two men headed through the town toward the house of Ahmal.

To Reuben's surprise, he heard the sound of singing and dancing coming from the house. A celebration of some kind?

Cautiously he pulled Tema back into the shadows with him and listened.

A man hurried down the street toward the house and Reuben stepped out and stopped him.

"My friend, we are strangers in Shechem. Can you tell me what is happening at that house? A wedding . . . ?"

The man peered at them curiously. "You must indeed be strangers not to know what has happened. The merchant Ahmal has returned after three years. His wife thought him dead. Not only has he returned, but he tells of being cured of leprosy by the Messiah. The same Messiah who came here to Shechem. He stayed with us two days and performed many miracles."

"Ah, they indeed have cause for rejoicing. Thank you, my friend."

The man nodded and hurried on his way. Reuben pulled on his beard. He could not see Tema's eyes in the darkness, but he sensed the fear of his servant, which echoed his own. He had not seen this Jesus himself, but even in Sebaste they were talking about the miracles. Why did he feel apprehension at the mention of this so-called Messiah?

"Master . . . ," Tema began hesitantly.

"Be still, Tema," Reuben growled. "I must think."

The man had not mentioned Ahmal's wife. If Ahmal had been the outraged husband, there would not be this celebration. If she had not told her husband, he would find out about Reuben in time. Marah would have to deal with it. Using his wits had saved him many times before. He stood quietly, listening to the laughter and music. After a few moments, he pulled his mantle closer about his face and turned back toward the inn. He could sense rather than hear Tema's sigh of relief.

"There are other towns, Tema," he said confidently. "Let us be on our way."

Author's Note

This book has been twenty-five years in the writing. When I read the story of the Samaritan woman years ago, it touched and intrigued me. I felt there was so much more to her than what first appeared, and God planted the seed of her story in my heart. I shared the idea and my first tentative chapters with the members of a critique group in the San Diego Christian Writer's Guild, founded by Dr. Sherwood "Woody" Wirt to encourage budding writers. I appreciate the group's encouragement and help over the years. At a writer's conference at Forest Home Christian Conference Center, I talked with an editor about the book. Her question, "But can you write it?" startled me and made me pause. My genre was poetry and short stories, not novels. Perhaps I could not. With the difficulties of a broken marriage and raising three children alone, the manuscript was shelved many times. During my own journey through those years, I walked my own paths and didn't seek God for what He had planned for me. Through my struggles and deep valleys, in bits and pieces came the story of Marah, the woman of Samaria. There were many revisions to the story.

During those years I was able to travel to the Holy Land and see the sights mentioned in the book including Jacob's well. In 1986, while working at Point Loma Nazarene University, I was fortunate to find an old copy of *The Samaritans, the Earliest Jewish Sect* by James Alan Montgomery, PhD. It covered the more current dwindling generation of Samaritans, but gave me depth and insight into the lives of the Samaritan people, the *Samarim,* whose customs have really not changed through the centuries.

In 1990, I remarried and we moved to a small mountain community called Lewiston, in northern California. With all the time to write, God began to nudge me again about the woman of Samaria, and I knew I needed to finish her story.

I would like to extend my heartfelt thanks to Mona Gansberg Hodgson, who first read and edited the budding manuscript through the Christian Communicator Critique Service; to my agent, Joyce Hart, for answering the cold call of an inexperienced but determined writer, for her encouragement and belief in the story, for keeping faith with me and becoming a true friend; to Jan Medley, who went through the manuscript with a fine-tooth comb and found things I couldn't see; to the ladies of my book club, Donnie Cramer, Betty Alman, Ricki Cokas, Ronnie Feehan, Claire Hughes, Phyllis Kaylor, Doris Kenyon, Joanna Ludwig, Mary Meisner, Sue Randerson, Joanna Schumacher, and Carol Simpson, who faithfully read the manuscript in one month, enthusiastically endorsed the story, and have held me up with their prayers and encouragement; to my daughter, Karen Penrod, for her insightful comments and suggestions during the latter stages of the writing; to Glenna Hess, assistant manager of our Family Christian Bookstore, who read the manuscript and told me, "Good as anything on the shelf!" at a time when I was discouraged; and last but not least, to my dear husband for his patience as I burrowed down under mounds of research books and papers and lived in front of my computer.

Finally, there is not a great deal written on the daily life of the ancient Samaritans, so I used the life of the Jewish people in ancient times. Where it was possible, I used a known custom. In other situations, forgive me for taking poetic license. I pray that as you read this story, you will see in the woman of Samaria what Jesus saw in her and what Jesus sees in us all.

Diana Wallis Taylor is an award-winning poet, songwriter, and author. A poet since the age of twelve, her collection of poetry, *Wings of the Wind*, came out in 2007. A former teacher, she retired in 1990 as director of conference services for a private college. After their marriage in 1990, she and her husband moved to northern California where she fulfilled a dream of owning a bookshop/coffeehouse for writers' groups and poetry readings and was able to devote more time to her writing.

The Taylors have six grown children between them and ten grandchildren. They now live in the San Diego area, where between writing projects Diana is an inspirational speaker for Stonecroft Ministries, participates in Christian Women's Fellowship, serves on the Board of the San Diego Christian Writer's Guild, and is active in the music ministry of her church. She enjoys teaching poetry and writing workshops, and sharing her heart with women of all ages.

Visit Diana's website at www.dianawallistaylor.com.

A SWEEPING BIBLICAL TALE OF PASSION AND DRAMA!

Against the backdrop of opulent palace life, raging war, and desert escapes, Michal deals with love, loss, and personal transformation as one of the wives of David. Be swept up in this exciting and romantic story!